THE NEW REALITY

AN ALEX PELLA NOVEL
STEPHEN MARTINO

To Pauline Vilain who believed in my work
but returned home before its publication

Acknowledgments

The Dalai Lama said that when you practice gratefulness, there is a sense of respect toward others. And thus my greatest respect goes to my wife for being my greatest partner in life and to my parents who taught me that the love of family, God and country are the three essential pillars to a successful life. Also, my utmost respect goes to Dr. Joseph Albanese and to Karen Nugent who, among others, were there for me when I needed them the most. I would like to give special thanks to Drew Sheinen who helped take my manuscript and create a readable novel. Lastly, I would like to especially thank Elizabeth Turnbull of Light Messages Publishing for believing in my work, editing it, and helping to bring it to publication.

"When government wishes to do the work of God, it becomes not divine but demonic."
Pope Benedict XVI

Map of the Middle East and Northern Africa

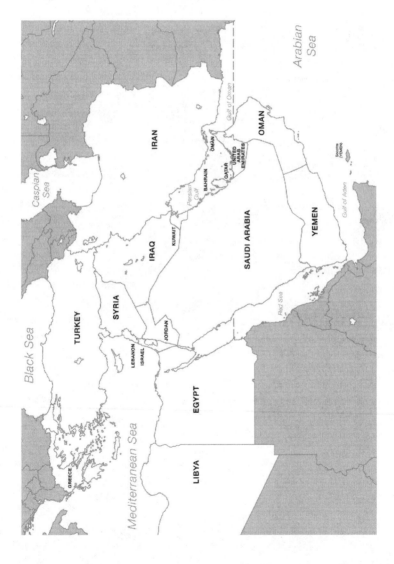

PROLOGUE

August 10, 2080

THE DIM LIGHT COULD NOT HIDE the surreptitious events occurring in the confines of a forgotten surgical room. Some would call it treasonous or state how it's an abomination to God. Still others might tout it as revolutionary. However, each surgeon knew their actions contradicted all ethical boundaries. While their surgical masks hid the faces of their shame, their eyes revealed what their souls were feeling.

"I thought we were going to stop at the tenth patient," hesitantly commented the curly redheaded physician.

No one responded.

It was what all four were thinking but were too afraid to state aloud.

Sweat began to drip down her fair-skinned face. Her brow glistened with mounting perspiration. Though a lone fan in the room helped cool down this underground facility, it was insufficient to douse her burning shame.

What was once promised to be the greatest medical

experiment of their careers had turned into their greatest nightmare. After their first ten patients died within months of the procedure, all thought the project would be terminated. It hadn't been.

Failure only meant more experiments. More experiments only meant more deaths. With this patient marking the fiftieth, they knew something finally had to be done.

Another one of the surgeons looked up after what seemed like an eternity to all those in the room. His furrowed brow and glaring dark brown eyes had more to say than any words.

After authoritatively clearing his throat, he distinctly stated through the surgical mask, "We all knew what we were in for at the inception of this project."

Without moving his head, he eyed each of his colleagues in a firm manner. "This is not a matter open for discussion nor is this the proper forum for debate." The gray-haired man should have dismissed his fellow redheaded surgeon right there without another word. All expected him to do so but he, too, experienced the same disgrace as the others. As the lead investigator of the project, he felt even more responsible than the other three.

"Dr. Christakos—," she began to say before being interrupted.

"Begin the infusion," he stated matter-of-factly, expecting to curtail all further commentary.

The patient lay flat on his stomach atop the surgical table. Though entirely draped in green linen, his back was uncovered and washed in a black solution. Eight small syringes protruded in a line along his bony spine. The orange-tinged fluid in each of the syringes had an eerie glow, making the surgical site reminiscent of a Halloween landscape.

Under the physician's guidance, each syringe emptied one by one into the patient's spine. Though only one of the surgeons administered the solution, all felt just as responsible. Accompanying her accumulating beads of sweat, tears ran down the redhead's cheeks.

The small room suddenly became claustrophobic. Dr. Christakos knew that he had most likely just condemned another innocent man from this island to a painful death. His breathing became more rapid while his pulse accelerated. Though blood was rapidly being pumped throughout his body, the doctor became cold and clammy.

The whitewashed stone walls of this underground room began to suffocate him. The scant light from the ceiling fixture suddenly became unbearably hot.

This is insane! Doctor Thompson is right. What are we doing? This experiment was supposed to help mankind, not destroy it!

Unable to stand any longer without passing out, he turned and abruptly marched over to the only door in the room. Unable to look his colleagues in the eye once again, Dr. Christakos simply told them to finish without him. The iron door swung open, leaving the final three surgeons to complete their assignment.

Outside the operating room was not much more aesthetically pleasing. Albeit better lit, the same whitewashed stone walls accompanied him down a long and dreary hallway. An old-fashioned elevator stood at the end of it. Though the year was 2080, this antique piece of equipment dated back to World War II. With a single rusty metal door waist-high in height, its squeaky hinges welcomed the doctor as he entered.

Ascending the shaft, Dr. Christakos recalled the history of this bunker, contemplating how its use had changed but its clandestine purpose remained the same.

During World War II, the British constructed many of these bunkers throughout the island. Astipalea, along with its sister Greek islands along the southeastern Aegean Sea, was once the site of a forgotten battle during the waning years of the war. After the surrender of the occupying Italian forces, the Germans quickly seized most of the Greek islands, denying the Allies both ports and airfields for operation. Under the command of Major General Brittorous, the British countered the Nazi's aggression by fortifying their own islands in the Aegean Sea.

Astipalea had bunkers constructed both for ammunition storage and bomb shelters. Some of these, like the one Dr. Christakos was exiting, were transformed into makeshift hospital wings for the intended military and civilian casualties.

Though German forces led by General Müller defeated the British, many of the defensive fortifications could still be found throughout numerous islands. Most were abandoned, but some still proved functional many decades after the war.

Dr. Christakos squinted as his eyes were flooded with the light of a bright midday sun. No longer feeling trapped in his previous cryptal environment, he exited the decrepit elevator and entered his office. With its numerous windows and wide-opened space, the room abated his previously suffocating claustrophobia.

The doctor took off his mask and surgical cap and let loose a long sigh of relief. *Time to see my morning patients.*

Immediately upon entering the hospital wing, Dr. Christakos was accosted by numerous nursing staff members and his personal assistant, Henry.

"Punctual as usual, sir," Henry quickly greeted with a Pilipino accent. "This is going to be a busy day."

Before Dr. Christakos could collect his thoughts, his assistant promptly escorted him to the first patient. Inside the glassed-off room a man was covered in blood-soaked bandages and lay motionless upon his sterile bed. The unbandaged skin appeared red and festering as if burned by a sun a thousand times brighter than our own. In excruciating pain, the sickly patient mumbled incomprehensibly to himself.

On the glass wall isolating the hospital room a three-dimensional representation of the man appeared. Most of his skin was red and transparent while the organs underneath were well visualized. Around this holographic figure were different illustrations of separate organs with numbers underneath representing the various bodily functions.

Dr. Christakos tapped a few spots on the glass. Four robotic arms appeared from underneath the man's bed and began changing his bandages. A swooshing sound emanated from the holograph, informing the doctor that the morning medications had just been administered.

"Mr. Milonas just arrived yesterday," Henry said as the doctor continued to work, "and his condition continues to worsen just like the rest. Despite all that we have…"

Henry continued to talk rapidly. His accent was so thick at times that his English became almost unrecognizable. By now, Dr. Christakos had stopped paying attention. He knew the scenario and it was the same for all the patients placed in this clinical trial: rapid breakdown of the muscle, which was followed in quick succession by internal organ failure, rashes, terminating in encephalopathy where in essence the brain shuts down.

Though Dr. Christakos repeatedly warned the sponsor of the trial about its dire results, he was reluctantly forced to continue. *The ends justify the means*, he was told.

Only Dr. Christakos and his three surgical colleagues knew about the clinical trial. The rest of the hospital and people on the island were oblivious to the truth.

"And the sad thing is," Henry went on to say, "his brother just passed away two weeks ago with the same thing and his sister is in the next room with an identical illness."

Dr. Christakos took his hand immediately off the glass and grabbed Henry's shoulder. "What? What was that about his brother and sister?" he frantically sputtered.

Startled, Henry relayed the same information, albeit a little slower and in a more enunciated manner.

Dr. Christakos quickly rushed over to the next room where the man's sister was located. Pulling up her schematics on the glass, he rapidly analyzed all the information.

Exactly the same. The two of them have exactly the same thing! This cannot be. Only the younger brother who died two weeks ago was part of the experiment! This is impossible!

Dr. Christakos knew his other patients involved in the experiment died as a direct result of his work. However, these two were definitely not participants and bore no marks of the procedure. It defied all medical knowledge. He and his medical team were not administering infectious agents in this trial.

Though perplexed, the doctor knew there could be only one solution.

"Sound the island's siren, and have every one of the island's 1,081 inhabitants here in the hospital auditorium for an emergency meeting in four hours." He pointed at Henry and shook his head as he continued, "Call in all the fishing ships. I want everyone accounted for before this emergency meeting begins!"

●●●

Never had four hours passed so quickly. It felt like only a minute ago when he had given Henry his orders, and now Dr. Christakos stood on a small platform in front of over a thousand scared people. He wished he had more time to determine what had afflicted the Milonas family. He wished he had more time to correct the problems with his clinical trial.

Right now, above all else, he simply wished he had time to say goodbye to his loved ones.

Dr. Christakos turned back and looked apologetically at his three surgical colleagues. It was at this moment that he noticed the natural beauty of the redhead. With glowing green eyes, long curly hair, and an attractive, petite figure, she was like an ancient Greek siren of the sea calling out for him. All the time he was here on the island he was too busy with his work to appreciate anything else, and now it was too late.

Dr. Christakos cleared his throat and almost instantly the frantic chatter around him abated.

Knowing that everyone on the island had been accounted for, he took a deep breath and began to speak, "Thank you all for your quick response."

He could barely talk over the growing lump in his throat. As time grew ever closer to 4:00 P.M. he wanted to say something to the people in front of him. Some were scientists or medical staff working at the hospital while others were native to the island and made their livelihood fishing in the sea. No matter who they were, they were all in the same place now.

Whether to say something uplifting or just tell the truth was the largest quagmire. Did these people need to know what he and his colleagues had been doing or was naiveté the most appropriate option? With his mind inundated with both guilt and sorrow, the doctor made up his mind on how to proceed.

"I have great news for everyone here!" he began with a forced smile.

3:59:45 P.M.

"Something fantastic has happened."

3:59:50 P.M.

The crowd was at the edge of their seats, grinning with great expectation.

"Today is the day we all leave behind our mundane lives."

3:59:55 P.M.

"And start a great new beginning!"

The end justifies the means.
4:00:00 P.M.

BOOM! The entire 37 square-mile island of Astipalea and all its inhabitants were instantly vaporized. The explosion lit up the sky and sent tidal waves to its neighboring islands along with both mainland Greece and Turkey. So great was the explosion, it could be seen and felt from hundreds of miles away.

Known only to Dr. Christakos, there were more than just old military supplies hidden in the island's underground bunkers. Stashed away long ago, an incendiary arsenal of weapons had been written off by the Greek military as properly disposed of. And disposed of is what the doctor hoped to accomplish with his final act.

CHAPTER 1

July 15, 2081

"Off to work again?" Suzan asked, both half-kidding and annoyed.

Her husband seemed oblivious to the question. Because he labored three weeks of double shifts and returned home from work only four hours prior, she thought he was going to at least have the rest of the this day off. Clearly that was not the case. With so many of his coworkers getting sick, it left only a handful of dedicated employees to man the local factory.

"They're working you straight into the grave," Suzan added. "They only care about money and not their employees. I don't know why you let them do this to you. Look at you." She pointed the dishtowel towards him. "You are an old man and your body can't do this anymore."

She was right. Berk was going to be 65 next month and his youthful veracity had been quickly dwindling over the past few years. As arthritis in his back and neck set in, he could do less physical activity, causing him to gain weight. No longer a strapping young man, he had acquired a large gut and two extra chins in the process. Berk's jet-black hair had also grayed precipitously since putting in all these extra hours at work.

"You worry too much," he cajoled with a cherub-like grin.

In fact, Berk had been the one doing most of the worrying. He was concerned not only for himself but also for his friends and family in this small town of Yakakoy. Located in western Turkey just off the Aegean Sea, the town's sole means of sustenance was its local factory. With fewer healthy employees remaining, it left only a handful of people to keep the business alive.

"If I didn't do the worrying, who would?" Suzan scoffed, while washing the pots in the sink.

Suzan was a sturdy woman, full of life. Accustomed to the hard work of living on a farm as a child, she had grown strong both physically and mentally. Though fifty years of age, she still retained her youthful glow and joked about marrying such an old man. She always responded that he was young when she married him, and now look what happened.

Berk tried to leave without his wife noticing, but she held out her cheek, expecting a kiss before his departure.

"I have to be at the factory," he curtly responded, while attempting to open the door.

"Oh, no honey. You're not leaving until you give your wife her proper goodbye."

Suzan grabbed Berk's wrist. To her surprise it felt warm and clammy, almost as if she were holding a wet snake. She then realized how red her husband's face appeared. It was as if he fell asleep in a tanning bed and forgot to wake up for a day.

Berk looked down, not knowing what to say to his wife. They both had witnessed at least half their town come down with the same condition. Whenever someone developed these symptoms, they were immediately whisked away, never to be seen again. Over the past six months Yakakoy had slowly dwindled down to a fraction of its original population. Berk hoped that if he continued working no one would notice his declining health. Failure was not an option for him, and the last thing he ever wanted was to be forced to leave his dear wife and town.

"They're not going to take you away, honey!" Suzan blurted with authority. "They will have to get through me first. Now you go upstairs and get some rest. You probably just have a fever from working too hard. I'll tell the factory that you sprained your ankle and will be there in the morning."

Berk knew excuses would not suffice. If anyone missed work or was late, the town police would immediately come to the house. With so many people in Yakakoy becoming mysteriously sick, the Turkish government had become adamant about removing anyone from the town with signs of *The Disease*.

The Disease is what the people called it. Since its appearance almost a year ago, it first spread quickly through Greece and Turkey, afflicting more of its population than either government cared to divulge. Scientists could give it no other name. No pathological organism for this new scourge could be found. Neither bacteria, virus, protozoa nor other infectious agent was ever discovered. Even rare pathogens such as prions, similar to those causing mad cow disease, were investigated but without any success.

Now as new victims began cropping up all over the world, humanity lay helpless at the mercy of *The Disease*. Without knowing the cause of this scourge or having any idea about the mode of its dissemination, humanity stood at the precipice of mass extinction. To prevent global chaos, there remained a total media blackout on the situation. All the general population of the world knew was that *The Disease* had been mostly confined to Turkey and Greece. Those that understood the truth were forced to secrecy.

"You know they'll come for me if they discover I'm sick," Berk said. "I have a thermos full of cold water and I just took two Tylenol. That should at least get me through the day."

"I bet it's just a simple fever," Suzan sputtered with false hope. "You'll probably be better tonight after work."

A deafening bullhorn from somewhere outside curtailed further conversation. Despite the volume, the rattle of helicopters flying overhead and what sounded like heavy machinery outside their door obscured its blaring noise.

Berk immediately dropped his thermos and ran outside. It was as if war had broken out without anyone telling them. Down the street he could see a desert camouflaged Altay III tank slowly lumbering up the dirt road towards him. Atop of it and adjacent to its Rheinmetall 165 mm gun stood the large bullhorn causing all the commotion.

Though recently commissioned by the Turkish government, the tank was unusually noisy for such a modern machine. Berk conjectured that by the time you could hear the Altay III it would probably be too late anyway. With that large gun and Kevlar reinforced armor, it certainly did not need to rely on stealth in the field of combat.

Behind the tank marched at least a hundred soldiers. Each of the soldiers wore desert camouflaged contamination suits covering their entire body. It was a hybrid uniform, where science met military. Able to see through a yellow-tinged transparent square on their hoods, the soldiers marched in unison with guns at attention, waiting for any excuse to use them.

"Get out of the street!" Suzan yelled. "Don't just stand there. Get in here!"

Suzan's pleas were drown out by the bullhorn and a helicopter hovering two houses down from them. As the tank and soldiers approached, Berk began waving his arms in the air, expecting some answers.

It was his town and he'd lived there all of his life. If there were any problems, someone needed to speak with him before parading any further through the streets. His arms began to wave more frantically the closer they came.

Other neighbors also came to their doors. A few, like Berk, went into the streets, hoping to accost their uninvited visitors. Many congregated together, but the noise made conversation impossible.

About ten of the soldiers, brandishing their weapons, immediately ran in front of the tank. Berk stood tall. Now he was going to get answers.

Before he could extend his hand in welcome, Berk was repelled to the ground by a barrage of bullets to the chest. Looks of horror filled the faces of the townspeople, and his wife let out a scream of grief that could be heard over the surrounding noise.

Their alarm was short lived as the soldiers summarily disposed of the townspeople with an endless volley of gunfire. Those who were not shot burned to death as each house was set to the torch by flame-throwers. Others who tried to run into the woods were gunned down by the helicopter roaming above them.

In a mere thirty minutes the town of Yakakoy was completely razed to the ground and its entire population decimated.

Modern science had failed them and all those afflicted with *The Disease*. There was no cure and more concerning there was no source. When science becomes God and science fails, fear and cruelty rush in to fill the void. Destroying this town and others like it would solve nothing. *The Disease* had affected them all, even those not afflicted by it.

CHAPTER 2

THE DECIBEL IS A MEASUREMENT unit used to quantify the intensity of sound. A normal conversation usually registers at 60dB while a subway car can reach up to 100dB. Pain usually sets in at 125dB. The scale, however, does not calculate the annoyance of the sound, nor in the case of a conversation, its irritability.

Thus, the decibel by no means could accurately quantify the ear-splitting sound of Samantha Mancini's voice. With its high-pitched shrill and intensity it could be heard clearly through a roaring jet engine.

Despite her voice, Samantha was an extremely attractive professional in her late forties with flowing brown hair, cut to shoulder length. Her petite size and gentle face caused many to underestimate both her mental and physical fortitude.

Samantha wore a red, high-cut skirt and matching tight blouse. High-heeled black boots completed the outfit, giving her an extra five inches of height in the process.

"I see you're exquisitely dressed again, Samantha," Alex Pella jested. "Just don't stand on the street corner outside

Neurono-Tek when you begin working."

"Work!" Samantha screeched. "You should try it sometime instead of dating a new bimbo each week or racing around on one of your aero-bikes."

Samantha was correct. Alex did enjoy racing and had a propensity for women. It wasn't that he preferred perpetual dating, but his work at Neurono-Tek had become all-encompassing. And he had convinced himself that he didn't have the proper time to commit to a long-term relationship.

"What does twenty dollars get me?" Alex continued to jest with an uncanny smirk that Samantha always found amusing.

"A punch in the nose," she rebutted, trying to hold back a smile. "You know I'm going to be very rich once that sexual harassment suit comes in."

Alex laughed aloud, knowing he might just get that punch in the nose if he continued teasing.

Despite the bickering, Samantha and Alex were very close and enjoyed the occasional banter between them.

Alex was impeccably dressed in his black pinstripe suit. Also in his forties, he looked no more than thirty years of age. With short jet-black, curly hair, vibrant olive skin and broad shoulders, he was a perpetual favorite among women.

His dark brown eyes complimented his suntan, and he had a smile that could turn any heated argument his way.

"What's with the stiff," Alex asked. "Did he arrive yet?"

"Yes, while you were doing God-knows-what in your office, security quarantined him in the level five Biohazard room in the basement. Now, he just awaits the *illustrious* and *famous* Dr. Alex Pella to examine him and save the planet from *The Disease*."

Samantha pointed to the elevators. "If you want to see the body right now, go right ahead. Humanity awaits."

Alex followed Samantha's finger, but when he turned

towards the elevator there was a different body that piqued his interest. She was about five foot eight, just like him, and was staring straight at them. It was as if nothing else existed for that brief moment in the vast Neurono-Tek lobby.

Her long brown hair, angelic face, fair skin and big, vibrant green eyes lit up the room. Alex was momentarily at a loss for words. He became only more dumbfounded when she walked his way. Her thin, yet muscular legs, long torso and compact figure tucked away in a tight brown dress made her appear as if she were a beautiful gazelle effortlessly striding through the brush.

If she were the gazelle, Alex would be all too happy to play the role of the ravenous lion.

Samantha succinctly snapped him out of his daze.

"Get your head out of the gutter and go over there and meet Marissa Ambrosia," she chastised. "She came with the body."

"She sure did!"

Samantha gave Alex that punch she promised him. Sparing the face, she got in a quick jab to his ribs.

"Dr. Pella," Marissa greeted, "thank you so much for letting us bring one of *The Disease* victims here."

As the two shook hands, there was an instant connection. It was almost as if he were welcoming an old friend. Alex did not want to release her soft, delicate hand and did his best not to seem overzealous by holding on too long.

"Call me Alex," he gasped, still out of breath from that blow to the ribs.

Samantha stepped between the two. "Now that formalities are over, why don't we move to the lounge area. My legs are getting tired standing in these boots."

Samantha led them over to the large arrangement of black leather couches and chairs in the middle of the lobby. No expense had been spared with the construction of the building, particularly this area. White marble floors speckled with green streaks, Victorian chandeliers hanging overhead, expensive works of art on the walls, and a priceless display of antique medical devices made the lobby the showpiece for all of Neurono-Tek. A woman dressed in a long, flowing white dress stroking a golden harp added to the room's ambience.

"So Marissa," Samantha asked, "tell me about the present you brought us in the Level Five Biohazard room."

"I'd like to thank you both again on behalf of The National Institutes of Health for accepting the body."

Alex kept his comments to himself this time.

"We at the NIH," she said, "are at a complete loss."

A waiter came to their sides and placed a napkin on a granite-topped end table next to each of them. He then poured them each a complimentary glass of champagne in a long fluted glass. This luxury was not theirs exclusively. All were welcomed with the champagne along with the open bar and complimentary café in the lobby.

"Would you like anything else to drink?" the waiter politely asked. "Or may I interest you with a menu?"

Each was satisfied with the champagne. The waiter went off to another couple sitting nearby and took their order.

Marissa turned to Alex. "We were able to obtain the body from Turkey. It seems that country has been the hardest hit thus far and is desperate to find answers. With *The Disease* continuing to decimate their population, they gave the NIH full access to all their medical information and victims' bodies."

"But why Neurono-Tek?" Alex asked. "Can't the NIH take care of this by themselves?"

"Unfortunately," Marissa responded, "the answer is no." She went on to explain how *The Disease* had stumped them all at the NIH. Located in Bethesda, Maryland, the world-renowned biomedical research center's months of research had failed to reveal any useful information thus far. The only definitive fact discovered was that each victim died of multiple organ failure. The question still remained: What was the cause?

Alex felt flattered but still did not understand why other research hospitals that treated general medical and infectious conditions were not approached first. It seemed only natural that they would prove a more suitable institute for such forensic matters.

"You are not only our best hope," Marissa went on to explain, "but you are our only hope."

"There you go Alex," Samantha chimed in. "You won by default."

"But I still won," Alex jested back, "and that's all that matters."

However, Alex did understand that although Neurono-Tek was mostly a neuroscience institution, it was equipped with the latest scientific and medical equipment. Plus, as the CEO and founder of the company, he was a world-renowned scientist. With a Ph.D. in both neuroscience and bioengineering, he had already discovered or created treatments for many of the most complicated neurological diseases. Other than his business partner Dr. Samantha Mancini, there was no one else as qualified to tackle such a difficult task.

Marissa continued, "Unfortunately, as you know, most of our greatest research hospitals are going bankrupt and are unable to treat even the most menial of medical or surgical conditions."

"See," Samantha interrupted, "I told you this is what would happen if the government became the country's only healthcare provider. Failure was inevitable!"

Always looking at the big picture, Alex cautioned, "But you do remember what got our country into the mess we are in right now?"

"Fat cat bureaucrats and a bloated IRS system," Samantha quipped.

"No," Alex rebutted. "Rising healthcare costs, decreased patient benefits, and private insurance companies that became too greedy."

"But look where most of the country is now. We went from bad to worse."

"And since Neurono-Tek is one of the only privately run hospitals and research centers left," Marissa interjected, "the world is relying on you."

Unfortunately, Alex knew she spoke the truth. He had watched the country's medical system rapidly decline and witnessed the substandard care most Americans had to endure. What was once advertised by the government as the solution to all healthcare problems became the greatest healthcare problem ever created.

Neurono-Tek, unlike other hospitals, was a fee-for-service institution. Unbound by oppressive governmental regulations, it thus flourished in the free market, maintaining the highest standards in medical care.

"How long has our Turkish guest been dead?" Samantha asked.

"Oh, no," Marissa corrected. "He's not exactly dead. While still in Turkey, I cryopreserved the entire body just before nature took its course. Though technically still living, he only has about a week before the body will start to decompose, making further analysis impossible."

Marissa looked over Alex's shoulder and noticed the driver of the medical transport team who brought her here walking out of the elevator.

"Excuse me," she interrupted. "It seems like my driver has gotten himself lost. I think—"

Just as Marissa began to stand, a deafening explosion

rocked the building and it began to shake with such vigor it seemed like the entire research facility was going to collapse.

Cement slabs from the ceiling crumbled down to the floor. Accompanying the debris, two of the huge chandeliers crashed down, instantly killing a few people in the lobby. The entire area became complete pandemonium. People were screaming, injured were pleading for help, and others just ran around in a frenzy, looking for an exit amidst the growing dust cloud.

Marissa was knocked to the ground and staggered to regain her footing. Still dazed, she did not notice the chandelier hanging precariously overhead. As a few aftershocks began to strike the building, the beautiful lighting fixture fell.

Almost out of pure instinct Alex jumped from his seat, grabbed both Marissa and Samantha and secured them under a long granite-top table, saving them both.

As some of the dust began to clear, the true damage from the explosion became apparent. What was once a beautiful lobby was now in complete ruin. Moans of agony pierced their ears and pulled at their hearts.

Alex wanted answers immediately. Focusing on the videre contact lens in his right eye, he brought up a schematic of the entire Neurono-Tek complex of buildings. No structure other than this one was affected, and it appeared that the explosion came directly from the Level Five Biohazard room containing the body. All the research facilities were destroyed in the basement. However, the subbasement containing the morgue and a bunker-like research facility were still preserved.

By focusing on different parts of his specialized contact lens, Alex immediately activated Neurono-Tek's security system and alerted the police, fire station, and governor's office of the apparent terrorist attack. He also alerted the security detail to detain Marissa and her driver for further questioning.

"Speaking of the driver," Alex said aloud.

Amidst the dust cloud, Alex noticed the man fleeing through the main entrance. Alex leapt to his feet in quick pursuit. Throwing down his sports jacket and removing his tie, he bolted towards the potential perpetrator.

CHAPTER 3

IT WAS A DAY LATER AND YAKAKOY'S buildings were still smoldering. Fresh tank tracts could be seen littering the dirt streets. Bullet riddled or burned bodies lay unburied throughout the town. The only signs of life now were the scavenging birds making a meal out of the carnage. Humanity had forsaken the town.

Despite all the bloodshed, one man had the courage to reenter Yakakoy. He was not a native of the town nor did he even possess a Turkish citizenship.

The man appeared unassuming and humble in nature. He was thin but not too skinny. Age had marked his fair-skinned face with wrinkles and matching age spots. His full head of gray hair was parted to the right side. Despite early signs of arthritis, the man walked with a zip in his step and seemed not to be slowed by his malady.

The man's name was Jonathan Maloney.

He kept a worn old leather-bound Bible to his side as he looked solemnly upon the corpses along the street. One body he found particularly interesting. It was a heavyset man who apparently died from multiple gunshots to the chest. He also looked badly sunburned, but as it had been cloudy for days, sun obviously was not the culprit.

Jonathan knelt down and examined the man. While doing so, he opened the Bible and leafed through the pages. *What does this all mean?*

Reaching into his back pocket, he pulled out a quarter-size disc and placed it next to the dead man's body. Immediately, a forty-letter by forty-letter grid of Hebrew letters holographically appeared.

After a few seconds of analysis, he used his right pointer finger to circle a few letters. On doing so, the grid immediately changed into a different configuration of letters. Over and over he did the same thing as he circled the same Hebrew letters each time.

Jonathan immediately took the disk and placed it in his back pocket. He had found what he was searching for. His job here in the town was complete. After saying a small prayer, he turned and briskly walked down the same road from which he entered.

The answer found in those Hebrew letters which brought him here would now guide him to a new destination. It was not a place this time but a particular person.

Alex Pella.

CHAPTER 4

HOW COULD I'VE LET MY GUARD DOWN! Alex lamented to himself. *I shouldn't have assumed the NIH transport vehicle and team weren't a possible security risk!*

Alex hurtled a long black couch in the lobby as if he were an Olympic athlete. Despite wearing designer dress shoes, he remained limber on his feet and able to scramble through the piles of debris with ease. The culprit had just exited out the main entrance, and he, too, ran like a track star.

The security guards at the entrance thought the man was just fleeing for his life and never made the connection between him and the attack. And to be truthful, Alex was not a hundred percent sure of the man's culpability. But his instincts told him otherwise, and his gut rarely led him astray.

While Alex raced out the exit, Samantha and Marissa tended to the injured. The emergency health services from the hospital had been activated and a few brave medical professionals trickled into the lobby despite the possible danger.

Marissa grabbed a bag from one of the EMS workers and tended to a woman with a crushed leg. The woman had tried

24

to crawl to safety, but the exhaustion and pain hindered further movement. She had a compound fracture in her tibia, which was causing excessive bleeding from her lower leg.

Marissa was well versed in emergency medical care. As a medical field operative for the NIH, she had come into contact with exotic illnesses, traumatic injuries, and other acute care circumstances. She usually carried a similar-type EMS pack on her during fieldwork and knew its contents well.

Marissa grabbed a narcotic-filled syringe and injected it into the woman's thigh. She needed the pain controlled before any other procedures could be performed.

The woman was losing blood fast. The fractured tibia protruded from her lower leg, causing life-threatening bleeding. Marissa tightly grabbed the woman's ankle and knee. With a quick pull she snapped her leg back into place, repositioning the tibia under the skin. Though the bleeding did not stop, it significantly diminished.

Marissa next grabbed a silver pen-like object from the bag and ran it down the woman's open wound. A red light glowed from its tip and wherever it came into contact with the skin the bleeding stopped. After the leg had been cauterized, the woman immediately fell asleep. Whether it was the narcotic, blood loss, or pure exhaustion, she needed the rest.

A Ph.D. and not an MD by training, Samantha did her part during the crisis. Because of all the commotion, dust and noise, it was difficult to generate any type of organization. She used her shrill-like voice to cut through the turmoil and commandeer the scene. It was as if her mouth were a bullhorn as she quickly organized all the medical staff entering the lobby.

"Prioritize!" Samantha yelled. "Tend to the sickest first. If they don't have a pulse, they don't need treatment."

She grabbed a white towel from one of the physicians and waved it in the air. "Place any sort of linen over the heads of the deceased so that we don't keep on checking them. Be efficient people!"

What was once a chaotic mess turned into an efficient and coordinated effort. Samantha gave each new person who entered a specific task and no matter who it was, they did it without argument.

Marissa went to the aid of another victim. He seemed to have suffered a head injury from falling debris and now appeared unconscious. His pulse was strong and his pupils were reactive to light.

Hopefully only a mild concussion.

She took out a two-inch-square object from the bag. It was flat with a clear center and a black strip around the edges. Placing it atop the man's head, she maneuvered the object over his hair, scanning the entire area. Through its transparent part Marissa could see a clear picture of the brain and its anatomy as if there were no skull in between.

No bleeding. He'll do fine.

Before Marissa could examine another victim, two burley-looking guards yanked her up by the arms. Each was dressed in the standard blue Neurono-Tek uniform and bore a striking resemblance to a really aggravated bulldog.

"What are you two Neanderthals doing?" Marissa yelled. "Unhand me!"

She tried to fight their grip, but to her dismay both men's strength matched their ugliness.

"You're coming with us!" one of the guards grunted. "House arrest."

The other man chimed in, "I think it's best you keep your mouth shut until we get things sorted out around here."

Luckily for the victims, more physicians and nurses flooded into the lobby, making her presence less urgent.

"What authority gives you the right… ," she attempted to

say.

"Dr. Alex Pella," one guard snipped, "and that's as good as the governor himself."

The guard did not overestimate Alex or his company's clout. As Neurono-Tek was Pennsylvania's most lucrative company and second only to The New Reality in the country's most successful businesses, the governor had Alex's back on most issues.

"Alex Pella!" she muttered. "I think I'll need to have a little word with him."

She looked over to the lobby's entrance, but Alex must have exited too quickly for her to notice.

●●●

Alex saw the man running ahead. His white scrubs with red NIH letters embroidered on the back made him conspicuous even through the growing chaos outside the main research building. Sirens blared as fire trucks, ambulances, police cars and a few military vehicles from the National Guard barreled through the streets.

Neurono-Tek had grown from a single building with an adjacent hospital into a modern medical mecca. Forty buildings in all, it was an architectural masterpiece laid down into a square-like grid.

Sneakers! Alex thought while still running full speed in his designer shoes. What I would give for a pair of sneakers!

The driver ran full speed in his pair of white running shoes. A police vehicle accidentally pulled in front of him, and he hurtled it without stumbling. Alex did the same and tried to pump his arms harder to gain ground. With a head start, the driver had a fifty-foot cushion.

Alex looked into his videre contact lens, and a satellite view of Neurono-Tek instantly appeared. He could see himself and the presumed terrorist running down the longest street in the complex, heading towards the hospital. There were a few buildings to each of their sides separated by dead-end alleys. The road split in front of the hospital.

Alex could see in his contacts a few fire engines driving in from the right.

If he goes right, they'll be blocking his way. If he makes a left, he will be able to take the road leading out of Neurono-Tek and escape into the forest.

Alex had hoped the police would blockade all the streets around Neurono-Tek, but with most vehicles already at the main research building and others too far off, he knew it was still too premature.

Plus, the presumed terrorist could have a getaway car, an aero-bike, or other vehicle waiting, Alex further contemplated. He did not see anything from the satellite but knew if this man were cunning enough to infiltrate the NIH and get through his security, anything was possible.

The driver looked back and gave Alex a sneer. Pride filled the man's face, and he seemed to lack any remorse for his apparent actions.

My gut was right!

Alex took longer strides and tried to make himself as aerodynamic as possible in order to gain speed. It worked. The distance between the two narrowed to less than thirty feet by the time the man reached the hospital.

Unfortunately, the blaring sirens from the fire engines to the right gave away their presence and the man quickly headed left. Alex anticipated this move and had darted down a dead-end alley. He noted that the gates at the end of it had been removed, providing a more direct path to his adversary.

Alex flew down the tight alley full of delivery vehicles and a few heaping dumpsters. The terrorist continued fleeing, oblivious to Alex's subversive maneuver.

A black aero-bike suddenly levitated out of the woods, awaiting the man's arrival. It looked like a motorcycle but instead of wheels, it boasted a flat bottom with cylindrical gravity dampeners along the sides.

Alex saw the bike and knew if the man became air bound, capture would be impossible.

He had it all planned out, Alex thought. But for what purpose?

Alex emerged from the alley like a ball shot out of a cannon. The terrorist was shocked to see his foe now an arm's length away, but he still smiled with contempt.

The aero-bike turned and faced away from them both. It then began to levitate backwards towards them. The terrorist obviously hoped to leap onto his bike like a bandit to a horse in an old western movie.

Alex would not let that happen.

Alex jumped forward and grabbed the man's legs as if he were a defensive tackle stopping a running back from entering the end zone. The terrorist fell forward, smashing his face upon the aero-bike's metal frame.

Blood poured from his mouth and oozed from his nose.

"You are not as smart as you think," the man turned and blubbered. "We will win. Oh, yes. The time has come for a great change."

The terrorist slipped a pill out of his back pocket and placed it under his tongue before Alex had a chance to stop him. Suddenly, his whole body became ashen in color and his veins began to pop out of his neck. After a quick jerk of the torso, the man's eyes rolled back and his body went limp.

Alex knew what he had taken: an autolysis pill. It was now the choice of all spies worldwide. The pill caused almost instantaneous death and eradicated all genetic evidence of the person who ingested it. By triggering the immediate release of calcium in all cells throughout the body, it triggered the liberation of toxic enzymes stored in special cellular vacuoles. Once released, the enzymes caused the cells to digest themselves and their DNA. All that is left after a minute is a crumbled mass of necrotic flesh clinging to a skeleton. No DNA signature or other forms of identification remain. *Perfect for hiding all evidence.*

Alex ripped off the man's shirt.

There has to be some identification here! A tattoo or maybe even a scar.

There was nothing. No mole, sign of surgery, or even a blemish could be seen. The man had no imperfection.

Time was running out. The terrorist's skin began to turn even grayer and flake away while all his hair fell to his side like a shedding dog. All evidence quickly faded away. An expeditious inspection of his legs also failed to reveal any conspicuous markings.

Just as the skin began to turn black, Alex noticed a small tattoo on the back of the man's head. Originally concealed by hair, it now became evident.

The tattoo clearly portrayed the outline of a falcon with its head turned to the left and holding a bundle of sticks with its talons. Alex blinked and the evidence disintegrated.

The symbol was unmistakable—one that Alex would soon never forget.

CHAPTER 5

THE AIR TINGLED WITH GREAT ANTICIPATION, and the stars shimmered above in the clear night sky. The only light illuminating the vast open arena emanated from an enormous ring of fire set above a barely visible marble platform.

The crowd stood in the darkness. Their excitement was palpable as they all waited for the culmination of the day's ceremony. The anticipation was overwhelming. A few even fainted as the expectation proved too much for them to handle.

No one spoke.

Most tried not to hyperventilate.

Two spotlights from the bottom of the stage suddenly came to life and revealed two long, yellow banners hanging on both sides of the emblazoned ring. Each bore the symbol of why they all assembled there that night.

The *falcon*.

It was a beautiful golden bird with its head turned to the left as if looking towards something greater than itself. The falcon's wings were held high at its side while its feathered talons tightly held a bundle of sticks underneath.

The crowd erupted immediately with joy as the roar of their adulation joined as one deafening sound . It was as if the individual did not exist and only the collective could be heard. No voice stood out regardless of how long or hard they cheered.

All were surrounded in a mystique of community that appealed to both their spiritual and visual senses.

These cheers and levity had enveloped the usually quiet desert city of Tabas, Iran all week. Once a year during the first full week in July, the government staged this enormous rally.

They spared no expense. Despite the marked decline in the economy, all attending had free accommodations along with full access to the weeklong festivities.

Aimed at glorifying the government, the rally and its activities had the same underlying message: Government can conquer all. All along the streets of Tabas, accompanying the falcon's emblems, quotes such as "Pray not to God but to the Malik", "We are all Children of the Malik", and "Malik is Hope" hung prominently.

The rally made all those attending feel as if they were a part of something momentous—something more significant than even themselves or their meager lives. It was as if their presence in this place made them even greater.

Amidst the endless cheers, Xenon arch spotlights began to shine straight up into the air, parallel to one another. In succession, beginning behind the stage, the spotlights ignited until finally, an entire oval-shaped cathedral of light encircled the arena.

To amplify the awe-inspiring site, docking planes hovering in the stratosphere amplified the light and reflected it in parallel lines to encircle all of Tabas. People hundreds of miles away could view the event. Even those who could not partake in the festivities felt as if they were there just by gazing at this magnificent spectacle.

A hush befell the crowd at the arena. The magnificence of the site made further cheering at the moment seem redundant. Goosebumps chilled their skin.

A deep voice echoed through the arena and brought the people out of their trance.

"Attention. The Malik is here!"

From one end of the arena a single man entered. Looking straight ahead towards the circle of flame and its accompanying banners, he sauntered straight towards the stage.

A band began to play. Each stroked a traditional Arab string instrument. Whether it was the *oud*, *rabab* or the *qitara* they played in perfect harmony. In a high-pitched tone a woman accompanied the music by singing an ancient love song known as a *ghazal* meant for the Malik.

A new round of cheers began to drown out the music. Women cried, men shouted. It was as if their favorite football team had just scored the winning touchdown in the last seconds of the game.

The Malik's name was Ari Lesmana, and he savored every second of this adulation. He donned a traditional Arab black robe known as a *bisht* with a golden embroidered collar running down the chest. The symbol of his power, the golden falcon adorned each of the sleeves. Atop his head he boasted a red scarf known as a *ghutra* that covered his forehead to the back of his neck. A golden band called an *igal* secured the *ghutra* along his forehead.

Ninety-thousand men wearing the same traditional outfit stood before him. Instead of the red scarves, they each donned a white one with a black band.

Upon reaching them, Ari stopped and began to look authoritatively at all in attendance. Above the highest level of seating, many huge three-dimensional screens encircled the area. Each displayed Ari from a view looking up at him. If the fifty-foot screens did not make him appear larger than life, the angle in which he was captured definitely completed the look.

Ari turned his gaze to the men in front of him and shouted, "One People! One Blood! One Nation!"

The ninety thousand immediately positioned themselves into perfectly aligned rows with a ten-foot pathway down the center so that Ari could walk unhindered to the platform.

The crowd once again hushed as Ari strutted through the mass of men as if he were Moses leading his people through the Red Sea.

As he passed, the person standing along the aisle would hold up a white flag with the golden falcon emblazoned on each of its sides. The others behind him would turn and follow Ari with their bodies while standing in place. As he passed, the crowd raised their hands above their heads to make an *O* as a sign of reverence and respect to their leader.

The *O* represented the sun. Ari was their sun and the man who would bring light back into their lives and their country.

Besides the Malik, his followers also referred to him as the Red Leviathan. The scarf that covered his head was red, while his larger than life persona made him a leviathan.

Ari reached the platform and climbed a small set of stairs until he arrived at the top. He walked behind a golden podium under the flaming circle and looked out into the crowd. Again, the screens above the arena showed his image as if all were looking up to him like the great messiah.

"We have all suffered," he said as his voice bellowed throughout the arena and broadcast across the entire United Arab Alliance (UAA).

A native of Indonesia, Ari was a thin man in his early fifties. He was considered handsome by his female swooners and debonair by his male followers. His dark eyebrows made his face look stern while his ears, which pointed outward, gave him a playful appearance. Because of his former tobacco addiction, faint lines ran down the sides of his face, and his puckered lips looked as if they anxiously awaited the next cigarette.

"We have been raped by the West!"

The crowd went crazy. Many yelled out *Malik* while others clapped so enthusiastically it appeared they were having a seizure.

"They have taken our oil and thrown us aside like a broken-down engine!"

Again he was inundated with accolades.

He pointed to the people. "Now is the time for change. Now is the time to hope for a better future for you and your families!"

The words resonated well among the crowd. Many were hit by especially hard economic times. With their country's oil reserves dwindling and unemployment or underemployment rising, they looked for someone, a savior, to bring them back to prosperity.

Ari despised Western society and found it both a convenient and well-deserved scapegoat for their problems. Capitalism and free markets sickened him. He viewed it as the most oppressive economic system ever implemented. Though it created great wealth, capitalism only made a small percentage rich while practically enslaving the rest, forcing them to work for a mere pittance .

He believed that only a powerfully managed government could provide a true utopia on earth whereby inequality would be eradicated. And there was no room for God in his government-run utopia. Praying to an unseen and presumed omnipotent being seemed to him as a childish and nearsighted endeavor meant only for the weak.

"First the West brought you despair. Now they bring you *The Disease*!"

The crowd hissed and booed. Others shouted anti-Western

sentiments.

"You all know of Tustegee!" he said with a sinister snicker.

There was no way to forget as he made a point to mention it each time he spoke publically.

Tustegee was the greatest blemish in the history of American medicine. Three hundred ninety-nine black sharecroppers from Alabama enrolled in the study. Each had previously contracted syphilis but instead of being treated by the Public Health Service, they were instead studied to obverse the natural history of the disease. Mostly a forgotten story, Ari dug up this skeleton in American history and acted as if it had just occurred yesterday.

The crowd all shouted derogatory statements towards the West while others just put their hands above their heads in the shape of an *O*.

"I am personally going to see to it that the United Arab Alliance shall not succumb to *The Disease* like Turkey, Greece, and other Western countries." He continued to boast loudly, "I will personally ensure that there will be food on everyone's table. That every able-bodied person has a job. And that the Arab nations once again rise to power!"

The crowd looked upon Ari as their savior and he upon them as his subjects. With a promise for change and a better future, Ari rose to power after successfully overthrowing their former leader. However, with no real political experience or leadership skills, he offered only good looks and empty promises.

He shook his head mockingly. "The League of Arab States has also forsaken you!"

Consecrated after World War II, The League of Arab States was designed as a loose association of Arab countries to promote common goals. It had no real authoritative powers, like the United Nations, and was frequently blamed for the ongoing misfortunes of its former members.

"Do not forget how they appeased the West by giving them our oil. They let them take it from us as easily as a baby sucks milk from his mother's breast!"

"It is out of these failures," he boasted, "that the United Arab Alliance was formed. One Government. One People. One Purpose!"

The slogans resounded well with the people. It restored memories of former greatness when they were the world's leading oil suppliers and economically rich. It also made them feel as if they were united, superior, and meant for greatness under the Malik's guidance.

Despite the rhetoric, the United Arab Alliance successfully joined the people under one central government. Iran, Iraq, Syria, Jordan, Yemen, Oman, Libya, Afghanistan, Egypt, Saudi Arabia, and the United Arab Emirates had all given up their autonomy and had become states within the UAA. Unlike The League of Arab States, it did have binding power and the ability to mandate control over its entire population.

"I need all of your help to restore our people! You must give of yourselves if we as a nation are to grow."

Another slogan followed, "Government First! Success to Follow!"

The crowd cheered and the band began to play. Ari soaked in all the accolades. Though providing only promises during his first four years as their Malik, he acted as if he had saved his country from the brink of despair and was single-handedly responsible for steering them back to a path of economic success.

The speech went on for another hour. Filled with more rhetoric, anti-Western jargon, and accusations, it provided the people with what they wanted to hear and gave them a convenient scapegoat during their continued economic hardships. Devoid of any real substance, the speech lacked any meaningful plan for their country's future. Oblivious to his real motives, all those in attendance continued to greet Ari as their messiah.

CHAPTER 6

"SO YOU LET THEM BRING us another body? Samantha screeched. "Did you happen to forget what happened here last week, or do you need another chandelier to almost kill us all before it jogs a memory?"

"Hey," Alex joked, "I told them at the NIH they can send ten more bodies as long as Marissa Ambrosia accompanies them. Plus, I'm good at dodging chandeliers."

Samantha scoffed as she threw a pillow in Alex's direction. "Dodge this!"

Though they laughed today, the last week had been an extremely stressful one. Ten people had died in the terrorist attack while another seventy were injured. Over half of the casualties were still in their hospital with a few remaining in critical care.

Plus, the attack had left their Level Five Biohazard rooms completely destroyed. The only place that could accommodate the body now was a subbasement research facility under where the attack had taken place. Fortified like a bunker, it had been designed for research even in the most inauspicious circumstances.

Alex and Samantha relaxed in the plush armchairs in Alex's office. After a week of total chaos, both leaned back and enjoyed the momentary silence. Too exhausted to continue with their banter, they each sat and tried to enjoy a quick nap.

The room was conducive to rest. With plush chairs and couches, soft music, and comfortable colors, it soothed all that entered. Once decorated with a more masculine flair, it now boasted potted plants and gentle pictures of the sky hanging on the walls.

The office also represented the change in Alex. No longer a man plagued by inner turmoil, he was at peace with himself, and his attitude toward this office and work personified this transition. He had only recently overcome the realization that he had been adopted and that he, somehow, was genetically unique. His parents had wished to spare him the truth and only recently informed him about the adoption. However, to his even greater dismay, they couldn't provide him with any other information about his genetics other than that he was unique. *But what did that mean?*

A voice, though pleasant, awoke both from their fledgling naps. "Dr. Pella, Dr. Marissa Ambrosia is here to see you."

Before Alex had a chance to respond, the door to his office dematerialized.

Marissa entered first. She was dressed in jeans and a flattering tight white shirt that accentuated her long torso and feminine curves.

One of the Neanderthal-like security guards that had apprehended her during the terrorist attack accompanied her into the room. With a stern look on his face, he bluntly stated, "Dr. Ambrosia's credentials check out and she's free of contraband."

He then grabbed the tip of his blue hat and left without

another word. The door materialized behind him upon his exit.

Alex quickly stood and offered Marissa a seat. Though not regretful for ordering her apprehension last week, he still wanted to be as accommodating now as possible.

She, too, held no grudge and was pleased to see that new security measures had been implemented.

"Don't let his looks or gruff nature fool you," Alex stated, referring to the security guard. "Phil's the absolute best. Not much for words, though."

Alex straightened out his sports jacket as he and Marissa took their respective seats. "I'm sorry about your two colleagues," he went on to say. "Further casualties of *The Disease*."

Alex referred to the two scientists that accompanied her when she delivered the body last week. Both were in the research room when it exploded and had been killed instantly.

"It's really sad," Marissa lamented. "Both Kathy and Sharon had recently been forced into retirement. Due to cutbacks at the NIH, they were let go from the agency but decided to continue assisting me on my fieldwork anyway and without pay."

She looked down with regret. "They would have done anything to find the cure." After regaining her composure, she turned abruptly to Alex. "What happened to the S.O.B. who did this?"

The police had suppressed the true nature of the attack as they progressed with a full investigation. To avoid igniting further panic amidst the growing angst of *The Disease,* the public was told only that there was an explosion at Neurono-Tek due to faulty wiring.

Alex did not mind taking the blame for the terrorist attack if it prevented public pandemonium, but he certainly hoped it would not compromise Neurono-Tek's reputation.

"The bastard tried to get away but killed himself before I

could apprehend him," Alex stated.

"Did he leave any evidence?" Marissa asked.

"He took an autolysis pill," Alex responded. "Wiped out all evidence. Forensics could do nothing with the body."

"Tell her about the tattoo," Samantha interrupted.

"I didn't forget," Alex said as he rolled his eyes towards his colleague. "There was a small tattoo of a falcon on the man's scalp just before the skin degraded. It—"

"The United Arab Alliance," Marissa blurted, instantly recognizing its significance.

Reminiscent of more promising times, the symbol had originally been used by Saladin when his army defeated the Crusaders and drove them out of Jerusalem. The bundle of sticks the bird held was a modern twist. It represented the individual states of the UAA and showed that when they stood together, they could not be broken.

"I've seen their men," Marissa went on to say, "at some of the mass graves in Turkey. I also spotted them in Crete and a few other Greek islands. Do the police have any other leads?"

"If they do," he answered, "they certainly haven't told me." Alex looked at both of them seriously. "And what still doesn't make sense to me is why the terrorist just didn't put a delay on the explosives or escape out of the loading dock. This may sound strange, but it almost seemed like he wanted to be caught."

Samantha threw her hands up in the air. "You're trying to make sense out of a man who knowingly just killed himself and a bunch of other people," she scoffed. "Maybe his mother didn't hug him or something. It doesn't matter anyway. He was nuts… really, all those damn terrorists are all nuts."

Despite Samantha's cajoling, Alex knew he was on to something. Destroying the body Marissa had brought produced nothing. More corpses mounted from *The Disease* by the minute. Plus, the terrorist had ample opportunities to escape. The only thing that appeared accidental was the fact Alex identified the tattoo. It must have been an oversight on the terrorist's part.

"Well, he's safely tucked away in our morgue," Samantha said, "and I seriously doubt he'll be giving us any more trouble."

"How'd this mole infiltrate the NIH anyway?" Alex asked.

Marissa shook her head, as she knew the truth about the NIH. Once a medical juggernaut, it was now a shell of its former self. Budget cuts, poor funding, and mediocre government support had almost made the organization defunct.

"We went broke," Marissa admitted. "In fact, the whole medical system went broke. We are just the tip of the iceberg. Because adequate background screens could no longer be afforded, the man just simply slipped through the cracks."

"See," Samantha screeched as if she had personally warned everyone herself. "That's what happens when you vote jackasses into government."

There was no argument from Alex or Marissa.

The European Union, China, and India, among others, had all fallen into the same predicament. Fiscal responsibility was something found only in older textbooks and definitely not practiced in the year 2081.

Samantha tried to bring some levity to the situation. "So, tell us what the NIH knows about all those dead people you've been collecting."

Marissa pulled out a small metallic tablet from her right pocket and placed it onto an end table situated between the three of them.

"Let me run down the natural history of the condition first," she said.

A holographic image of a muscle came into view. It was a thinly-sliced section of the tissue showing its different pink bundles surrounded by bands of white connective tissue.

Marissa touched one of the bundles and it grew in size. "You see this muscle here?" she pointed. "Look how distorted it appears."

What should have been a clear pink circle with strands of white tissue surrounding it looked more like a deflated beach ball.

She then touched it again and an oval, blue organelle in the muscle expanded in size. It had what looked like haphazard steps along with black spots inside of it.

"Is that supposed to be a mitochondria?" Samantha asked.

"It is the mitochondria," Marissa answered. "You see how disfigured it has become. We believe that the primary target for *The Disease* is within this organelle."

"Have you found any source?" Alex asked. "A virus, bacteria, or prion? Anything?"

"Nothing. All we know is that the condition begins with general malaise and weakness and that the muscle is the first to be affected."

"Sounds like the flu," Samantha chimed in.

"Yeah," Alex commented, "except the flu doesn't kill everyone it comes in contact with."

The holographic picture changed into a figure of the small intestine. Wrapped in coils, it looked like a long strand of red sausage.

"Next affected is the gut," Marissa said. "Through malabsorption, some affected people literally begin to starve to death while others begin to bloat and retain fluid."

She then placed her hand on the figure and two microscopic pictures appeared. The pink-colored cells on the left had flowing undulations at their top while the ones on the right were rectangular and half the size of its counterpart.

"Look here at what happens to the gut cells," she said,

pointing to the figure on the right while explaining what it meant.

Marissa then went on to describe the other manifestations of *The Disease*. From the gut the condition can spread to the liver and kidneys in a characteristic fashion. Once the body was about to shut down, she showed how the mutated mitochondria caused the skin to turn red in a failed attempt to replenish itself. The brain was last to be affected, with confusion, seizures, and ultimately death.

Holographic micropathology slides of the affected organ accompanied each description. Lacking, however, was any true explanation of the cause. Despite months of research, little tangible knowledge had been gained. Alex knew the information Marissa presented could have easily been determined at Neurono-Tek in about a day's time.

The door dematerialized, and behind it a familiar face again came into view: Phil, the security guard. He stood there frozen in place, showing his characteristic level of exuberance. Waiting permission to talk, he stared at Alex in full attention.

"Yes, Phil?" Alex asked.

Usually the responsibility of his secretary, Phil had made it his personal duty to oversee Alex's personal schedule. As head of security, he took his job seriously and felt that if any harm came to Alex, he would be personally liable.

"Dr. Pella, sir. Your 8:00 A.M. appointment has arrived."

Alex had lost track of time but immediately remembered who he was meeting. Last week his office received a call just after the terrorist attack. The man claimed to have vital information regarding *The Disease* that no one else could provide.

Most of the unsolicited communications received by Neurono-Tek recently had been from pranksters or mentally deranged people. Some claimed the apocalypse was upon them, while others did their best to voice their theories about *The*

Disease. Space aliens, increased cosmic rays, ozone toxicity, and flesh-eating bacteria from Mars were a few of the gems fielded by the PR department.

Sparing any details, Phil simply stated, "He checks out—"

Phil exited and an unassuming man entered the office. With a smile on his face and dressed rather casually in jeans and a simple red-collared short-sleeve shirt, he greeted them all with a, "Good day."

Usually not responsive to unsolicited communications, the staff at Neurono-Tek felt it necessary to grant this man dedicated time with Dr. Alex Pella. Though all he brought with him was the promise of valuable information, his sincerity and simple charm did convince Alex's secretary that his intentions were completely genuine.

After some minor pleasantries, the man took Alex by the hand and said, "Dr. Pella, I would like to introduce myself. My name is Jonathan Maloney and I've traveled a long way just to meet you."

"Sir," Alex responded, "the pleasure is mine."

"I am not a kook, nor a run-of-the-mill psychopath," Jonathan went on to say with a pleasant yet slightly rushed cadence, "but I have some information to tell that you may find hard to believe."

Looking at the sincerity on the man's face, Alex promptly said, "Have a seat and tell me what you've got."

CHAPTER 7

THE RALLY IN TABAS WAS LONG OVER and the immense clean-up job was practically finished. The desert city had finally returned to its usual state of solitude and now tended to its usual business.

After a massive earthquake in 2073, the entire city was rebuilt with a palace erected at its center. Other Arab leaders had vacationed here, but when Ari came to power he took control of the entire city and estate for himself.

He then transformed Tabas into the capital of the UAA and vastly expanded the estate to meet his own personal specifications.

The motive for moving the capital to Tabas was a direct snub at the West. In 1980 the United States had attempted to rescue 52 hostages held at their embassy in Tehran. The mission was a disaster from its inception. The operation failed miserably and needed to be aborted just outside of Tabas, making the city the focal point for the new UAA.

Amidst the sprawling palace in this desert city was a man-made oasis that would rival the Hanging Gardens of Babylon.

Beautiful fountains situated among palm trees and numerous flowering plants made it a heaven on earth.

A holographic image of an unnaturally thin and balding elderly gentleman appeared in the shade underneath one of the palm trees. The holographic image looked red and grainy to ensure both its secrecy and privacy.

"Ari," the man in the holograph said with a raspy voice, "I am very pleased at what you have accomplished with the UAA. You have single-handedly brought your people out of despair and escorted them into a new future."

Although not truly improving the lives of anyone under him, Ari did believe that without his leadership the country would have fallen into a morass of chaos. "Yes," he boasted, "the UAA has come a long way since my inauguration four years ago."

The man in the holograph was Albert Rosenberg, CEO of The New Reality. A company originally known for its virtual reality product line, The New Reality had branched out into different economic endeavors with high-end banking being its most lucrative enterprise. In fact, it was the major lender of money throughout the world, and as a result, every country owed a substantial debt to them.

These debts reached such magnitude that most honest economists believed they could never be paid off. However, the countries across the globe avoided this obvious conclusion and continued borrowing money from them with reckless abandon.

Unfortunately, The New Reality was no charity.

"You are vital to the stability of the area," Albert went on to say. "Without a strong UAA the Middle East would crumble, leaving the entire area in economic chaos."

Albert gave out a large cough and a young attendant came to his side to wipe his mouth. Though the image was grainy, Albert appeared ill. Sunken eyes, wrinkled skin, and multiple blemishes only added to his cadaver-like appearance.

"It would be like dominoes," he said. "If you were to fall, then so would the world. We must keep you strong and see to it that the UAA prospers."

"It will," Ari said with a swagger. "There has been a rebirth in this country. No longer do people cling to their guns or religion for a false sense of support. The change they need has come. Now they are embracing the government instead of themselves or their simple family ties for a better tomorrow."

"And that is why I will continue to pledge my economic support to you and your country. Remember to be true to yourself and follow your beliefs. Compromise is not an option."

"Nor is it something I ever intend to do," Ari said as the holograph vanished.

"Do not cater to him!" a strong female voice bellowed in the most demeaning fashion from behind. "Do not forget who you are," she chastised.

Ari turned, and the fury in her eyes immediately immobilized him. It was as if she were Medusa and had turned him to stone. He felt frozen in his shoes, unable to answer.

The woman was tall and looked as if she were chiseled from black marble. Though thin in figure, she had strong, sharp features that accentuated her underlying muscular tone. Long black hair, accusing eyebrows, and a prominent forehead completed her look. Wearing red lipstick and a long red dress to match, she appeared like a Greek goddess straight from Hades.

Ari tried not to swallow his manhood, responding to her in the most masculine tone he could muster.

"Woman, hold your tongue. You know as well as I, we can't survive without his monetary support."

"But he is from the West! Mark my words Ari: He plays you like a fool!"

Mistrustful of everyone, Ari Lesmana's wife made no

qualms about making her feelings known. Skepticism, deceit, and ruthlessness were her mantra, and she wanted no person to interfere with their rise to greater power.

Ari finally let out a smile and took his wife's hand. Gently caressing it he said, "Don't you see? Albert recognizes what I—"

He paused. "No, what we are doing here. He, apart from all the other Westerners, recognizes what we are attempting to achieve here."

Ari led his wife to a gazebo next to one of the area's beautiful fountains. While sitting there, he pulled out a book from underneath his *bisht* and held it against his heart.

Written by his favorite philosopher, Freidrich Nietzsche, the book provided insight into the author's existentialist outlook on life and morality. Instead of any religious text, Ari turned to the man's writing for personal inspiration.

"Remember what Nietzsche has taught us," he preached. "We define our own existence. Without support from Albert we would not have the funding needed to define our government. And without government, we are nothing."

"I still do not trust him!" his wife blurted.

Her name was Masika, which meant "born during a monsoon". Delivered during an extremely violent storm that killed most of her village including her mother, she had been named by her father. However, this was much more than simply a name as it exemplified her very essence. Strong, powerful, and with the wrath of a Level Five hurricane, she was a formidable force few dared cross.

When she met Ari in college, she found a soul mate that shared her same existentialist views and anti-Western sentiment. Fueled by drugs and cigarettes, they would stay up late at night with their friends pontificating on how the world would be better if they ran it.

She lost touch with some of these friends, but the most

radical ones had been placed into key positions within the UAA to ensure that Ari's fascist wishes were precisely followed.

Ari stood and looked out upon the beautiful garden. He recanted the words of *Daybreak* through his mind and reveled in their brilliance. "I am Nietzsche's personification of the Übermensch," he said, speaking as if the author had written the book solely about him.

He looked at Masika to reiterate, "I am the man who has risen above the rest. I am the chosen one, and Albert can clearly see that."

Masika was proud to see the fire in her husband's eyes. Her blood ran hot and her skin became alive with goose bumps. Nostrils flared and breathing heavily, she stated through clenched teeth, "You are the Malik!"

Just then a group of 24 staff members approached the gazebo. They were Masika's personal attendants. Each greeted Ari with a bow and placed their hands above their heads in the shape of an *O*.

Ari acknowledged them with a quick nod.

Masika looked down upon them and thought of these creatures not as attendants but servants. Ari, too, saw the UAA citizens as subjects to be used for the greater good. He and his wife were the ultimate leaders. And just like God, they could both give and take away just as easily.

After she barked out a litany of new orders, Masika told her staff to be off and not to return until all the work had been completed. There would be no thanks given nor an accommodating smile.

"Man reaps what he sows," a voice said from behind the gazebo. "You preach self-sacrifice yet live extravagantly."

They both turned, already knowing who had arrived.

Masika glared condescendingly. Though she could speak her mind to her husband, it was not her place to voice an opinion openly in Arab society. If she did, Ari could be seen as weak, and those who coveted his position could use it as an opportunity for a coup.

He identified himself only as SattAr and headed Ari's elite police force. A native from the Arabian Peninsula, he had honorably served many previous leaders across the Middle East over the past twenty years.

He wore a baggy military green shirt that buttoned down its center along with baggy pants to match. With a finely trimmed black mustache, and a clean-shaven head, he looked both sophisticated and lethal. A dark green beret completed the military mystique.

"I think you should stand down soldier," Ari said.

He did not appreciate criticism from anyone, especially from his subordinates. However, SattAr was different. All others would have been summarily dismissed from their ranks or sent to prison. But because of his high regard among the military elite, any punishment bestowed upon SattAr by Ari would produce serious repercussions.

Plus, SattAr's service to Ari bolstered his legitimacy as the Malik. The man was a highly-decorated veteran, former commander in the army, and extremely nationalistic. Wounded over six times in battle, he had proven his love for his country and his willingness to make the ultimate sacrifice. Without him, Ari could lose backing from the armed forces. No military support meant instant political death.

SattAr greeted Ari in the proper fashion but held his tongue further. As a true Arab nationalist, he respected the title of the Malik.

"Our country has come to a great crossroad," Ari said. "To achieve our goals we must take every advantage we can of *The Disease.*"

SattAr showed no signs of emotion. Though curious about

the Malik's words, he kept his feelings to himself and stood tall without expression.

Ari walked out from the gazebo. Without making eye contact, he looked straight ahead and said, "We must be the first to find the cure."

SattAr knew a cure would serve his country well as *The Disease* had already taken the lives of many thousands of its citizens.

With total control over the media, Ari had suppressed any knowledge of its spread to the public. All those who had succumbed to the illness in his country had been immediately cremated and their medical records burned. Sometimes all records of the person's existence were totally eradicated in order to hide the truth.

"Yes," SattAr said, "a cure will serve our people well."

Ari held his tongue. His main concern was not for the citizens of the UAA but for himself and his power. He knew the person who had the cure for *The Disease* had a commodity more valuable than any diamond, gold, or even air that they breathed—and that meant power. And if he didn't have that power, no one would.

A holographic image of Alex Pella appeared in front of them.

The image was smaller than Ari, and he looked down upon it with distain.

"As of today, you must guarantee that Alex Pella never finds the cure for *The Disease*, and if he does, you must steal it from him. Follow him. Track him. Do what you must."

Even though SattAr had already heard of Alex Pella, Ari went on to inform him of Neurono-Tek and what information the UAA had already gleaned about their involvement with both *The Disease* and NIH.

Though meager in nature, the information was sufficient

enough for SattAr to start. With his keen military senses, he needed little to accomplish a lot. Ten years previously he and only a handful of other commandoes under his command single-handedly undermined the entire rebel forces of Libya and brought an end to the country's dissidence and political opposition.

"One of our men has already infiltrated Neurono-Tek," Ari went on to say. "His sacrifice will serve us well."

Ari held SattAr by his shoulders with outstretched arms. "This mission is vital to our country, soldier. Do not fail the UAA or me."

"Yes Malik!" SattAr responded.

CHAPTER 8

THE MORGUE WAS COLD AND DRY. Its gray walls and floors gave it an uninviting atmosphere while the dim lighting above cast an eerie glow to the surroundings.

The morgue's occupants had no complaints. Most were the casualties of the terrorist attack. The police had sequestered them there while they completed their investigation. Tucked away in individual drawers, the bodies lined the walls as if they were all placed in a large filing cabinet.

The Biohazard rooms above had been almost completely repaired. In addition, construction of the building's lobby and scientific research rooms neared completion. Fortunately, the structural integrity of the building, along with most of its electric and plumbing remained intact despite the impact of the blast.

Alex had been promised that after another week of construction the building would pass final inspection and return to full capacity.

There would, of course, be the memorial services. Flowers, wreaths, and other reminders of the terrorist attack had already been placed in front of the building. There had also been a few candlelight vigils during the nights and at least one religious ceremony during the day.

The body of the terrorist had also been cloistered in Neurono-Tek's morgue. It was not uncommon for criminals or victims of deadly crimes to be placed there at least temporarily.

Because of the morgue's state-of-the-art forensics lab, all nearby hospitals and most police autopsies were completed there. As a way of building good will and currying favors, Neurono-Tek routinely donated its services for this task.

With all living tissue on the terrorist degraded by the autolysis pill, the only thing that remained was a heap of necrotic material surrounding the skeleton. Death had been almost instantaneous and occurred without suffering—in stark contrast to all those effected directly or indirectly by his terrorist act.

Death usually meant the end for a person. But in this case, death was just the beginning for this terrorist's legacy.

A white sheet covered his body. A Pennsylvania State Police stamp had been sewn onto it as a reminder of the man's criminal actions.

Like the Biblical Lazarus, the terrorist began moving from underneath the sheet.

Rising from the dead?

The whole body was involved. It almost seemed to be dancing to some macabre song. It rattled the claustrophobic storage cabinet in which it had been placed.

At first the sound was soft, but then it began to echo throughout the morgue, drowning out the hum of the sterilizing lights.

No one was there to hear it. The morgue remained completely empty as the building had still not been cleared for full operation. Other than the arrival of the new victim from

The Disease, there had been no medical or scientific work accomplished during the past week.

The cabinet drawer suddenly flew open and the white sheet fell to the ground. Riddled with small holes, it looked like a piece of Swiss cheese.

As the sheet fell, a cloud of dust accompanied it to the floor. The cloud was composed of former skin, muscle, and internal organs. It covered the sheet and coated it with a faint brown coloring.

All the rattling instantly stopped, returning the morgue back to its sterile quietness.

Without introduction, a small bug-like creature scurried out from the cabinet and began climbing up the wall. In a few moments, another one decided to exit and followed the first.

What was once a trickle became a flood. Hundreds of these creatures began to rush out and pepper the walls.

The entire cabinet was full of them.

Spawned out of death and created for destruction, they were like little demons sent to unleash horror onto the unsuspecting world.

Their one-centimeter, oval-shaped bodies had tiny little spikes adorning their back, resembling some ancient type of armor. Their heads were like something seen in a horror movie. Four red eyes, two beaded antennae, and an elongated jaw full of serrated teeth with two large fangs along the edges made it a formidable sight.

These creatures created a clanging sound like falling rain upon a tin roof as their multi-jointed six legs sputtered across the wall.

The bugs did not seem completely organic in nature. Their bodies appeared to be constructed from a black metallic substance while their movements at times looked more mechanical than biologic. They were certainly not of any species a trained entomologist could identify.

It was not long before the entire cabinet had been vacated, leaving only a clean white skeleton behind.

The bugs scurried haphazardly along the walls and on the floor. Without immediate direction, they frantically moved their antennae, attempting to gain some bearing.

One of the bug's eyes began to glow bright red in intensity. As it did, the others stopped moving erratically and headed towards its direction.

Like a self-proclaimed ringleader it marched up the wall, followed closely by the others. The bugs then began to encircle the rectangular cabinet drawers, which held the hospital's other corpses. Only those containing a body attracted them while the others were left alone.

Working together, they began to pry open the drawers until they created just enough room for them to fit through. One by one, the drawers cracked open and the bugs seeped in. Like tiny little grains of salt in an hourglass they spilled upon the unsuspecting bodies inside.

All fifteen occupied drawers soon became inundated with these monstrosities. Death for their occupants would now take on a new meaning—one much more morbid than they could have ever imagined.

Those bugs that did not enter the drawers followed their leader's new direction. From the wall they scurried down to the floor.

Ahead stood the forensics lab. Packed with tables full of microscopes, laboratory equipment, and high-tech machinery, it would prove to be their next area for assault.

Specific lab equipment immediately drew their attention. Whether it was an incubator, centrifuge, or mass spectrometer, as long as it was powered by electricity, the creatures seemed interested. The equipment that did not have an electric source was summarily overlooked.

A few of the bugs took special interest in a proton accelerator. At first they scurried around the foot-long oval machine while examining it with their antennae.

One creature crawled to the machine's underbelly. After wedging its two articulated front legs adjacent to where a small wire inserted into the proton accelerator, the bug began to glow brightly with a blue hue that could have blinded some unsuspecting onlooker.

Within a second, a light at the top of the proton accelerator turned green, signifying that it had been activated. The machine then began to emit a low rumbling noise that initially scared the bugs surrounding it. They jumped back but after a brief pause slowly edged their way towards it.

Other pieces of electrical equipment in the lab also came to life. Before long, the entire area became alive with the lights and sounds of modern technology. It was a chaotic harmony, which only the bugs could appreciate.

As the bugs continued to interfere, much of the equipment began to short circuit. Some began to catch fire. Others spun out of control until their motors burned out or knocked to the floor, braking upon impact.

As one piece of equipment failed, the bugs turned to something new. The cycle continued until everything lay in ruins. Within a quick span of fifteen minutes, millions of dollars of equipment had been rendered useless.

The destructive powers of these creatures were immense and their appetite for trouble seemed insatiable.

Once they destroyed the lab's entire stock of electrical equipment, the bugs crawled back on the floor, searching for their next target. Frantic once again, they scurried around with no apparent direction. Without any further electrical machinery to attack, they held their antennae up high, hoping to sense their next prey.

One of the bugs stopped moving as it detected something interesting.

An air duct.

It was located on the ceiling just above them. Infusing the area with fresh air, the duct helped prevent the atmosphere from becoming stagnant in the morgue.

The bugs quickly ran across the floor and up the walls.

Instinct or programming? It was uncertain.

As if it were a race, each scampered as quickly as their little legs would take them. Running over one another, cutting each other off, or simply pushing another away, the bugs did their best to be the first to arrive.

Upon reaching the air duct their eyes began to glow.

Freedom.

The duct led out of the room and connected to the rest of the Neurono-Tek building complex.

With only a quick pause, the bugs were moving again, scurrying up the air duct and out of the room.

Neurono-Tek's Achilles' heel had been found and the bugs were more than happy to pierce it.

CHAPTER 9

JONATHAN MALONEY SAT at the edge of his seat, excited to divulge all he knew but hesitant to do so because of its delicate nature.

"You see," he began to say, "ever since the outbreak of *The Disease*, I've been following it. From the Dodecanese Islands of the Aegean to Bodrum in Turkey, I have personally seen the destructive path of this illness."

These particular places Jonathan mentioned were the most devastated by *The Disease*. With their entire populations wiped out, they had become universally synonymous with *The Disease's* destruction . Like a tornado, it had the ability to demolish everything in its path.

Marissa was particularly intrigued. Because the places Jonathan mentioned were off-limits to even the NIH's staff, she definitely had her curiosity piqued by what he had seen.

"And there was one thing in common about all of these places," Jonathan said. "Death was the inevitable outcome: red, bloated, and stiff. That's how I found many of their inhabitants. It was a shame to see such a tragedy."

"But all of those places had restricted access," Marissa finally blurted, unable to sustain her enthusiasm. "How did you gain entrance to them?"

"You aren't some kind of spy?" Samantha exclaimed.

Jonathan smiled.

"No, no. I've been called a lot of things in my day. Many of them I vowed I would never repeat. But a spy? No, I can assure you I am not that."

Alex, too, remained skeptical. He knew there were certain hot spots that both the Turkish and Greek governments deemed restricted for foreign access. The Dodecanese Islands and Bodrum were at the top of this list.

"Let me just clarify something first," Alex said. "Were you actually at these particular places or just surveying them remotely from an aerial view?"

"No, I was there," Jonathan answered nonchalantly. "I touched the ground, smelled the air, and walked amongst the buildings. Beautiful as they were, death overshadowed all their aesthetic qualities."

"Then, are you a governmental agent?" Alex asked.

"I have no governmental ties," Jonathan said with his usual quick cadence, "nor do I have any relationship with the Queen of England or the Prince of Monaco. I am just an ordinary man on an extraordinary mission."

Despite the circuitous answer, Alex did believe him. A good judge of character, he felt Jonathan was true to his word and had more to offer. They just had to have a little patience.

Jonathan looked at each of them before talking. "You just assume that I went there after these places had been totally quarantined. The truth of the matter is, I was there before their governments fully realized what had occurred. A simple visa was all I needed."

"Are you some sort of psychic then?" Samantha joked.

"I have no extraordinary powers," Jonathan admitted, "I am just a regular guy who has been blessed with a little knowledge."

Jonathan took out his leather-bound Bible and held it out in front of him, tightly within his left hand. As if drawing strength from the book, his pale freckled face seemed to become aglow in its presence.

"You're not some religious nut?" Samantha scoffed.

"A Millerite to be correct," he rebutted.

"That's it!" Samantha blurted. "I'm outta here."

She immediately stood up and began to walk to the door.

"I know what happened on Astipalea," Jonathan finally said in a direct manner.

No longer roundabout in nature, he knew a direct approach would be needed in this situation.

"Can you just take a seat and let the man talk?" Alex said. "I thought patience was one of your virtues."

"I'll give you patience," Samantha said. Begrudgingly, she finally sat.

"Despite what you have heard on the news," Jonathan said after he had everybody's full attention, "Astipalea was not a military testing facility nor was it consumed in some underwater volcanic eruption. Its destruction was no accident, but the scourge it bestowed upon the planet was."

"Are you implying Astipalea is the source of *The Disease*?" Marissa asked.

Though the NIH acknowledged Astipalea could have also been infected with *The Disease*, they had made no connection with it as its epicenter. They were just like the general public: at the mercy of the media for information regarding the island's destruction.

Marissa felt as if she could kick herself. What appeared unlikely only a minute ago seemed all too obvious at the present time. The thought had briefly crossed her mind, but she had been too involved with the details of her work to see the big picture.

"As you may or may not know," Jonathan explained, "Astipalea was once just a simple island where fishing and tourism provided the mainstay of its sustenance. In fact, I signed on as a fisherman before *The Disease* ever came to fruition."

"Then you knew about *The Disease* before it started?" Alex asked.

"Not specifically, but I knew something was on its way. And that something could change the world as we know it."

An aerial image of the butterfly-shaped island before the entire area had been vaporized appeared in front of them.

Samantha had pulled up the image from their central data banks. Still skeptical of Jonathan, she wanted to confirm his testimony.

Under the image were bold titles such as Location, Animal Habitat and Mean Temperature. Samantha scrolled through the words with her hand and touched those that she wanted to read more about.

The conversation stopped as she did her own investigation.

"Says here," she interrupted, "prior to Astipalea's destruction it had become a volcanic research facility."

Samantha looked at Jonathan, "I thought you said you were a fisherman."

Jonathan thought of his words to be exact. "We are all fishermen of men, but in fact I was simply doing as I said, catching fish."

"He got you there," Alex commented. He then scrolled through the titles and came to Exports. "You see here. It says the major export of the island was fish."

"A fisherman I was," Jonathan added, "however, the island did indeed become a research facility, but not for volcanism."

"But it says right here—" Samantha insisted.

"Do not blind yourself with the obvious," Jonathan rebutted, "for sometimes the answer you seek can only be found in the most inauspicious places."

He placed his prized Bible on the end table and gazed upon it as if it contained the answer.

"So what research were they doing?" Marissa asked.

"The funny thing is I never exactly discovered everything they were doing. The answer eluded me the whole time I was there, but I can tell you this: they had no interest in volcanoes."

"Then what was it?" Marissa asked again. "What were they studying? Some plant or a sea creature?"

"It was not a tree, beast of burden, or some other animal native to the island. Man was their sole and only test subject. Their volcanology project provided just a cover, a ruse to hide the truth."

"And how do you know this?" Marissa asked.

"Though at times I kept myself inconspicuous, I made myself conspicuous enough to uncover a few answers. You see, I spoke to many of the people seeking medical help from their hospital."

Jonathan paused a second. The faces of both friends and acquaintances he had made on Astipalea briefly ran through his mind. These were difficult memories. He had trouble focusing, knowing they had all met a premature death.

"I worked with most of them and knew their families," he went on to say, holding back a lump in his throat. "They all visited the hospital for different reasons: broken bones, backaches, or even the common cold. The odd thing was that some of them left with bandages in seemingly random places on their body."

"What do you mean bandages?" Marissa asked.

"There was nothing elaborate about the dressing. However,

what intrigued me was that they were there. I may not be a physician, but I do know that you should not enter a hospital with the sniffles and leave with dressings along your spine, skull, and abdomen."

Alex turned to Samantha. "Does it say who was funding this research? Is there a name behind this volcanism project, even if it was just a façade?"

Samantha scrolled through the data on the holographic image. Despite her speed-reading, she could find nothing.

"'Private Donation' is all it says," Samantha responded.

"Did you see any cargo ships with a logo?" Alex asked Jonathan. "Or was anyone on the island wearing something that could identify the source of the funding?"

Jonathan shook his head. He then allowed a little smirk. "And there was no tell-tale sign of that little UAA falcon either," he then said to keep their interest.

Alex and Samantha leapt from their seats almost immediately. Instead of blurting out what they knew, both kept a calm composure and let Jonathan continue speaking.

But how did he know about the falcon?

"Though I did not see the bird on Astipalea, I did manage to notice a few men bearing the emblem while in Turkey and Greece."

"Nothing on the island though," Alex conceded, without giving Jonathan the response he was most likely expecting. "Dead-end. How about your friends? Can you give us any more information about them?"

"At first they started missing work. I just assumed they had been drinking too much or had been partying until the wee hours of the morning. It was not an uncommon occurrence. A fisherman's life was a difficult one, and many turned to the bottle as a result.

"But they weren't drunk," Marissa said. "What did you see?"

"Their work ethic suffered first. Usually a bunch of hearty men, they began to slow down and complained of muscle aches. Many, in fact, went back to the hospital, but those who decided to fight through it turned red throughout their body, like they had been baking in the sun for too long."

Jonathan shook his head. "That was just before they died."

"But you survived?" Alex commented. "How come you didn't get *The Disease* or die in the island's explosion?"

Jonathan glanced over to the Bible. Though it could not speak, the book obviously held more answers than he let on.

"Well, let's just say this," he explained briskly. "I just knew my time was up and my visit to the island was complete. Three days before its explosion I left for Bodrum, Turkey, never to return again."

This information given to them by Jonathan was a start. Alex now surmised that *The Disease* must have been man-made and the island may have been intentionally destroyed to prevent its spread. But who designed it and why?

It was also obvious to Alex that the UAA must have been asking the same questions. He knew that its leader was a classic narcissist who held himself higher than his people. If the UAA were able to discover the answer before anyone else, its leader, Ari Lesmana, could capitalize on it for his own dangerous purposes. The world's suffering would be his gain.

Alex also realized the UAA would do anything to stop their competition. The terrorist attack at Neurono-Tek had been a testament to that fact. He and his company would have to be extra vigilant. Not only was time against them in finding a cure, but now an egotistical narcissist hell-bent on stopping them would be interfering with their research.

Just the kind of challenge Alex Pella relished!

"Too bad everyone died in the explosion," Marissa lamented. "It would have been nice to have at least one person with some inside knowledge."

"And that is the main reason why I've requested your assistance," Jonathan emphatically responded.

"Someone survived!" Marissa shouted in pure excitement.

"His name is Guri Bergmann," Jonathan said. "I neither know what his role was in the experiment nor his relationship to Astipalea. What I do know is that he is in Crete and will most likely give us some answers."

Before Alex could say anything, Samantha already had Guri's picture holographically displayed in front of them.

The man could by no means be considered handsome. Nebbishy, troll-like, and homely were a few of the first adjectives that came to mind when looking at him.

He wore silver rectangular glasses, and his eyes almost closed during the contrived smile he made for the picture. With a slightly chubby face, salt and pepper colored beard, and a highly greased comb-over, he was a man who could not easily be forgotten.

Even Jonathan said, "I think I would have remembered him if I'd seen him on the island."

"Take a look to see where he is on Crete," Alex said.

"Well, I can take a guess it's not on a date," Samantha responded.

They all could not help but chuckle slightly at Samantha's candid remark.

A map of Crete appeared with a star located at its northeastern tip on a town called Sitia. Samantha touched the star, and a larger map of the boating community came into view. A small red dot discernibly overshadowed one of the houses.

"Well, there you go," Samantha said. "Ask and I shall deliver."

"How about you get me some coffee then," Alex joked.

"Very funny!"

"I wonder what he knows?" Marissa said aloud.

"Well," Alex responded while standing up abruptly, "we're going to find out right now."

He looked back towards his desk and said, "Phil!"

A holograph of the man appeared where the map had been. "Yes, Dr. Pella?"

"Could you have Tom make preparations for the Stratoskimmer? My friends and I need to take a little road trip."

"Yes, sir!" And his image disappeared.

"Samantha, I hate to say this," Alex said as her gave her a wink, "but I'm going to have to leave you here with the corpse."

"Good," Samantha said, "it'll probably provide me with more mental stimulation than you ever could."

Despite Alex's excitement about this adventure, he did realize the risks of traveling to Sitia.

He turned to Marissa and Jonathan.

Looking at them both seriously he said, "I want to let you both know that if you come with me it could be dangerous. Besides being at an increased risk of acquiring *The Disease*, we may have some unwanted company from the UAA."

As Alex spoke, Marissa and Jonathan were already on their feet. Staring him straight in the eyes, both looked as if to say, "What are you waiting for?"

CHAPTER 10

THE AIR-CONDITIONING DUCT barely made the hot and muggy air tolerable. Sweat clung to their skin like a wet towel. It was like being in a sauna but without the luxury.

They were two miles under the eastern coast of Yemen in a poorly lit cavern that contained just enough oxygen to breathe. The working conditions were so deplorable that the heat made the Sahara look like an oasis.

"So water from the Arabian Sea is scheduled to fill this entire cavern tonight?" Ari asked with his usual swagger. However, wearing a heavy hard hat and stiff blue coveralls made his usual fluid motions seem almost mechanical.

"No, sir." The foreman answered, "We plan to slowly let water inundate the entire area beginning at 6:00 A.M. tomorrow morning."

Ari knew the final preparations were being made for the completion of his bunker but did not know the exact details. Though in construction for over six months and costing the UAA trillions that they did not have, this massive endeavor hadn't attracted any of his attention recently as it neared completion.

A large crowd of the laborers had congregated near him. All looked the same way: cachectic, dirty, and drenched in sweat. Working under these harsh conditions had obviously taken its toll. It was the type of labor that no matter how much water or fluid a person drank, it just wasn't enough.

Despite the dehydration, they all looked energized to see the Malik. Wide-eyed and smiling, the workers pushed up next to one another just to catch a glimpse of their leader. Being so close together made them even hotter. However, all their misery seemed to dissipate in Ari's presence.

"At what rate would you prefer the water to enter?" the foreman asked. "The Minister of Construction, Razmi, said you would make the final decision after this inspection."

Ari had no clue how to answer the man. Though sanctioning this project and overseeing its leadership, he knew none of the specific details. He was above these trivialities and, in fact, felt offended by such questioning.

"What rate would be expected to produce the quickest results?" Ari asked, not wanting to commit to any decision.

The foreman went on to give a lengthy answer to his question. Speaking of the water release mechanisms, pounds per square inch, and the Bernoulli's Principle among other things, he provided a comprehensive response.

Ari became lost within the first few words. His mind was on greater things at the moment as he imagined how this massive bunker would provide his ultimate salvation from the ravages of *The Disease*.

Ari had come a long way since his childhood. Abandoned by his alcoholic father at a young age, he had always felt alone and dejected. Like most kids, he wondered if it was his fault his dad left and at other times believed that maybe his father was too ashamed of him to stay.

Whatever the cause for the man's departure, it had left Ari with low self-esteem. His mother did nothing to bolster his blossoming confidence. Working abroad most of her life, she lad left Ari to be raised by her parents. Though loving grandparents, they were not the same as his true mother and father.

Depressed and lost in a self-proclaimed meaningless world, Ari found no solace in either religion or friendship. Turning to narcotics and alcohol, he attempted to drown away his sorrow in a drug-induced stupor.

Things changed for him upon entering college.

Ari was fortunate to be accepted into a prestigious school. With poor grades and below-average aptitude test scores, he had managed to gain entrance not by merit, but through his grandfather's influence.

While in college, he was exposed to a world much larger than he had ever known. The constant barrage of fascist ideals from both classmates and professors alike inundated him.

He was taught about the West's hypocrisy and their ardent belief in capitalism. It was like a love story between the hedonistic Western society and their economic system. He finally understood that utopia could only be orchestrated from the government. People were too mentally unfit and materialistic to be left to their own devices. Their greed and pursuit of material goods not only created an unjust social hierarchy based upon wealth, but it also created a sense of individualism instead of nationalism.

While in college, he also inundated himself with existentialist readings. It was the ultimate epiphany. No longer seeking the meaning of life, he realized that it was his duty alone to create it. His future wife, Masika, also shared this existentialist view.

They met in college and made an instant connection. Both shared the same anti-Western sentiment and prayed not to a God but to a reality, which they created for themselves.

The foreman brought Ari out of his trance when he asked, "So what type of adjustments should be made when we apply Bernoulli's Principle?"

He looked at the man and gave an answer that only a politician could provide.

"When you apply the principle to this situation, there is only one conclusion that can be made. And that conclusion is the precise method by which to proceed. Do not deviate from this course or second-guess these results."

The foreman ultimately had been left with making all the decisions himself. Asking further questions would only prove to irritate the Malik. Instead, he responded as if Ari had given him an abundance of information.

"Thank you, sir," he said, bowing and making the symbol of an *O* above his head.

Ari smiled with confidence knowing that, as the population above dwindled into extinction, he would be safe from *The Disease* in his bunker. He was bound to win no matter the circumstances. If he found the cure for this scourge, he would be the most powerful man in the planet. If not, he would rise from the ashes of humanity like a phoenix and take control of a shattered world, creating an international fascist utopia.

CHAPTER 11

MOSTLY ABANDONED, THE COASTAL CITY of Sitia lay dormant. Its beautiful beaches were devoid of its usual outpouring of sunbathers while only a few ships dared traverse its port.

Sitia, along with most of Crete, had been evacuated early since *The Disease's* outbreak. It was not mandatory to leave the island but most had in fear of contracting the fatal illness. A few, however, stayed on the island, neglecting any risk to their health.

Guri Bergmann was one of them. A hermit by nature, he enjoyed the solitude and relative lack of human contact.

Alex looked down at the calculator-shaped device in his hand and inspected the intricate display upon its faceplate.

"This DNA tracker shows with a 99.8 percent probability that Guri should be in that brick-colored apartment building up the road."

Marissa leaned against Alex's shoulder. She had never seen a DNA tracker before and was interested in its capabilities. She considered its potential applications and thought it may prove useful during her field work.

Alex could not help but appreciate Marissa's soft touch and the coconut scent in her long brown hair. Her distraction was not unwelcome.

Though truly interested in the DNA tracker, Marissa, too, found herself attracted to Alex. She stayed close to him and examined the device in his hands with a little added interest.

Alex wanted to stay focused. He knew this endeavor could be dangerous and felt responsible for their safety. Now was not the time for petty self-indulgences.

Turning back to the group, he said, "O.K. everybody. Let's not forget the potential dangers. I have the whole city currently being evaluated by our Neurono-Tek satellite. Everything seems quiet now, but things could change rapidly."

"What do you mean *change rapidly*?" blurted a voice next to Alex. "I hope you're talking about the weather!"

Since leaving Neurono-Tek, they had acquired one more guest. Alex's entourage was no longer limited to Marissa and Jonathan as he invited an old college friend to join them.

Dressed as if he had just climbed out of bed, he wore a wrinkled white polo shirt, and instead of pants, he donned equally wrinkled blue shorts. An unflattering pair of brown sandals capped the entire ensemble. Because of the man's size, albeit not entirely from muscle, no one dared comment on his clothing selection.

The baseball cap on his head had the semblance of once being red. Now brown with dirt and most probably some other mysterious substances, it appeared as if it might sprout legs and walk off of its own volition. Well worn, only the letters *G* and *R* were decipherable above its brim. Although awkwardly dressed, he was a handsome man in his forties with fair skin, blue eyes, and a Hollywood smile.

The guest's name was William Fowler, and he boasted a

long and accomplished career as a virologist. Once working for the American Academy of Medicine, he had taken his talents into the private sector once the public one began to crumble.

"I'm just saying," Alex responded, "because of the UAA's terrorist attack on Neurono-Tek, we must be careful."

"Terrorist attack," he repeated in a trembling voice. "I thought that was a gas leak!"

Sweat began to soak his face and saturate his armpits. Though appearing big and tough, his exterior demeanor was nothing more than a façade.

"Gas leak, bomb, what's the difference?" Alex said nonchalantly. "They can both cause an explosion."

"I swear to God," William sputtered, "if you get me killed, I'm going to beat your ass."

Alex laughed to himself. He had known William ever since they roomed together in college. Though a nervous man and prone to fits of panic, he was a person of strong character and integrity who Alex could depend on no matter what the situation.

"I'll keep that in mind," Alex said. "But for now let's walk up the road here to find Guri."

Empty cars littered the street and not a single voice, laugh, or even shout could be heard along its path. Sitia had become a modern ghost town.

Quaint multilevel buildings painted white, tan, blue, and red bordered them on each side of the road. Because of their differing architectural designs, it gave the city a unique appearance not seen in the conformity of modern architecture.

Jonathan kept quiet, soaking in the city's beauty. Though silent, Alex knew the man had much more to say but kept it to himself. He just wished he could tease some more out of him.

"Jonathan," Alex said, trying not to act too inquisitive, "back at Neurono-Tek you mentioned something about being a Millerite."

"You are an astute one," Jonathan replied. "That is indeed what I said."

Jonathan was not oblivious to the fact that Alex presented him with an open-ended question. He also knew there was much more that he needed to tell them if they were successfully going to find a cure for *The Disease*.

"You see," Jonathan explained, "the term Millerism originates from a 19th century gentleman by the name of William Miller. It was his belief that the Bible held the clues to the second coming of Jesus Christ and the ensuing rapture."

Marissa leaned closer to hear what he had to say. His unpretentious manner, captivating way of speaking, and gentle smile gave him a grandfatherly-like demeanor that she certainly appreciated in such a stressful outing.

"So when did he predict the second coming?" Alex asked.

"Between the years of 1843 to 1844."

"I'd say he was a little off that one," Alex responded.

"That was called The Great Disappointment," Jonathan explained. "He, like many of his day, believed that there were clues hidden within the Bible, and if one knew how to interpret them, they could predict the future."

Jonathan pulled out his Bible and quickly opened it to the book of Daniel.

He read, "Unto two thousand and three hundred days; then shall the sanctuary be cleansed."

Jonathan closed the book and held it tightly to his side.

"Though this passage appears somewhat vague," he said, "it provided the cornerstone of William Miller's beliefs."

Music began to play.

Dreamer, you know you are a dreamer. Well, can you put your hands on your head. Oh, no I said…

Jonathan stopped talking and turned to see where the

music had started. Marissa also began to look for its source.

Alex, however, knew all too well where it came from. "William?" he asked inquisitively, without even looking at him.

"It's Supertramp," he answered. "You know I need to play it when I get nervous. It calms me down."

William then began to close his eyes and sing along in a soft, yet totally out of tune pitch, "Dreamer. You know you are a dreamer…"

"Did this William Miller predict out-of-date 1970s music?" Alex joked.

"Nothing of the sort," Jonathan responded, smiling.

"Unto two thousand and three hundred days," Marissa repeated, somewhat annoyed at William's interruption.

"Yes," Jonathan said. "There was a popular belief in the 19th century called the day-year principle. It was not uncommon to interpret each Biblical day to represent a year in actual time."

"How did they manage to come up with that math?" Alex asked.

"It was actually used by some 4th century Christians but popularized by more contemporary Protestant reformers."

Jonathan looked at Alex and Marissa and quickly added, "With a start date 457 B.C. when Jerusalem was ordered to be rebuilt, William Miller calculated judgment day to be around the years 1843 to 1844."

He waved his hand in the air and said nonchalantly, "Yes, the years passed without repercussion and many of his followers were rightly disillusioned. However, many continued to believe there was a secret code to the Bible and continued searching."

Alex interrupted, "And I guess they're called Millerites."

"You are a smart man, Dr. Alex Pella," Jonathan stated. "But as enthusiasm in religion has greatly diminished since the time of William Miller, there are but a few of us left."

"And is that what led you to Astipalea originally?" Marissa

asked.

Jonathan pointed to the brick-red building they were standing next to and responded, "And that is what has led us now to Guri Bergmann."

Alex knew there was much more to Jonathan's story, but now would not be the time for any fireside chat. Looking through his right videre contact lens, he could see a three-dimensional infrared satellite view of Sitia.

The city appeared relatively free of any human inhabitants. A few stray dogs and cats roamed the streets, but otherwise he could count its inhabitants on two hands.

Alex looked down at his DNA tracker and compared the results to the satellite image.

"He's on the third floor. Other than him this place appears empty."

Alex had come appropriately dressed for this excursion. Instead of the designer suit and dress shoes, he now wore his running sneakers along with blue jeans and a thin, white-collared shirt. He wouldn't be caught off-guard again if he needed to run.

Alex opened up the building's glass door and pointed down the hallway. "We'll have to take the stairwell. We don't want to find out somebody didn't pay the electrical bill the hard way."

The music stopped playing to everyone's delight.

"What do you mean third floor?" William blurted. "Is this some sort of triathlon you're dragging me on?" Once an all-state football athlete, he had long since left the daily rigor of a two hour workout in the gym at 5:00 A.M. for sleeping in late and a few cups of strong coffee in the morning to get him going. Still an extremely hard-working man, he would rather be up to his eyes in his work than pumping heavy weights these days.

Though moaning and groaning the whole time, William managed to follow the group up the stairs. With a little help from the railing, he ascended the last step.

"Marissa," Alex asked whimsically, "you wouldn't have anything in your bag to help out my friend back there?"

"I have just the thing," she said, opening up the black pack hanging from her shoulder.

Sweating and out of breath, William expected a power vitamin, a quick shot of adrena-boost, or at least a cool drink.

Marissa handed William a small green piece of plastic in the shape of a spool of thread.

Enthusiastically taking it, he looked down to read what he had been given.

Deodorant.

"Make sure you apply it at least three times a day," Marissa joked.

Though annoyed, William quick-wittedly responded, "Thanks, I won't need to shower for another week."

Alex stood in front of a finely-polished oak door with the number 57 glued to its exterior. He then took out what appeared to be a glass monocle from his shirt pocket.

He placed his fingers up to his lips, telling them all he needed silence and handed Jonathan a black playing card.

With the monocle up to his eye, he looked through the door. He could see the inside perfectly. It was a stuffy room with no decorations. Two brown couches and an ugly orange throw rug were all it had to offer.

"There he is," appeared on the card as the other three read Alex's mental transmission.

"Sitting on the couch trimming his toenails. He doesn't suspect a thing."

Marissa made a gagging face.

Alex pulled out a pocketknife-type instrument and flipped open what looked like a rectangular circuit panel. He placed it against the steel lock next to the doorknob.

"When I say GO the door will immediately open. I'll bum-rush the room and tackle Guri before he attempts to escape. William, you take my back."

William was ready. After wiping the perspiration from his face with the bottom of his shirt, he stood behind Alex, set for action.

"GO!"

Alex rushed the room as the door flung open. Guri was so frightened he could muster only a meager yelp. Before he could shout another sound, Alex tackled him to the floor and placed his hand tightly against his mouth.

"Are you Guri Bergmann?" Alex asked forcefully.

The man did not answer. In shock, he kept his eyes wide open and didn't move a muscle.

"Are you Guri Bergmann?" William reiterated.

Guri's eyes moved over to William's direction. The sight of the large figure instantly frightened him to rigorously nod his head yes.

Marissa and Jonathan entered the room. Inside there was not much to see. Guri did indeed live like a hermit. With gray walls and absolutely no décor, it appeared just as boring and bland as Guri himself.

"Now I'm going to take my hand off your mouth," Alex said distinctly and softly, "and I want you to slowly get up and sit on the couch without saying anything."

Guri again nodded his head, albeit slightly slower.

Alex did just as he said, and Guri moved cautiously to the couch, looking at everyone in the room as he did.

The picture they had seen of him did not do him justice. Dressed in a gray corduroy sport jacket and baggy brown slacks, he appeared even more nebbishy and troll-like than expected.

"What do you know about *The Disease*?" Alex asked while maintaining eye contact with the man.

"I don't know what you're talking about," he said in a nasal voice.

William stood behind the couch and placed his hand upon Guri's shoulder. "You heard Dr. Pella."

Alex looked over to his friend as if to say: *Thanks for the anonymity. Maybe you'd like to give him my home address, too?*

Marissa sat on the couch next to Guri and offered him a sweet smile. Somewhat disapproving of Alex and William's gruffness, she thought politeness might prove the most effective path for an answer.

"You do know millions, if not billions, of lives are at stake," she said very pleasantly. "We just want to know what your connection is with the experiment on Astipalea."

Her method certainly eased his tension. Feeling a little more relaxed, he squinted and pushed his glasses higher on his nose. Although at first wanting to remain quiet, the burden of his knowledge had been weighing on him like a bag of bricks for some time. The mental anguish it eventually caused felt overwhelming. Instead of facing his problems, he sequestered himself from the rest of the world, hoping the problem he had helped create would resolve on its own. Unfortunately, that was not the case.

"The thing is," Guri answered, relieved to finally tell someone, anyone, what he knew, "I was there for such a short time, and I never suspected anything like this was going to happen."

He looked at Alex and said, "You have to believe me. This whole thing is just crazy. People dying, the island exploding, it's like a bad dream. No one was supposed to get hurt—let alone lose their lives."

Alex became instantly distracted. In his videre lens a flurry of infrared figures jumped out of two manholes outside their building. Zooming in, he could see they were all dressed in military attire and carrying automatic weapons.

"Alex?" William asked, noting his apparent lack of concentration.

"Do you have any metal pots or pans?" Alex blurted.

Didn't see that question coming, Marissa thought.

"Yea," Guri said, now even more perplexed. "Over there in the kitchen. If you're hungry, I can get—"

Alex grabbed Guri and turned to the rest of them. "Come with me. It seems we have a little unexpected company."

"Company!" William stuttered. "I hope you mean like a pizza delivery man."

"I don't think pizza men carry automatic weapons," Alex said as they ran into the kitchen.

The small kitchen had only one folding chair and a TV-dinner table. It was the type of room that even an ardent bachelor would be ashamed of.

"There's only one pot here," Jonathan said, taking it out and handing it to Alex.

"I hope it will do."

The armed men began to storm the building. Alex could see their infrared images ascending the steps and pouring out onto the third floor. A few muffled voices could be heard down the hallway along with the shouting of commands by a loud voice.

"This doesn't look good," Alex said.

Supertramp again began to play. *Dreamer, you know you are a dreamer. Well, can you put your hands on your head...*

CHAPTER 12

IT WAS LATE AT NIGHT, but Samantha Mancini still worked diligently in her office. With Alex unavailable, the brunt of Neurono-Tek's managerial responsibilities became hers. In addition to these extra duties, she still had long hours of research to perform on the body Marissa had delivered.

The lights in the three-story building outside her office began to flicker and slowly turn off one by one until it went completely dark.

That's odd.

Samantha stood up from behind her desk and went to the window. The building was completely dark except for a few red emergency lights scattered along the different levels. She looked up and down the street. The rest of Neurono-Tek did not appear to be experiencing any electrical problems.

I guess it's up to me to see what happened.

She went back to her desk and asked, with a long sigh, for security. She waited a few seconds and when no answer came, she requested their presence a few more times.

Nothing. No response.

She tried to contact anyone, but it appeared all communications at this time were completely nonfunctional.

First the building and now I can't talk to anyone? What'd they make this place out of? Paper mache!

Samantha felt disgusted and needed to leave the office.

Filled with multiple and flowering plants, the room was reminiscent of the ancient Hanging Garden of Babylon. Each year she had added more vegetation until the whole place became a veritable rain forest.

Samantha cautiously walked through the foliage to the office door.

It did not dematerialize. Frustrated, she slapped it a few times in a futile attempt to activate it. The door remained solid, blocking her exit.

What's next! If the coffee machines goes, I'm outta here!

She then grabbed the manual disengage handle and turned it. The door snapped open, and Samantha stormed out of her office. Inconveniences and long hours of work did not mix with her.

Samantha marched down the stairs in her high-heeled boots and out of the building. She dared not attempt the elevator or Silidome. If she encountered another mechanical failure, she may end up in a padded room restrained in a straight jacket.

Outside people began to congregate beside the darkened building. Most were janitorial staff but a few other hospital employees working the night shift came out to see what had happened.

"I hope this isn't another gas leak," Samantha overhead someone say. "I hope Neurono-Tek isn't going broke like the country and couldn't pay the electric bill," another joked.

Before she could talk to any one of them, she felt a tap on her shoulder.

"Dr. Mancini," a booming voice declared from behind her.

She turned and saw it was the director of night security, Gill. Phil's identical twin brother, Gill had inherited the same set of Neanderthal-like characteristics. Though difficult to look at, he proved just as efficient a security guard as his brother.

"I was trying to reach you, but I got no response," he said. "I ran right out to see if you were O.K."

Though a feminist by nature, Samantha did enjoy a little chivalry.

"What's going on around here?" she asked.

"The power grid has gone haywire for some reason. I'm no electrician, but I've never seen anything like this before."

"Did our maintenance staff have a look at it yet?"

"They've been working on it for the last two hours."

Samantha looked over at the darkened building next to her and said, "Well, I can tell you this. It doesn't appear they're making much headway at the moment."

"No ma'am. It doesn't."

Samantha agreed with Gill. She, too, had never seen anything like this before. The power grid of Neurono-Tek had been assembled with so much redundancy that problems like this shouldn't occur.

She might have simply ignored the issue a month ago, but with the recent attack on Neurono-Tek, she had a lingering sense of suspicion something was awry.

"Gill," Samantha said, "I think we need to go have a little talk with the maintenance crew."

"I'll lead the way."

The two walked down the street. Fortunately, the rest of the Neurono-Tek complex remained well lit. Beautiful lanterns on either sides of the street illuminated the area well.

Next to the main research building ahead of them stood the central power building. Maintenance vehicles still remained along the sides of the street as the final preparations were being completed for the reopening of the research building. Even into the night, people worked diligently inside finishing the job. Alex wanted no delays and had the crews staffed 24 hours a day.

The longer the building remained nonfunctional, the more money Neurono-Tek lost by the day—a certain economic conundrum Alex could not allow.

The central power building was an unassuming structure in this modern institution. Converted from an old factory, the red-brick construction boasted multi-paned glass windows and an old-fashioned ironclad front door.

Before Samantha entered, she noted that the lights in another building up the street began to flicker and fade away into darkness.

"You wouldn't happen to have about an extra million candles handy?" Samantha asked, already becoming discouraged.

"No ma'am," Gill answered matter-of-factly.

Samantha tried to joke, but this was no laughing matter. Because the 800-bed hospital at Neurono-Tek also had been integrated with the central power system, she understood many lives could be at risk if it lost its power.

Already thinking ahead, Gill added, "I already put our five neighboring hospitals on alert and have both air and land transport on stand-by, just in case of any further problem at Neurono-Tek."

This was no easy task. Because only one other hospital in Pennsylvania remained, Gill needed to contact New York, New Jersey, and Delaware for support. The governmental-run health program had essentially placed all private hospitals out of business. Only a few hospitals throughout the country remained and just about all of them were government-run.

"I'm impressed," Samantha said. "I guess you security guys aren't just sleeping and drinking coffee all night."

Gill grunted. Not one for humor, he rarely ever appreciated

Samantha's jokes.

Like a gentleman, however, he pushed open the door and let Samantha enter first. The ground floor was not nearly as spectacular as the one in the main research building. Mostly composed of office space, a small lobby stood before them with one elevator to their right and other to their left.

Samantha, again, did not trust any electrical equipment and chose the steps instead of any modern convenience. As they walked down, an acrid smell with an unusual metallic scent caught their attention.

Samantha stopped and took in a deep breath, hoping her senses were wrong. She knew the smell all too well and realized what lay ahead.

She grabbed Gill by the arm. Her grip was surprisingly strong for such a small woman.

"Ma'am?" he asked, surprised by her reaction.

"There's been an accident down here," she warned. "Be very cautious."

The two slowly went down the last few steps and opened the door to the central power grid. Samantha gasped at the sight. Even Gill could not believe what he saw. Usually a strong man, his hand trembled while holding the door.

Like a modern crime scene, the floor was scattered with bodies. The five maintenance workers who had been sent to fix the grid had all been burned. Charred beyond recognition, their corpses simmered after an apparent electrical assault.

The power grids along the sides of the walls sparked and sizzled while metal from their wires dripped on the floor.

"I think we need to have the hospital evacuated," Gill said with a quiver in his voice.

Even Samantha found herself at a momentary loss for words. After taking a big gulp she said, "Let's not stop with the hospital. All of Neurono-Tek needs to be cleared out, and now."

Gill immediately shut the door. Calling a doctor at this point seemed redundant. The two quickly made their way up the stairs and walked out of the building.

"Gill," she said with her usual spunk. "Get the police here immediately. I think this whole thing's tied in with that terrorist attack, but I don't know how."

She made a wide circle with her hands. "I want this place completely evacuated within the hour. No one is to stay. No excuses."

"Yes ma'am," he responded. "Me and my men will get on it at once."

"He looked at Samantha and asked, "Will you need a personal escort?"

"Me?" she quickly responded. "I'm not going anywhere. There's a company to look after and a corpse special delivered here that needs to be examined."

"But I insist."

"Gill!" she yelled. "I don't care if this is the damn Titanic sinking to the bottom of the Atlantic. If it is, I'll make sure I'm at the bridge whistling Dixie the whole time while it sinks. Now let's get started."

"Yes, ma'am!"

CHAPTER 13

"YOU AMONG ALL OTHERS, President Vasilios," Albert Rosenberg said in a weak, raspy voice, "you have disappointed me the most. Your country was once the cradle of democracy, the source from which Western Society based its ideals."

Despite his sickened and frail state, Albert appeared disgusted.

"Look at you now."

This small burst of emotion caused Albert to have a fit of coughing. His two young, female attendants were at his side. One smacked his back to clear up any phlegm while the other placed a small, white plastic stick under his nose so that he could breathe better.

Albert took a large breath and exhaled with some authority. The coughing spell had quelled, but his disgust lingered.

Unable to make eye contact, President Vasilios said in a Greek accent, "Do not cast dispersion on the man who stands humbly before you now, for he has inherited all the follies of his predecessors."

Albert laughed aloud. He was too amused at such a simple and nearsighted statement to even comment upon it. If this man was that naive, why bother wasting the few worldly breaths he had left with a response. 90

Albert took a handkerchief from one of his attendants and wiped the phlegm from his mouth.

muscle wasting, sunken eyes, and a gray hue all added to the sickly appearance. The full set of teeth he boasted was the only semblance of health he retained. It was as if Albert died two weeks earlier, but no one had told him what happened.

He had certainly lived life to its fullest, and as the end drew near, he had no regrets.

There was, however, just one final bit of business he had to accomplish before his passing. Only then could he rest in peace knowing he had achieved all his goals.

"Your debts to The New Reality are insurmountable," he went on to say, "and your interest payments have become greater than your country's entire GNP."

With the assistance of his attendant, Albert sat up straighter in his hand-carved mahogany chair. He needed a new position in order to say what he needed to without getting out of breath.

Though markedly ill, he still insisted on wearing a blue, double-breasted suit. As CEO and president of The New Reality, he considered any lesser attire to be unprofessional.

"Plus," he said, "your constant failure to make the needed economic decisions in the face of imminent bankruptcy tells me that your government is too inadequate to run even a simple lemonade stand, let alone an entire country."

President Vasilios was not alone. Both the presidents of Iceland and France were also present for Albert's admonishment.

All three had been sent by their prospective countries to ask for forgiveness and for continued economic support from The New Reality. Without the quarterly blank checks sent to them with Albert Rosenberg's name written upon the bottom, they would have gone bankrupt years ago.

"Yes," President Vasilios said, "as leader of Greece I am personally here to apologize for our financial situation."

He extended his arms and placed a big smile on his face as

if they were best friends. "But I must also thank you for your continued financial assistance. Our people are indebted to your great generosity."

President Vasilios thought his trip to America would be just a simple PR endeavor. His advisors had instructed him to appease the old man from The New Reality and leave with another trillion-dollar loan. In fact, the president had only scheduled fifteen minutes for the meeting. The rest of the time had been blocked out for a tour of New York City. Fine dining, a Broadway play, and some high-end nightcaps were his main agenda.

Albert slowly stood up from his chair, revealing its gold-embroidered, red cushions. His aged joints cracked while his legs shook under the stress. His attendants attempted to help him, but he waved them off as if shooing away a fly.

Aided only by adrenaline, he slowly regained his composure. No one takes him for a fool.

"When I was young," Albert said with a little more baritone in his voice, "I learned many good lessons. One was how to balance a checkbook and another was to never underestimate your opponent."

Albert looked at the three world leaders and scoffed, "You obviously have failed to learn either lesson."

President Fornier interrupted with a thick French accent. "We are not foes but friends, Mr. Rosenberg. I am offended that you think of the French people as your opponent."

The French president stood indignantly and stared at Albert from the tip of his nose. He acted as if his country were doing The New Reality a favor by taking their loan checks.

"I know why all of you are here today," Albert said. "This trip was meant only as a mere social calling. No one here has made any concerted plans to balance your budget or orchestrate some financial means to pay off your debts."

The three leaders feigned a look of surprise and laughed at the accusations. They were all good actors but unfortunately for them, Albert did not like to be patronized.

He turned to President Bjarnason and asked, "So how has Iceland decided to erase their debts? A balanced budget act? Maybe a plan to curtail their spending?"

"I can assure you," the president authoritatively said, "Iceland has full intentions of paying off their entire debt. Financial independence is our government's utmost priority."

Albert shook his head. He had heard these promises before. It was like a broken record played whimsically to him each time these world leaders arrived.

"It's not that I don't believe you President Bjarnason," Albert said, "but numbers don't lie. Let me reiterate the figures I received from Iceland's finance minister from last year: salaries for government employees up 20%, jobs in the private sector down 8%, governmental spending up 22%, and overall economic growth index down 1%."

"But Mr. Rosenberg," President Bjarnason responded, "the most effective method for reducing debt and preventing a recession is by increasing governmental spending."

The other two leaders nodded their heads in total approval as if this were sound economic policy.

However, President Bjarnason's statement was both an offense to the hard-working people in his country and an insult to Albert. It was the type of unaccountable, financial wisdom adopted by far too many of the world's governments.. Albert fully understood economics and knew that such policies created only excessive waste, while simultaneously strangling any hopes for a prosperous financial future.

"That is why we require your further financial support," President Fornier insisted. "You must understand. We need to spend more in order to reduce our debts."

Albert had had enough of this charade. With his legs failing and heart pumping, he slowly walked back to his chair and collapsed down onto the well-padded cushions. He exhaled loudly. Though his mind remained intact, his body could no longer take the strain.

He looked up at all three in disgust.

"I'm sure you are all aware of the stipulations attached to your loans," he said, knowing fully that the three presidents were not attentive to these details. "To summarize one particular clause: *If the interest of the debt accrued by the country becomes larger than the GNP of the preceding year, The New Reality has the right to assume control of your government and all financial institutions.*"

"That is but a technicality," President Fornier stated, waving his hand in the air. "It is not something that is meant to be taken literally."

President Bjarnason reiterated as if speaking to a senile old kook, "These statements are just mere formalities."

Albert certainly did not appreciate their condescending demeanor, which made his decision even sweeter.

He pointed out his bony finger and said, "Enough! As of right now I am calling in all the loans to your countries in full. No longer will you or your governments continue their careless ways. Herein, I am assuming full control of Greece, France, and Iceland."

"You cannot do this to the French people!" President Fornier demanded.

"What about *The Disease*?" President Vasilios questioned. "Now is not the time for such bold maneuvers. Our countries have been afflicted by this illness and are currently at a significant disadvantage."

On the contrary. Albert understood that this was an impeccable time to call in the debts. With *The Disease* causing disarray in most countries around the world, they were all too preoccupied to mount any significant resistance to his takeover.

The Disease had given him the perfect opportunity, and he certainly would not ignore it.

Security guards marched into the room and seized the three presidents.

The same guards who had escorted them from their perspective countries now held them in hand as if they were common thugs. No longer working for France, Iceland, or Greece, these men were now employed by The New Reality.

"During our little discussion here," Albert said, "I took the liberty of having my staff inform your countries about my takeover."

"Get your hands off me!" President Fornier shouted.

The guard only held him tighter.

"My first order of business," Albert said, "is to remove all three of you from office. Your services will no longer be needed."

"This is an outrage!" shouted President Vasilios.

President Bjarnason agreed, "You will not get away with this!"

Albert smiled to himself as the guards unceremoniously escorted the three men out of the room. It was something that their people should have done years ago.

Albert understood the significance of what he had just done. Today marked the last day of wayward spending and the beginning of The New Reality Empire.

CHAPTER 14

ALEX EXAMINED THE AERIAL MAP of the city on his videre lens. He counted ten men in total assaulting the building. There was no evidence of any backup nor did it appear they had secured a perimeter. Either an amateur conducted this raid, or they clearly underestimated Alex.

Marissa hit William's shoulder. "Will you turn off that music," she whispered. "They're going to hear us."

William quickly complied. If he could have his life prolonged, even for an extra second, he would oblige.

The soldiers' voices became louder.

Crack! Crack!

The doors down the hall smashed open. The sound startled them all as they listened to the demolition.

The soldiers ransacked each apartment after their unauthorized entrance. Everything in them was destroyed as they frantically searched for their target.

"What's the metal pot for?" Marissa asked.

Alex slowly crawled on his knees to the edge of the kitchen. Holding the handle of the pot with one hand and his pocketknife-like device with the other, he peered around the corner into the living room. *Just as he feared.* The door to the apartment was left ajar, a dead giveaway of their location.

"Alex," William frantically said as sweat poured from his brow and saturated his dilapidated cap. "I hope that you're not trying to whip them up a batch of macaroni and cheese to win them over."

Jonathan fully understood Alex's concerns. Without warning, he leapt over Alex and ran up against the door. Pushing with the side of his body, he slowly shut it without making the slightest of sounds. The automatic lock set with its closure.

His actions definitely impressed Alex. Jonathan was certainly not the meek gentleman he appeared to be.

Before he scurried back to the kitchen, Alex gave him a quick nod of appreciation.

A few more doors smashed open. Alex had counted twelve apartments on this floor and after the eleventh one had just been entered, he knew they were next.

Placing his device against the back of the pot, he held it up and pointed it to the door. A barely audible hum could be heard resonating from the cooking device, producing a harmonic-type field not obvious to those behind it.

"I'm waiting," William said impatiently.

"Shush!" Marissa mouthed.

"Hell," William grumbled, "if Alex isn't going to do anything practical with that pot, I can at least use it to shatter the window in here so that I can jump out."

The door to the apartment smashed open and splintered onto the ground in pieces. A few soldiers ran into the room with their guns in hand. Though there was very little to destroy, the men did their best to lay waist to everything there. They began in the living room and proceeded into the bedroom like a mini tornado. They even smashed the windows with the butts of their guns.

"I hope they don't destroy my comics," Guri whispered.

"Comics!" William lipped. "We're about to all die here and you're worried about your comics. I swear to God if we get out of here alive, I'm going to wipe my ass with every last one of those comic books."

Marissa turned to them both. "Will you two cut it out. The last thing I want to hear right now is about you wiping yourself."

"I… I… just… ," Guri began to sputter.

"Zip it," Marissa snipped.

SattAr entered the apartment last. He confidently walked into the living room as if a welcomed guest. Wearing his usual green fatigues and beret with the UAA emblem, he looked around the room without saying a word. His men continued to ransack the apartment without disruption.

Alex knelt steadfast as SattAr watched his men reconnoiter the room.

William looked directly at him as his image burned into his head. The cold, calculating eyes, finely trimmed mustache, and air of superiority made it a face not to be forgotten. But why was he not alerting his men?

It did not matter. If these were his last moments, he would not go down without a fight. William grabbed the sole chair in the kitchen. Before he could lift it, Jonathan placed his foot upon the seat.

William looked at him with disbelief. What was this man doing? Did he just want to stand there and get gunned down like a horse with a broken leg?

Jonathan placed two fingers up to his eyes, pointed at SattAr and then shook his head.

William finally understood. Whatever Alex was doing with that metal pot, he must have created an illusion that had fooled all the soldiers. *Simple yet effective.*

The soldiers came out of the bedroom and shrugged their shoulders. Hoping for a fight, they all looked greatly disappointed. SattAr pointed to the door and barked a few more commands. The men responded and quickly marched out of the room.

SattAr turned and followed his men out the door, totally unaware of how close he was to capturing his prey.

After about a minute of heart-wrenching silence, Alex turned back and looked at William. "What was that about macaroni and cheese?"

"Listen Alex," he said while wiping sweat from his brow, "I don't know how you pulled that one off but whatever you did, it worked."

"Great job," Marissa agreed. She placed her hand upon his shoulder in a gesture of gratitude. Though subtle, she ran her fingers slightly into his hair.

Alex gave her a hint of a smile. Slightly embarrassed, she pulled her hand to the side.

"How did you know?" Alex asked Jonathan, still whispering.

"I was once an electrical engineer in my former life. And that pot was a dead giveaway." He waved his hands nonchalantly. "Apply an electrical signal, amplify the response, and create a one -way holographic image. I learned that my first year."

This is certainly no simpleton, Alex thought. Whatever he's hiding, I'd like to find out soon.

"So, now what?" William asked.

Alex responded, "I can see them on the roof. They obviously know we're here but appear to be blindly assaulting the building, searching for us haphazardly."

"'Respect your enemies,'" Jonathan quoted. "'Never underestimate him.' Sun Tsu."

"I bet they thought we were just a bunch of science geeks,"

William scoffed.

"We're not out of here yet," Alex cautioned before anyone felt any further relief. "While the rest of the soldiers are going up to the roof, they left two men on this floor to guard the stairwell."

Alex set down the metal pot and turned to Guri. "Where's the climate control panel?"

Guri sheepishly pointed to the wall in the kitchen. A small, rectangular, white box without any decorative accouterments stood where he gestured.

Alex grabbed the box and yanked it from the wall. Underneath was a black electrical board with little green flashes of light frequently racing across it. Alex threw the box on the floor and attached a quarter-sized disk directly onto it.

Before them, a three-dimensional holographic image of an architectural map of the building, detailed with all of its electrical circuitry, suddenly appeared. Thin red lines, representing the wiring, could clearly be seen throughout the blue structure.

"All the doors leading to the stairs," Alex said aloud, "appear to be magnetically activated."

Jonathan added, "It looks like an older version of our modern doors. Instead of dematerializing, they simply glide open and closed with the littlest of pressure. You would never know they weigh a few hundred pounds."

Alex nodded his head and smiled. "Exactly!"

"Does that pocketeer come with an electrical conduit?" Jonathan asked.

Short for pocket and engineer, the pocketeer was the pocketknife-type instrument Alex had used to enter Guri's apartment. Equipped with a multitude of miniature electrical devices, it was both an engineer's and modern spy's best friend.

"One step ahead of you," Alex said, taking the instrument

out of his back pocket and placing it up to the circuit board.

On the holograph the only door exiting to the roof turned red, while the others remained blue in color.

Jonathan inspected the image and then the kitchen wall. Turning to William, he said, "You may use the chair now," and pointed to a particular spot on the wall.

"With pleasure," William responded as he grabbed the chair and gleefully impaled one of its legs through the wall, creating a small fist-sized hole.

Jonathan quickly grabbed wires out from the hole and yanked them until he had about ten feet of excess. Taking one of them, he attached it to the pocketeer and stepped away.

Alex twisted the devise along the panel until the door on the roof turned purple. "Got it. That thing's sealed tighter now than if I welded the whole thing to the frame. Unless they jump or get air support, they're not coming off that roof any time soon."

"We'll also need that bipolar wire," Alex said.

Jonathan quickly complied and yanked the other wire over to the pocketeer. "You know I don't approve of this."

Nor did Alex, but there was no other choice. If the stakes had not been so high, he would consider an alternative. However, millions if not billions of lives depended on their success. There were no other options. He attached the wire to the pocketeer.

Suddenly, a blast rocketed down the hall. They all jumped at the sudden jolt.

The holographic image of the building showed that the door leading to the stairwell on their floor was no longer present. They all surmised what had happened but the question remained: What about the two soldiers?

"Let's go," Alex said, placing the pocketeer and quarter-shaped device back into his pocket. Unlike the others, he knew the answer. His videre contacts' infrared imaging showed that the two men standing next to the door had quickly died as a result of the electromagnetic blast.

Alex led the group into the hallway. The whole area was black and smoldering with pieces of the two soldiers' bodies strewn throughout the rubble. Thankfully, their escape down the stairs would not be hindered as the rest of the soldiers were on the roof; trapped behind the door that Alex sealed shut.

"Do you think we can find one of their guns?" William gasped, trying not to step on anything organic.

Alex shook his head. "I don't think there's anything left to find."

Alex led them down the stairs to the front door. Just as they arrived, he held out his hand to stop any further progression.

"I can see them on the roof. They're all looking over the side, ready to shoot anything that moves."

Alex did not have to say anything more. Just as he finished speaking a stray dog wandered out of an alley next to their building. The poor animal immediately got gunned down the instant he entered the soldiers' line of sight.

"Let's send Guri out first," William untimely joked.

Guri instantly turned white with shock. "I think it's best," he stuttered while pointing at Alex, "that we let that man right there decide what to do. He seems to be in charge."

Alex knew he had to make a decision quickly. It would only be a matter of time before help arrived for the soldiers trapped on the rooftop. However, he had only one option, and it was drastic.

Alex looked Jonathan in the eye, as if asking forgiveness for his next action. Again taking the pocketeer, he jammed it into the door's control panel. At first the green lights on the panel flickered, but after a few seconds the whole thing glowed red.

The building then began to hum and vibrate synchronously.

It was if everything in it had become a musical instrument and produced its own unique sound. The harmony created an eerie rhythm that gave them all a little quiver.

"I'm not familiar with that feature," Jonathan commented.

"Let's just say this isn't your usual pocketeer," Alex noted. "I made a few adjustments to it, if you know what I mean."

The panel in front of them began to smoke as did most of the building's vents and electrical fixtures. Crackling noises could be heard throughout the structure until finally sparks began shooting randomly out from the walls and the panel in front of them.

"That will just about do it," Alex said while removing the pocketeer.

Within a minute, the entire building began to catch fire. What started as a few flames became many and soon fire totally surrounded them. The smoke it produced became insufferable. They all placed their shirts over their noses, waiting for Alex to give them the signal to leave.

"When I say go," Alex shouted from underneath his shirt, "we're all going to run out of here to our right. There's a white building with a red roof two streets down. I've contacted Tom and he has flown our Stratoskimmer next to it."

The smoke billowed throughout the lobby until visibility was reduced to about a foot. After checking the satellite view of the building, Alex shouted, "*Go!*" as loud as he could muster.

They all ran out of the flaming building as quickly as their legs would take them. Though the fresh air brought them relief, the possibility of being shot curtailed any of their contentment. They all felt the same ache in the small of their back. It was as if they were expecting a bullet to enter in that precise spot and pierce their spines.

Fortunately, only a few scattered shots were fired, each missing their mark. No one was injured and the sight of the

Stratoskimmer brought them as much joy as a lighthouse would to a sailor caught in a raging storm.

Many considered the ship the most aerodynamic vehicle of its day. With two large cylindrical engines in the rear and a curved tail fin running the length of the oval-shaped ship, it gave the clear impression that it had been built for speed.

A side hatch opened and turned into a set of stairs. Usually slow in its decent, the stairs dropped to the road, creating a loud clanging noise in the process.

Alex stood by the stairs and watched everyone run up them. William, holding Guri by the arm, was the last to pass. As they did, Alex could hear some whimpering coming from Guri about his comic book collection.

Flames engulfed the building. Alex could see the dark smoke filling the sky, creating a black cloud above them. Fortunately for the soldiers, a small rescue vehicle hovered above the structure. There was too much smoke to see its success, and Alex didn't want to wait around any longer to find out.

Alex ran up the stairs and into the Stratoskimmer. The door shut behind him with an unusual clang. Inside, the décor sharply contrasted with Guri's Spartan apartment. Wall to wall carpeting, leather couches and chairs, and a wet bar constructed from mahogany wood gave the ship's interior an air of elegance.

Though Alex could now buy one for himself, an old friend gave the ship to him before his career at Neurono-Tek came to full fruition. It was an extremely expensive way to say thank you, and Alex could do nothing but accept.

"Tom!" Alex shouted. "Get us the hell out of here!"

"You got it!" promptly responded a deep voice emanating from the walls.

The ship instantly took flight. Despite the rapid acceleration, all those on board felt as if they were barely moving. The

Stratoskimmer's gravity dampeners certainly made the ride both a quick and luxurious one.

Exhausted, they all lounged on the couches and chairs. At first no one wanted to speak of what had just happened as the shock of the situation set in.

However, they needed to move forward.

Alex was the first to break the silence. After walking over to the bar, he asked if anyone would care for a drink.

William sprawled himself out on one of the couches. He had taken off his sandals to save the leather furniture. Looking up at Alex, he said, "One cold beer."

"Can I have a Shirley Temple?" Guri asked, while raising a finger.

"Make that two beers," William said. "One for me and one for our new friend over here."

"But… but my irritable bowel," Guri tried to spit out.

"Drink up," Alex agreed. "You're going to need it."

Alex handed out a drink to everyone. As the beer sounded appetizing, they all partook in its hops-filled flavor.

After finishing their beverages, Alex and William sat on either side of Guri. Feeling a little claustrophobic, he kept his arms close to his side and took quick sips from the beer bottle.

"Guys," Marissa warned, "Guri is a guest with us now and we must treat him as such. Play nice."

"Tom," Alex asked, "could you connect us with Samantha back at Neurono-Tek? I think she also needs to hear what our new *guest* is dying to tell us."

CHAPTER 15

SAMANTHA FOUND HERSELF ALONE in the gray and uninviting bunker underneath the main research building. It was the type of place that almost made her want to be back on the earth's surface, no matter what the circumstances.

"They could have at least put one potted plant down here!" Samantha said aloud. No one was there to listen, and her voice echoed throughout the room.

"I bet a man designed this! No paintings, gray walls, and sterile lighting. I've seen prisons with more décor than this place!"

Though correct about the room's decorations, its purpose was never meant to showcase the business or entertain guests. The facility had been placed securely under the main research building to be utilized only in a time of emergency. As *The Disease* threatened to wipe out mankind and as Neurono-Tek faced another possible terrorist attack, that time had certainly come.

The bunker was spacious, however. It boasted a complete forensics and chemistry lab, storage facility, and living quarters that could accommodate at least ten people. Plus, there was a separate and sterile autopsy area enclosed in glass that currently held the body Marissa brought to them for study.

Samantha went over to a long, clear desk full of multicolored, yet translucent, buttons etched into it. She was familiar with the layout and knew exactly how to activate the system.

She placed her two hands upon a green circle on the desk and kept it there until it turned red. It was a painful process as tiny laser beams pierced her palms, obtaining thousands of microscopic blood samples while also checking her venous fingerprint.

Samantha removed her hands. Her palms appeared slightly red. The laser had cauterized all the capillaries, preventing any further blood loss.

The entire room began to activate, starting with the labs and then moving over to the living quarters and storage facility. Finally, the lights in the autopsy room began to brighten.

The body lay on a table inside. It was obviously a young woman and a well- preserved one at that. Blankets covered her above the chest but her bare neck and head were visible. She appeared more asleep than dead.

Her skin was still red from the later stages of *The Disease,* but her long red hair looked as if it had just been combed.

Samantha walked over to the glass encasing the autopsy room and looked into it.

"I guess it's just me and the stiff over here," she said irreverently. "I'm at least glad it's another woman."

Painted along the walls were light gray rectangles about seventy inches wide and fifty inches high. It took a little squinting but an astute eye could differentiate the subtle color difference.

These light gray rectangles were the last to activate in the bunker. Made of phosphorous-based polymers painted onto the wall, they assembled with a simple electrical charge to create an exquisite picture. Separate live feeds of the entire Neurono-Tek facility instantly displayed on them.

Samantha looked at the screens around the bunker. The mass exodus of the complex had almost been completed. Police vans and a few fire trucks replaced all the medical vehicles. Most had been stationed outside the main power building but a few others remained next to the hospital.

"I sure hope these guys are getting paid overtime! Twice in a week. That's two times too many!"

Though Samantha joked, she felt upset inside. The sight and smell of the dead maintenance workers, the recent terrorist bombing, and whatever now was happening became overwhelming. At this point she wasn't sure if she should just ignore it all and continue with her work or simply pack up and leave to preserve her sanity. A Broadway play along with a nice Italian restaurant seemed mighty tantalizing right about now.

The decision required little thought. She belonged at Neurono-Tek, and she certainly had no intention of leaving. The company, if not the world, needed her where she was at this moment.

Samantha sat down behind the long desk next to the autopsy room. It faced the body and had the same layout as the one she just activated. Clear with translucent multicolored buttons, it looked comparable but had a completely different function.

"Samantha?" a voice reverberated in the room. Again there was a *Samantha* but no picture.

Samantha swiveled her chair around towards the control room desk. Just as she turned, a holographic image of Alex and the rest of the group within the Stratoskimmer appeared. She instantly noted them all drinking beer and lounging on the couches.

Before the picture became clear, Alex alarmingly asked, "What happened? Why are you in the bunker? Is there a problem?"

Alex knew the bunker was off limits—even for Samantha. He had quarantined the area until he personally felt it safe for anyone to enter.

Samantha took a deep breath and succinctly told Alex what had happened. Though completely frazzled by what had occurred, she needed to keep calm and show Alex she had things under control.

It definitely explained why it had been so difficult to find her as it took over fifteen minutes just for Tom to make the connection.

Alex had only one response, "Necroids!"

No one knew what Alex insinuated. Even Jonathan seemed confused. The term was nothing he or any of them had ever encountered.

"What's a necroid?" Samantha asked skeptically.

"This all makes perfect sense now. The assault on Neurono-Tek last week was just a ploy. The real attack came not with the bomb but with the bomber."

"Are you insinuating it was a suicide mission?" Samantha said.

"I'm not insinuating anything. It *was* a suicide mission. The UAA must have known that the body would be stored at Neurono-Tek. Plus, they must have surmised that with the commotion caused by the attack, we would be spending all of our time cleaning up the mess and trying to bolster our security. The thought of a necrotic corpse would be dead last on our minds."

"But how come we didn't notice any of these necroids at the autopsy?" Samantha asked.

"Because we never did a genetic analysis. The autolysis pill degraded all the proteins into simple amino acids. Since DNA has innate instability, it was the first to break down. Because the terrorist's genetic blueprint had been lost, the forensics team decided to forgo any further detailed DNA studies. So, unless you're looking for a necroid, you would never think to run a magnetic scan."

Marissa interjected, "But I must ask. How'd you know so much about these necroids?"

"Theoretical anatomy," Alex answered. "It's a little-known scientific specialty where researchers devise certain biological possibilities that could exist on other planets. One of the most debated topics recently has been what they called a necroid."

Samantha raised an inquisitive eyebrow.

"The interesting thing," Alex continued, "is that a Saudi Arabian scientist wrote a paper two years ago stating that he actually created a whole species of these self- replicating necroids."

"Interesting," Marissa commented.

"The author recanted the paper a month later and was never heard from again. It was like he vanished. There were no interviews and his entire lab had been vacated. It's been a mystery that has haunted the scientific community since, but I'm certain that this is the necroid species he created."

Samantha quickly surmised the necroid's engineering. "So what you are trying to say is that the basic building block for these necroids is not biological but mechanical."

"Exactly. Instead of DNA they have ME-DNA, standing for mechanically equivalent deoxyribonucleic acid. It's structurally similar and has the same configuration and electrical charges but is constructed from a silicone-iron backbone. Essentially it's nondegradable and designed to assemble an entire necroid using only simple amino acids and the enzymatic components at each end of the ME-DNA."

"So," Samantha asked, "how do we stop them?"

"I don't know."

Samantha rarely heard Alex say that term and now, especially, was the one time when she wished he hadn't uttered it. "Well," she said, almost exasperated, "can you at least tell me how your little adventure went on Crete?"

"Let me introduce you to our new friend, Guri Bergmann," William interrupted. "He was just about to tell us about his involvement with *The Disease*."

"Well, I… a… ," Guri said with a nasal voice, pushing up his glasses. "I was sworn to secrecy. However, I think I may have had something to do with *The Disease*. But this whole thing was never supposed to happen."

"You started it?" Marissa said.

"I wouldn't exactly say that I, personally, started it. But what I would say is that something definitely went wrong with the project on Astipalea."

"Now there's an understatement," Samantha blurted.

"Let's just hear him out," Alex interrupted. "What were you involved in? I researched your work, but you've not published anything for years."

"Well, I was not allowed to publish anything. About five years ago, The New Reality hired me as a genetic engineering consultant and our contract stipulated that all my work was their property. Since they decided not to publish anything, I really could do nothing about it."

Alex wasn't surprised. The New Reality had branched out into a myriad of endeavors with genetic engineering being its most clandestine. Somehow this enterprise must have inadvertently spawned *The Disease* pandemic.

"What were you researching?" Marissa quickly asked.

"This may seem difficult to believe but they wanted me to

find the greatness gene. You know. The gene that may trigger a cascade of events that makes a particular person stronger, smarter, quicker, or even braver."

"Well, look no further," William said with his arms wide open. "Lucky for you my greatness gene also came with stunning good looks."

Ignoring William, Guri responded, "The main thing about the whole project was that The New Reality provided me with twenty separate DNA samples all believed to contain the greatness gene."

"Did you ever question whose DNA they were?" Marissa said.

"No," Guri responded succinctly. "I just took the samples and began my research."

Marissa knew the answer but had to inquire. Guri did not seem like the type to make waves or ask questions. Both brilliant and naïve, the man was destined to create something so revolutionary that he would be too dim-witted to foresee its consequences.

"What did you do with them?" Samantha eagerly asked.

"I began analyzing the DNA but found nothing unusual. I then compared their DNA to specific types of people: rich, poor, smart, dumb, famous, and even infamous. Again, there was nothing outstanding. In fact, I almost found no difference at all."

William looked skeptical. Though only about two percent of human DNA actually coded proteins, he understood enough about genetics to ascertain that certain gene variants would be more adventitious than others.

"You obviously found something," William rebutted sarcastically.

"Well, sure. But that wasn't until I cultivated the DNA itself."

Guri went on to explain how he engineered different cell lines from the samples of DNA given to him. Muscle, liver, brain, and kidney tissues were all grown from each of the original twenty cell lines and then compared to those samples cultivated from ordinary people. Anal retentive by nature, he didn't neglect a single detail.Jonathan commented first, "I guess you then just reverse engineered your results to ascertain the proper gene."

"You were following that?" Alex asked, surprised.

Jonathan laughed. "The human body is not that much different from a machine. Sure, the parts have different names and the pieces are different, but the end result is the same." He gave Alex a smile, "No need to overcomplicate the situation."

Alex agreed.

"Well," Guri said, "reverse engineering is rather an oversimplification. After an exhaustive search of the proteins, we discovered that the cells deemed great produced a distinct variant of the bcl-xl protein."

Samantha immediately understood the implications. She then went on to describe how bcl-xl was responsible for determining the energy-producing capacity of all human mitochondria. Because these are the main energy-producing organelles in the cell, more efficient and powerful ones would prove adventitious.

"Exactly," Guri concurred. "When we went back to find the gene that coded this protein, we found that everyone had the same one on chromosome 16 and that they were all basically the same, regardless from whom they came."

"You mean we all have the same gene for this protein variant?" Marissa asked.

"Yes," Guri said while caressing his beard with his hand.

"The gene's imprinted, isn't it?" Samantha concluded aloud.

Guri nodded in agreement and then went on to detail

the genetic imprinting concept. He explained that humans obviously have one set of genes from each parent. 99% of the time both sets are coded, but in less than 1%, only one or neither are translated into proteins. These are the imprinted genes and harbor a special carbon-based cluster called a methyl group attached that make them unusable.

He went on to clarify that those people considered *great* did not have the bcl-xl gene imprinted and were able to produce this special protein.

"So I understand why you didn't find the answer through simple DNA analysis," Alex commented. "Because we all have the same gene, each of our genetic profiles would look the same."

"And my last step, "Guri explained, "was to create a specific DNA enzyme to activate the bcl-xl protein."

He looked a little perturbed and uneasy with what he had to say next and paused before he again began to speak.

"I told The New Reality that it would take time and at least a year of further research before I could deem it safe for human trials."

"Who did you tell?" Alex interrupted. "Who was your contact person? Do you have a name?"

"Dr. Christakos," Guri blurted, glad to finally say the man's name. "But he's dead now! Incinerated immediately in the explosion, along with all of our work!"

Guri's display of emotion was uncharacteristic and short-lived. Just after this small outburst he settled back into his crouched position and pushed up his glasses as if nothing had occurred.

"Was anyone else privy to your discovery?" Alex asked.

"No one," Guri replied. "Because of the project's secrecy, not even Dr. Christakos or his associates knew any specific details. After receiving my bcl-xl activating enzyme, The New Reality immediately shut down my lab, and Dr. Christakos started human experimentation on unsuspecting people entering the hospital at Astipalea."

Jonathan cringed at Guri's admission. The lack of scientific method and the blatant disregard for humanity appalled him. Those were his friends who died back there on the island. And for what? Was it to save time or money or was The New Reality too impatient to proceed with proper scientific protocol? These thoughts infuriated the usually stoic man, but he knew lashing out on Guri would be pointless. Though responsible indirectly, he was not the one to blame.

"The bcl-xl protein definitely explains why the mitochondria appeared the way they did in those people who died of *The Disease*," Marissa said.

Alex commented, "But it still doesn't explain why it's lethal or how it spreads." He looked over to Samantha. "We're going to have our work cut out for us. After I drop off my colleagues, I'll meet you in the bunker before the police place a full quarantine around Neurono-Tek."

Jonathan raised an eyebrow. "Alex," he said with his usual demeanor, "we're just beginning our journey. Finding Guri here was only the first step. We have a long way to go. I can't promise the path to find an answer will be fun, interesting, or even safe. But what I do promise is that if you want to find the cure, then you'll have to follow me. And I'm going to Megiddo."

"That's it," William said frantically, "I'm bailing. I'm sorry Alex, but I belong on a couch and not in front of some nuts with guns. If you could please tell your pilot Tom to drop me off at the nearest place where I won't get shot, I'd be especially grateful."

Guri held up a finger, "If you could also drop me off. My sinuses are getting clogged with the air here on the ship."

Alex leaned over and placed his hand on Marissa's knee.

"So, you up for a little more adventure?"

Marissa tried to hold back a blush as she placed her hands over his. "I'm in."

Jonathan nodded in agreement. "The world's counting on us."

Alex turned to William and said emphatically, "Yes, the world is counting on us. Plus, you are the best virologist I've ever known."

William shook his and let out the biggest shit-eating grin he could muster. After a brief pause, he threw up his hands. "I guess you can count me and Guri in for this little excursion, too. My couch can wait."

"But… but… ," Guri tried to say.

"How nice," Samantha said, rolling her eyes. "While you all are singing "Kumbaya" and drinking your beer, I'll be here, alone, also working to find a cure for *The Disease*. Oh yeah, and I'll also try not to get eaten alive by those necroids."

She waved to them and said as their transmission ended, "Au revoir."

Alex bit his lip, knowing Samantha's situation was precarious at best. Though he wished he could be there to help, he knew that his duties lie elsewhere.

CHAPTER 16

"DID YOU SAY MEGIDDO?" Alex asked. "Isn't that the site of earth's final battle in the Book of Revelation?"

"'They then assembled the kings in the place that is named Armageddon in Hebrew,'" Jonathan quoted, "Revelation 16:16."

"What's Armageddon and Megiddo have to do with each other?" William quickly inquired. "I thought Armageddon just meant the end of the earth?" Jonathan answered, "Well the word *Armageddon* is actually derived from two different Hebrew words. *Har* or *tel* meaning mount and *Megiddo* representing the city. When you put them together, you get *Har-Megiddo* or more commonly pronounced *Armageddon*."

"I don't like the sound of this!" William said.

Already nervous, he grew that much more concerned after learning they were heading straight for the Biblical apocalypse. With *The Disease's* grip on humanity growing tighter every day, it almost seemed as if Armageddon had already begun.

Jonathan wanted to put William's mind at ease. He noticed the man's internal tension and knew his stress would accomplish nothing other than to weaken his mind and spirit.

He said to William, "You need to focus on positive things instead of the negative. I see you sitting there fretting and over what? A name?"

He looked into William's eyes. "It reminds me of when the ancient Spartans went to battle. Many of their enemies would cower in fear or even run once they saw the Greek letter lambda painted on their shields. Do not follow in their footsteps, my friend. Megiddo is just a name of a place. Do not waste your time and energy in worrying. You're going to need all your strength."

"Megiddo does have an interesting history though," Alex said.

A history enthusiast all of his life, he was fascinated by the ancient world. From the Greeks to the Romans up to the Middle Ages, Alex was like an encyclopedia of facts. He also boasted one of the largest private collections of ancient weaponry. Swords, arrowheads, and even the remnants of a two-thousand-year-old chariot were in his possession.

Alex added, "Megiddo used to represent a very strategic location in the ancient world, guarding a narrow pass along the western border of modern Israel that connected the ancient superpowers of Egypt and Assyria."

"Yes," Jonathan agreed. "That's the precise reason why the city saw so much conflict over the years. In fact, the first documented battle ever recorded was at Megiddo in 1478 B.C. The records are still visible in hieroglyphics on the walls of Pharaoh Thutmose III's temple in upper Egypt."

"Didn't General Edmund Allenby also defeat the Ottoman forces there in 1918 at the end of World War I?" Marissa asked.

Alex's interest in her went up a few notches. Not only was she beautiful and intelligent but she was also a history buff.

"It was the battle which solidified the British conquest of

Palestine," she added.

"You're interested in World War II?" Alex inquisitively asked.

"I do find it fascinating, but my real passion is in ancient Greek and Persian history. I actually minored in the subjects while in college."

It was a match made in heaven.

"I'm also… ," Alex began to say just as the Stratoskimmer took a noticeable dip in altitude. Despite the gravity dampeners, the momentum was sufficient to almost knock everyone off their couches.

Alex rushed over to the cockpit and pushed open the door separating the two compartments. Behind him he could hear Guri complaining about there being no seatbelts and William grumbling about the beer spilled over his shirt.

"Tom," Alex asked. "What is going on up here?"

The pilot sat behind the intricate control panel, hands clenched onto the steering wheel. His grip was so tight that his veins popped out of his hands and wrists. He barely noticed Alex's entrance as he fought to keep control of the ship.

A few red lights flashed on the control panel while a low buzzing echoed throughout the cabin. Alex immediately sat down in the copilot's seat and grabbed hold of the other wheel.

Alex was a world-class pilot and had flown many different types of planes and airships during his spare time. Clocking in over five-hundred hours of airtime behind the Stratoskimmer, he was certainly not a novice to this particular vehicle.

They were flying twenty miles above sea level, just above the ozone layer. Because the Stratoskimmer usually cruises at thirty miles, Alex realized they must have taken a tremendous descent, enough to overpower the gravity dampeners in the cabin.

Tom finally realized he had a guest. Though in his early

sixties, the man barely looked his age. With a full head of thick, black hair, tanned skin, and a boyish grin, he was sometimes mistaken for a cadet and not a seasoned flying veteran.

"We were just hit by a long range magnetic cannon blast," Tom finally said. "It almost fried our entire electrical system here. Thank God for the redundant circuits or we'd be swimming with the fish."

A three-dimensional holographic image of the ship that fired the blast appeared at the bottom of the windshield. Despite being over twenty miles in distance, the image remained crisp and appeared as if taken from a close distance.

The ship had no markings to delineate its origin, but Alex knew it had to be UAA. It must have been spying on them the whole time while on Crete and had just broken its geostationary orbit to attack.

It was a commercial XR-2 class ship designed for low-altitude space flights. With an elongated white-colored body, short wings to either side that ran most of its length, and a small double tail fin, the vehicle did not appear threatening in nature.

"Do you have us in stealth?" Alex asked.

"Of course," Tom grumbled.

Tom banked the Stratoskimmer hard to the right, trying to place more distance between the ships in hopes that the stealth device would work better.

"Incoming!" he yelled.

The XR-2 had just unleashed another shot from its magnetic cannon. With a forty-mile conical spread of distribution, they were still well within its field of fire.

They're not going to like this one, Tom thought.

The Stratoskimmer suddenly took a nosedive. Alex could hear the beer bottles and the glasses from the bar smashing against the walls in the cabin. He also noted the cries from Guri claiming he was going to throw up and the prayers from

Jonathan saying the Lord's Prayer. William also chimed in with a few *this is its* and *we're all done fors*.

Despite their ship being directly in its path, the magnetic blast unexpectedly passed by them without causing any noticeable damage. The Stratoskimmer rocked only slightly, revealing the blast's presence. It was like a small wave flowing by that had yet to crest.

Tom continued their rapid descent. The nose cone of the Stratoskimmer heated up until it began to glow red with friction. The ship was not made for such drastic maneuvers, but he had no qualms about pushing it to the limit.

Tom leveled off the Stratoskimmer only a few hundred yards above the Atlantic. With such a vast ocean underneath them, the stealth device had a much higher probability of concealing their presence.

The ship suddenly buckled and swerved back and forth.

"You doing that?" Alex asked.

"I wish I were," Tom responded. "The Stratoskimmer here hasn't behaved well since departing Neurono-Tek. The blast from the magnetic cannon didn't help anything either."

The ship continued to fly erratically, and despite its computer-guided systems, it became more difficult to control. At one point they were only a foot above the ocean, skimming its surface.

William stumbled up to the cabin. Appearing much greener in the face, he obviously did not appreciate the accommodations thus far. "What in the world is going on around here?" he sputtered.

Alex's eyes were continuously locked on the image of the XR-2. While holding the steering wheel with one hand, he used the other to point to the offending ship. "Our friend here just hit us full blast with his magnetic cannon."

"But that's just a commercial spacecraft," William said.

"What do you mean it fired on us?"

Tom looked over at William, "That ain't no ordinary XR-2. That baby comes with an extra punch, and I don't think it's carrying any civilian passengers."

Before he could respond, Alex signaled him to go back into the cabin. "You better sit back down. We may have to make a crash landing. I don't think this ship has much more flying time left."

Crash and *landing* were two words William never wanted to hear together.

He jolted back to the cabin. Instead of telling the others to remain seated, Alex could hear him yell in a boisterous voice, "O.K. everyone! I just talked to Alex and he said we're all going to die!"

That went well.

"I think we lost him," Tom said while nodding to the XR-2. "It looks like the ship's heading back up into the mesosphere and in the opposite direction. Maybe he thinks we crashed or something."

Unfortunately, Alex knew that might not be too far off from the truth. If they didn't reach land soon, there was a chance they would have to abandon the Stratoskimmer in the middle of the Atlantic.

"Nice flying," Tom said. "What was that thing you did when the second magnetic blast came our way?'

"It was a trick I learned when aero-bike racing. I just reversed the magnetic polarity of the Stratoskimmer."

"You what?" Tom asked, flabbergasted. "That could have gotten us all killed. That's the first thing you learn not to do in flight training. Don't reverse the polarity of the ship!"

"Well, the other option of getting hit with a full blast from a magnetic cannon didn't seem much better."

Tom nodded his head in approval. "You know, I knew I

liked you for some reason. That was a pretty bold move. How'd you know it would work?"

"I didn't," Alex answered, shrugging his shoulders. "When I saw the magnetic blast had only a monopolar field, I figured if I reversed the polarity of the Stratoskimmer to match that of the incoming pulse, it might pass by without causing any harm."

"That's one for the books!"

The satellite map on the control panel showed they were not far from an island called Madeira off the western coast of Portugal. It was their only option.

"You see that?" Alex asked, referring to the island.

"I heard they have good wine there."

"Let's just hope they have a place to land."

Tom and Alex continued to fly the injured ship towards Madeira. The usually smooth ride was interjected with dips, bumps and uncontrolled swerves.

Within minutes, the beautiful landscape of Madeira came into view. There were lush mountains full of green vegetation and exquisite coastlines. The sight seemed especially breathtaking as it also represented their only salvation from a watery grave.

"Let's set her down in the opening in the forest next to the mountain peak," Alex said. "We'll hide there for a day while fixing the ship."

"Will I be able to get some wine?"

"If we're able to land this thing, the first bottle's on me!"

CHAPTER 17

THE MEN STILL GASPED FOR AIR. Soot filled their lungs and blackened their faces. Their green uniforms were singed and now charcoal in color.

These maladies were the least of their troubles. After having lost four of their elite soldiers on what should have been a mundane mission, they felt humiliated. Death at this point seemed a more viable option than living with disgrace.

SattAr, however, knew this recent debacle had been entirely his own fault. He was unprepared for the assault. He thought he could just walk into the building with a gun at his side and Alex Pella and his colleagues would surrender without a fight. He had not realized what a formidable force they would be. In fact, he had witnessed less resistance when he once squashed an entire Egyptian revolution.

"I underestimated Alex Pella," SattAr said, while gasping for air, "and... all of them escaped. This... is entirely my fault."

He continued to suck vigorously on the oxygen pellet, trying not to get lightheaded when talking. The oxygen diffused quickly into his bloodstream and down his lungs, making it somewhat easier to breathe.

SattAr and his men were sprawled out on the deck of a small UAA transport boat. Designed to appear as if it were a simple fishing trawler, it was large enough to accommodate all of them.

"So you're trying to tell me they all got away," Ari Lesmana said.

His red, holographic image was barely visible on the secure line, but his voice retained its boisterous nature and the air of self-promotion.

"Malik, I am sorry. My resignation will be sent to you immediately."

The news did indeed disappoint him, but failure was no reason for dismissal. Just like in other governmental positions, shoddy work ethics, sub-par outcomes, and a poor attitude were not grounds for getting fired. In fact, the only person Ari had asked to leave was actually superb at his job. However, he hated the man's criticism, even if it was made "off the record".

"That will not be necessary!" Ari exclaimed. "What I do need, however, is Alex Pella and the cure for *The Disease*. Where is he now?"

"The XR-2 that transported us here attempted to bring down their Stratoskimmer but lost them somewhere over the Atlantic. I have sent out two of our spy planes to aid in the search but for now I have heard nothing."

"Then I want you and your men on full alert. If those planes cannot find them, then our inside sources may be able to. Be ready for action soldier."

● ● ●

Ari was no longer two miles underground and had joined Masika in the foreman's quarters. Cool air-conditioning and breathable air were a welcome change from the hellish conditions he had just left.

The Minister of Construction, Razmi, had joined them to finalize the last details for their bunker. The man wore the traditional Arab garb with a white *ghutra* on his head. Razmi reminded most people of a weasel. With a thin face, narrow eyes, recessed jaw, and scruffy goatee, even he could not deny the resemblance.

"You must understand Minister Razmi," Ari went on to say in a boastful tone, "this bunker is of the utmost importance to the UAA."

"Yes Malik!" Razmi responded in an unusually high-pitched tone for a man. Still not understanding the need for such an extensive bunker, he obeyed orders without hesitation.

"Because much of our country's valuable resources and manpower have been filtered into this project over the last six months, its success is vital. Show me what's left to be done."

Above the circular table loaded with papers and binders a holographic image instantly appeared. "This is where you just were, Malik," he said while pointing to a large oval-shaped space on the hologram. The entire image showed a cross-sectional view of where Yemen met the Arabian Sea. The rocky crust of the land appeared blackish-brown in color while the water was deep blue. Multiple tunnels within the crust running both perpendicular and parallel created an enormous checkerboard pattern with the oval tunnel at its very bottom.

"The foreman stated that this space will be inundated first thing in the morning," Ari said.

"Exactly at 6:00 A.M. the aqueducts will begin to open," Razmi responded, pointing towards the hologram.

Water from the Arabian began to slowly fill the oval space with its blue hue until it completely filled the area. The process appeared effortless, but the technology and manpower behind it was incredible.

"The whole procedure will take about a day," Razmi went on to say. "This water will then circulate throughout the entire two mile deep bunker, creating a simple method for both cooling and heating the entire complex.

The audacity of the project certainly impressed Ari. He had never imagined how colossal the undertaking had become. His wife was in awe. She savored Razmi's words, imagining at each step how she and her husband inched that much closer to achieving world domination.

Born into nothing, she always aspired to greatness. She swore to herself that she would never again be that poor little girl in a desolate village with no hope for a future or possibility of getting ahead. Though her father tried to adequately support his family, each day was a difficult undertaking just to survive.

At the age of only twelve, Masika left her home in search of a better life. Never looking back even to contact her family, she found a way, no matter how despicable or demeaning, to survive and eventually pay for school.

When she finally went to college and met Ari, she knew that he would be her ticket to success. Her survival instinct took over and by the end of their first year of dating, she had managed to obtain a marriage proposal from him.

Fortunately for Masika, it did not take much convincing. Both shared the same fascist and existentialist views of life. Like Nietzsche's master morality theory, both adhered to the belief that wealth, strength, and power were the strong Homeric traits that should be emulated. They created and judged their own actions and if the outcomes benefited them or increased their stature in any way, then it was deemed positive and moral regardless of the consequences.

She knew that one day they would be in charge and the future was theirs to take.

"And the last step," Razmi finished explaining, "will be to

create a shallow lake three by two miles wide just above the bunker. It will serve to help both cool the bunker and conceal it from any sort of unwanted intrusions. Then, my Malik, the bunker will be fully operational."

The holograph then depicted blue water from the Aegean Sea flowing along the surface of the bunker, creating the lake Razmi had mentioned.

Blood pumped vigorously through Masika's body and her eyes widened with anticipation. She could barely hold herself still, thinking of what the future held for both her and Ari. It did not matter that billions would die from *The Disease*. It was their destiny, and they were meant for greater purposes.

Ari kept a cool demeanor and with a presidential air said, "Minister Razmi, I must say that I am very impressed. This project is the culmination of everything that I and the UAA stand for. The world will not forget your name, Minister Razmi."

CHAPTER 18

THE LEAGUE OF WORLD LEADERS (LWL) had been assembled on an urgent basis at Albert Rosenberg's request. Notably absent were France, Iceland, and Greece while the remaining 84 members attended.

Even Ari Lesmana was present. With a smug look on his face and an air of superiority, he already knew the motive behind the meeting. Just a few hours prior, Albert informed him of his intensions, and assured Ari that the UAA would be exempt from the meeting's outcome.

Though Albert called this conference on short notice, many of the world leaders had already been meeting in private. The fallout from The New Reality's financial takeover of three countries was far-reaching. Similar to a large surface earthquake in the Pacific, it generated enough momentum to cause a tsunami-like effect around the world.

The LWL met in a virtual arena created by The New Reality technology. Holographic images of the 84 world leaders were set against a backdrop similar to an ancient Roman forum. With white pillars, arches, flowering plants, and statues depicting ancient Gods, the setting appeared both beautiful and awe-inspiring.

Discussion spread immediately throughout the crowd. Worried, the members spoke collegially amongst themselves. Never before had an assembly of world leaders been so cordial or accommodating to one another. Sometimes it takes the worst to bring out the best in people.

The image of Albert appeared in the center of the Roman forum. The leaders from the other 84 countries sat in inclining, circular rows behind this central arena. His appearance brought an immediate silence to the crowd. Most tried to appear presidential and confident while a few carried their worries like a scarlet letter.

"I'd like to thank you for convening on such short notice," Albert said in a strong, loud voice. "I understand the importance of your busy schedules and thus appreciate your promptness."

Despite Albert's recent reputation as a ruthless businessman, he always kept an accommodating and affable air himself. He was the type of guy who would rob an unsuspecting stranger blind but do it with a smile on his face.

Albert holographically presented himself to the forum with a previous, healthier image of himself. No longer cachectic and balding, he now boasted a full head of white, curly hair and a vibrant face. Plus, his previously strong build was evident as he filled out his black pinstripe suit like a man half his age.

Not unique to Albert, many of the other world leaders did the same. Wrinkles, skin blotches and extra pounds had a way of disappearing every time they met for an LWL conference.

"The world has entered disturbing times," Albert went on to say.

The leaders from the various countries all nodded their heads in agreement. Hoping the subject concerned *The Disease,* many spoke of it in hushed voices, eager to lead the topic in that direction.

Albert looked around in a panoramic view to capture their attention. "What I am here to discuss with all of you today is an affliction far worse than *The Disease* which has strangled the life out of some of your countries while threatening others."

The mumbling had ceased as the attendants waited like wayward school children called to a scolding from the principal. Each leader had the same question: *Was what happened to France, Iceland, and Greece just a warning, or was it an omen for the future of all of their countries?*

"Irresponsibility," Albert said, and took a pause before continuing. "It's a simple word, but it has far-reaching implications. In school, I was taught to avoid it, and in business, I learned it would get me fired."

Albert made a pondering gesture and placed his left hand under his chin. "So what happened?"

The world leaders kept quiet. The longer Albert stared at them without speaking, the more their angst grew. The question resonated throughout the room as they each asked themselves: *What happened?*

"The New Reality," Albert finally said, "has not only loaned each of you here a substantial amount of money, but it has also donated large sums of currency to all of your countries. And for what? To be spent frivolously? To be used in creating more governmental jobs that fail to foster economic growth in any way? Or just to be allocated in such a way as to get you all reelected?"

The Mexican president was the first to interject. No longer able to tolerate being chastised like a child, he wanted this indignity to cease. "We have not come here to listen to a lecture Mr. Rosenberg!" he boldly stated in broken English upon rising to his feet. "This assembly of world leaders was created for the sole purpose of political discussion and not for accounting purposes. If you have any further economic concerns, please discuss them with the appropriate party and do not waste our valuable time."

Some members kept quiet while others shouted disparaging remarks at Albert and feigned leaving in response to these offensive accusations.

Unfortunately for them, Albert was not a novice in either economics or world politics. He had anticipated such a response and scoffed at their feigned rebuttal.

"President Delgado," Albert said in a stern voice, "your country is at the brink of financial collapse, your streets are overrun by drug lords, and your people are risking their lives to flee your borders. Sir, you need to sit down and listen to what I have to say!"

He glowered at each of them with the sternest of stares. Even his most vehement detractors were left paralyzed. Unable to respond, they all returned to their seats with the proverbial tails between their legs.

"You *all* need to listen to what I have to say!"

Albert's initially affable tone had turned into a disciplinary one. He had no time for further distractions.

"What I have seen throughout my tenure with The New Reality," Albert said, "is rampant irresponsibility. Not a single one of you here or your predecessors has made any strides to foster an independent and strong economy."

Albert slammed his fist into his hand.

"The time is up! I am calling in all the loans!"

An audible gasp could be heard throughout the room. Fear and surprise had replaced the former looks of pride and dignity.

"I'm sure you all are familiar with the content of these loans," Albert commented, knowing full well they had signed the contracts in desperation. "And as of right now, I plan to exercise the clause which states that each of your countries has to ante up one third of your debt in seven days or be in default on all your loans."

Albert's message was short but to the point. They had all borne witness to the consequences that had befallen Iceland, France, and Greece and none had doubts about his sincerity. No longer taking a strong stance, the world leaders began to plead and implore Albert for mercy. Some blamed their previous leaders, while others openly chastised their cabinets or economic counselors.

"Mr. Rosenberg," one voice rose up amongst the commotion. "Surely you do not believe that such a request can be met on such short notice. I do appreciate you and your company's generosity, but in these times a demand like this is unquestionably impossible to accommodate."

The gentleman distinctly articulated what the rest were thinking. As speaker of the LWL, the English Prime Minister, Thomas Harrison, held a particularly powerful position and attempted to use this influence to persuade Albert into a more lenient position.

"Prime Minister," Albert said to the distinguished Englishman, "let me briefly reiterate myself. Seven days."

These two words had never carried such a powerful meaning as they did now. In a mere week, the balance of world power would be changed irrevocably.

CHAPTER 19

THE HOT SUMMER AIR laid over them like an unwelcome blanket.

Alex and the team had hidden their Stratoskimmer not far from Megiddo in one of the forests scattered across the landscape. Though Israel was known for its harsh desert climates, this area near its western Mediterranean coast had lush vegetation and green grasses. It was the last oasis before entering the eastern sand-stricken scenery.

William panted as sweat made large stains under his armpits. Not one for exercising, he certainly did not enjoy the mile-long walk just to get to the ancient city of Megiddo. He much preferred his air-conditioned office with all the modern conveniences the 21st century had to offer.

"You do realize I'm not having fun here," William complained. "Alex, would it have killed you to stay an extra day at Madeira? I mean, if I wanted to be stuck anywhere, that's the place I'd want to be."

The Stratoskimmer had taken less damage than expected. Only the navigation and magnetic stabilization systems were affected and their refurbishing took less than half a day to complete.

Thus, Tom was not only able to enjoy two bottles of Madeira's famous wine but he also saw the island's magnificent fireworks display. He enjoyed himself so much that Alex teased him that he had planned to crash-land there the entire time.

Alex, however, did not partake in any of the festivities. His thoughts were on the necroids back at Neurono-Tek. He knew they must have fully infiltrated his company and were most likely sending confidential information back to the UAA.

It would provide the only feasible explanation as to why the UAA was waiting to ambush them in Crete. Neurono-Tek was hardwired with the latest spy-ware technology; nothing had been stolen or leaked for years as a result. Simply, it was the modern equivalent to Fort Knox.

While the emergency detour to the island had given the team a much-needed break, they knew they couldn't risk staying put for long. Though admittedly a little hungover, the team set off for Megiddo in the Stratoskimmer at dawn.

"This isn't *tel* Megiddo," William continued to whine, "this is *hell* Megiddo."

Guri fared no better. Out of shape and refusing to remove his sport jacket, he slowly walked with William along the dirt road, at least twenty feet behind Alex, Marissa, and Jonathan.

"You were explaining to us about the Bible code back on Crete," Alex said nonchalantly, turning to Jonathan.

Though acting casual about the subject, he had been deliberating upon it ever since they were interrupted on Crete. Marissa, too, had remained curious but after their near-death experience, she did not have an appropriate opportunity to ask any further questions.

Jonathan responded, "Well, since I've already almost gotten us killed, taken you to Crete, and now have brought you here to the Biblical site of Armageddon, a full explanation only seems fair."

The sweltering heat did not hinder the quick cadence of his response. In fact, he seemed to enjoy the weather. Though red in the face and sweating, Jonathan appeared energized by the heat and ready for a full day of activity.

He took a swig from his water bottle to moisten his palate before continuing. "You see, William Miller once considered himself a Deist and believed that God was a distant being, far removed from all human affairs. But after partaking in the Battle of Plattsburgh in the War of 1812, all that changed. Though vastly outnumbered by the British forces, the Americans were able to overcome the assault and claim victory for their country."

William interrupted from the rear with an, "Are we there yet?" like a discontented youth.

Marissa rolled her eyes, and Alex smirked in agreement.

"And you know what he concluded?" Jonathan asked aloud before taking a dramatic pause. "That only a Supreme Being could have brought them victory that day. It was a telling statement, but I sincerely believe the man was correct."

Alex had to ask, "So how do you explain *The Disease*, genocide, or natural disasters?"

"I do not have all the answers, nor do I claim to fully understanding the inner workings of God's mind," Jonathan said. "What I do know by reading the Bible is that God has helped man many times in the past, and that the Bible code is a tool which he has bestowed upon us to help ourselves."

"'He who walks wisely will be delivered,'" Marissa said. "Proverbs 28:26."

Alex and Jonathan were both silenced by her quotation. Not many people in these times were still able to quote the Bible, especially a more esoteric verse such as this. In the fast-paced modern world, religion was considered by many to be a relic or an outdated tradition clung to by the old, disenfranchised, or poor.

Marissa slightly blushed, surprised by their response. "What can I say? I'm a Sunday school teacher. If I'm not out on location, I make a point to spend time with the kids in my parish."

Beautiful, intelligent, and wholesome, Alex thought. Now if she could only cook…

"You must understand," Jonathan continued, "that the Bible has time-locked hidden messages within it that will only reveal themselves to us when we cross a certain threshold of technological and intellectual advancement."

"I can assume that you have crossed that point?" Alex commented.

"I have crossed *a* point, but the significance of the point to which I have crossed is uncertain. You see, the code is like an onion. There are many layers to it, and all that I have done is just uncover one of these layers. Will it provide us with an answer, or will it lead us to the next layer? I cannot say."

They had arrived at the base of Megiddo and waited for both William and Guri to join the group under a large palm tree. Both men appeared to be nearing heat exhaustion and stumbled to the ground upon reaching the tree.

"Are you two O.K.?" Alex asked, wondering if they could take the heat much longer.

"Just need to catch my breath," William responded, beet red in the face.

"With my breathing condition," Guri tried to say in his usual nasal voice before William interrupted with a stern look.

They all drank from their canteens and enjoyed the reprieve provided by the shade for a few minutes.

"What exactly are we supposed to be looking for in this

hellhole anyway?" William asked. "If it's heatstroke, then I found it and we can go home."

They all looked towards Jonathan, expecting an answer.

"I can only tell you that as part of our journey," he answered spryly, "we must be here. What we're supposed to find is unknown but will become known when we find it."

"So you don't know," William blurted. "That's great! Just great." Marissa whispered to Alex, "And why did you invite him along? I assume it wasn't his charming personality."

"He's just blowing off steam. I'd be more concerned if he weren't saying anything. Then we'd be in real trouble."

Alex took William and Guri by the hands and lifted them back to their feet. "Time to act like tourists."

Alex led the way as the group began the ascent up the original seventy-foot ramp to the city. Once able to accommodate horses and wagons, the road was now full of rubble and stones that had fallen from the city's crumbling outer walls. Grass grew alongside the ramp, and a few more palm trees greeted them along the way.

At the top of the hill, the extent of the ancient city could be visualized. Much of it lay in ruins, but the remaining stones gave a skeletal impression of how Megiddo appeared in the past.

A tour guide saw their approach and waved them over in his direction. Already surrounded by ten people, he was glad to welcome a few more.

"The tour is just beginning," he said with a hint of a Hebrew accent. "Come join us. Come."

Alex shrugged his shoulders and turned to the rest of them. "It's probably the best way to see the city."

Jonathan and Marissa nodded in agreement while Guri and William appeared too exhausted to put up any argument.

The tour guide wore khaki pants and a short-sleeved, collared blue shirt. He also donned a cowboy hat and a large pair of sunglasses that seemed to overwhelm much of his bearded face. The rest of the people surrounding him looked like classic tourists. With large sun hats or baseball caps, Hawaiian shirts and sandals, they waited eagerly for the tour to commence.

"My name is Hillel," the tour guide announced with a large smile, "and I will be personally guiding you through the magnificent ruins of ancient Megiddo. If you don't already know, this is not just one city but a total of twenty-six different cities layered one upon the next."

He pointed over to the ramp. "You may not have recognized it upon entering the city, but you have already passed through several of the original gates which once stood here."

The pile of stones and rubble provided a glimpse of Megiddo's former glory. Though only stone walls on either side of the path remained, one could imagine how great arches would have connected them, allowing chariots, horses, and people to pass into the city.

"These security gates," he went on to say, "along with a strongly fortified wall that surrounded the city helped protect Megiddo from unwanted visitors. And as the word *Armageddon* originates from this particular place, I can assure you it has seen more than its share of hostilities."

Alex did find the tour interesting but kept his attention towards the ruins rather than to the tour guide. Rocks, rubble, and dirt surrounded him. An occasional palm tree livened up the monotonous scenery, but otherwise, there was not much more to see.

An aerial view of the city didn't seem to offer much more help. Alex had been examining the layout from the satellite pictures provided on his videre lens and was at a loss to find anything of significance.

Did the city layout represent some hidden message? Was it somehow meant to guide them to a different location? The more Alex pondered these questions, the more frustrated he became. Thousands of archeologists had excavated Megiddo in the past and there was never any mention of any hidden code or a strange artifact being found.

"The city was ruled by many of the great superpowers of their day," Hillel said. "From the Egyptians, Canaanites, and Assyrians to the Israelites, Megiddo has been occupied by many different civilizations."

They walked farther into the city as the tour continued while Guri and William relaxed next to a shaded wall.

Alex turned back and gave William a look as if to say, *What are you guys doing?*

With a loud, boisterous voice William pointed to a pile of rubble next to him. "Guri said he found something rather interesting within these rocks. I thought we should stay back and give it the proper inspection that it deserves."

Guri squinted and pushed back his glasses. "I said nothing of the sort."

Alex kept on with the tour as the two squabbled between themselves while he left. After seeing how exhausted they both looked, he knew letting them rest a little was probably the best thing to do.

Marissa whispered to Alex, "You find anything interesting around here yet?"

Alex looked towards Marissa. Seeing her in tight blue jeans and a white halter top that revealed a hint of her midriff made him think he was standing next to the most interesting sight the city had offered in years.

"Not a thing," he finally said. "And the rocks are beginning to hypnotize me. It looks like there's nothing here."

Jonathan overheard their conversation and leaned towards them, "Do not be discouraged. Sometimes one will find what they are looking for in the most inauspicious of places."

"Does the Bible code give us any specifics as to what we are looking for around here?" Alex asked, trying not to sound overtly skeptical. "Because everything's starting to look the same."

"As I have told your companion, Mr. William Fowler, it only points us in the right direction. The rest is up to us."

Though Alex believed Jonathan, he had begun to become a little doubtful about the authenticity of this Bible code. *William Miller was wrong about the code almost three hundred years ago. Could Jonathan be wrong about it now?*

While contemplating this possibility, Alex began to examine a raised circular structure about ten meters in diameter.

Noticing his interest, the tour guide Hillel said, "I see you found the ancient pagan altar here at this site. You know, when they first excavated it, archeologists found remnants of animal bones and ashes, leading us to believe it was once used for sacrifices."

"Or a good pig roast," William commented a little too loudly, bringing scowls from the tourists.

"How nice of you and Guri to join us again," Alex said. "I guess you didn't find anything interesting in those rocks back there?"

Though prone to complaining, William did feel as if he were letting everyone down by relaxing under the shade. Alex had brought him here for a reason, and he certainly didn't want to disappoint him or somehow hinder their overall mission.

"Just needed a quick break," he finally admitted.

Their conversation was interrupted by four long-haired, bearded men wearing tie-dyed shirts and bandanas accompanied by two similarly dressed females hitting bongo drums without any semblance of rhythm.

"The world is going to end!" shouted one. "*The Disease* is going to kill us all!" yelled another.

They also held signs with a peace symbol painted on it and slogans such as "Make Peace not Death" or "Let's All Make Love Before We Die" written poorly underneath.

Hillel gestured over to a few rows of stone and said in a loud voice, hoping to speak over the interference, "If you would look over to the pillars in front of you, it is believed that this section of the city was once used as a stable. Those stones with circular holes at the top are thought to be where the horses were tied while the others that look like bathtubs were considered to be the troughs where the horses ate and drank.

"So rude!" Marissa said, referring to the group wearing the tie-dye shirts and making the commotion.

"Focus," Jonathan reminded.

He was right, but Alex found it increasingly difficult to concentrate the more he heard those drums beat and the mindless chants. He grew even more frustrated when he noticed a new pack of eight more men wearing tie-dyed shirts congregating around one of the stone pillars in front of them.

Does it ever end?

Alex picked up a rock and pantomimed as if he were going to throw it at one of them. Marissa smirked and nodded in agreement.

Fortunately, the new group of eight men sitting around the pillar boasted no musical instruments nor brandished any annoying signs. They were quiet and seemed to be peacefully partaking in some type of sit-in event.

As Alex walked past them, he noted that although they donned tie-dyed shirts, these men all had short hair and wore black marching boots.

Something did not seem right. Also uncharacteristic was the fact that most appeared cleanly shaven. Plus, they all looked as if they were a copy of one another. Even the tie-dyed stains on their shirts were identical.

Before Alex could alert anyone in his group, one of the men turned and looked his way.

He instantly recognized the man's face. The cold, calculating eyes and finely trimmed mustache made his identity undeniable. SattAr had found them.

"It's the piece of crap!" William shouted at the top of his lungs while pointing directly at him.

Believing William had discovered something interesting, the tourists all began moving toward the direction he pointed. Their enthusiasm became instantly tempered when one of the men in the group arose, brandishing a semiautomatic machine gun.

Well I guess a subtle retreat is out of the question now, Alex thought. In disbelief, he quickly determined that the UAA had somehow once again uncovered their location. Options were limited.

Alex took the rock already in his hand and threw it directly at the UAA soldier with the gun. The man's head violently jerked backwards upon impact as he fell limply to the ground in a concussive state. His body jerked a few times, but otherwise, he lay motionless with blood dripping profusely down his brow.

The other seven, including SattAr, immediately began to rise in unison. Also with machine guns, they were certainly not going to let this injustice go unpunished again.

CHAPTER 20

THE BODIES WITHIN THE MORGUE lay dormant no longer. Nesting within them, necroids feasted, devouring their prey. The cold air preserved the bodies' flesh and created the ideal temperature for the necroids to proliferate.

No longer restricted to consume only simple amino acids from their original, terrorist host, they now incorporated complete proteins from these bodies into their system.

The first casket snapped ajar, exposing it to the morgue's stale air. Within minutes the others clicked open in a sound reminiscent of falling dominoes.

Like Frankenstein rising from the dead, the newly created necroids flowed out from the caskets. No longer a centimeter in length like their predecessors, they were now at least four inches end-to-end, which made their protruding fangs, spiked body, and red eyes that much more terrifying.

As they escaped from the cabinets, the original necroids also slowly followed. Like in some type of macabre parade, they marched in line up the walls to the ventilator shaft at the top of the room. As if programmed from their parents, they knew where to go and what mission they were created to accomplish.

Because of Neurono-Tek's power grid failure, the fans and dehumidifiers had not been working, leaving the air in the dark shaft damp and stagnant.

The necroids had no need for ambient light. With their glowing eyes and internal radar they were able to negotiate through the dark unhindered by any obstacle.

They all continued scurrying through the shaft in a straight line. Although there were many branch points along the way, they all headed in the same direction like ants marching to a feast.

They climbed vertically towards the top of the building. A single fan at the very end of the shaft lay dormant, and the necroids crawled between the blades to freedom.

It was a clear night. Because of the nonfunctioning lights at Neurono-Tek the stars shone brightly, unhindered by any man-made florescence. The glow from the bugs' eyes cast a faint, yet eerie shadow on the rooftop like a red beacon of death.

The necroids all congregated at the top of the main science building until they numbered a few hundred. Their eyes blinked as if in Morse code, signaling to one another their next plan of attack.

Below, police vehicles, fire trucks, and a full bomb squad regimen had assembled. After an exhaustive search of the premises and the power grid, they found nothing out of the ordinary. The electrical failure and the deaths of the maintenance workers were deemed accidental, and the conclusion was that there had been no unusual activity at the Neurono-Tek complex.

Unbeknownst to them, the necroids that originally destroyed the power grid had been charred beyond recognition during their assault. Their small bodies were unable to compensate for such high voltage and had been destroyed as a result. Their remnants were considered pieces of the power grid and eventually discarded as unwanted debris.

The only reason both a police and fire department presence still remained at Neurono-Tek was due to Samantha's urging. Despite their conclusion that the blackout was due to a simple electrical failure, she insisted they refrain from leaving, stating the trouble had just begun.

Samantha would not take no for an answer. With her high-pitched voice and persistent manner, she forced them into submission. Plus, because of Neurono-Tek's continued financial benefit to both the local and state economy, they could not deny one of its top executives.

The law enforcement and fire department staff all stood outside their vehicles. Most drank coffee or ate a late night snack while others laughed with one another. There was certainly no sense of foreboding or belief another terrorist attack could be imminent.

Because electrical power had not returned, the hospital and entire complex had been fully evacuated. Samantha remained as the sole Neurono-Tek employee. Even Gill was forced to leave.

The necroids began crawling down the building. Their eyes, which once boasted a red glow, had turned black like the rest of their bodies to help keep them camouflaged in the night's darkness. The sound of crickets and other wildlife drowned out the noise of their legs clicking against the windows and metal façade of the main science building.

Upon reaching the ground, the bugs began to scatter. They had a full oasis of modern technology in front of them and did not wait to devour their unsuspecting prey.

The warm engines of the fire and police vehicles were the first to garner their attention. In the dark night, most of the devilish bugs began racing to these cars and trucks. A feast awaited them.

The assault went quickly and silently. The necroids scurried by the unsuspecting police and fire officials without bringing any attention to themselves. The stealth and rapidity of their attack would have impressed even the most elite of warriors.

Within minutes, the twenty running vehicles on the premises had been secured by the necroids. Another hundred necroids chose not to join the assault. They remained preoccupied at the base of the building in search of an even greater power source. They could feel its presence oozing out from underneath them, deep from within the earth.

A few of the necroids scurried around the building looking for the source but to no avail. It seemed to be well hidden and without a viable entrance.

A flashlight from one of the policeman suddenly bore down upon the bunch. The necroids all stopped moving and turned each of their four eyes to the light source.

"What the--?" the policeman gasped. Stunned by his discovery, he could not utter another syllable.

His partner turned and also caught sight of the ghastly view. This was no cockroach nor did it appear like anything they had ever seen before. The necroids' red eyes suddenly came back to life. Their glow shocked the two interlopers and made them jolt slightly back.

"What are they?" one asked.

"The spawn of Satan!" the other responded. "Go get the spotlight while I keep my light on them."

The necroids again began blinking their eyes in unison but remained still, seemingly hypnotized by the flashlight.

While the one policeman brought the spotlight, his other colleagues all congregated around it in disbelief at what they saw. Overpowering the flashlight's meager light, the spotlight bore down upon the necroids, illuminating them so brightly that they almost seemed to glow.

The police and fire officials mumbled to one another, unsure of how to handle the predicament. Though their training and manuals encompassed a vast variety of situations, there was certainly nothing written about how to properly approach a bunch of frighteningly large insects.

One of the policemen stepped out from the group. Holding a broom in one hand and a bucket in the other, he thought capturing one of these creatures would be the most logical first step.

"Be careful, Todd," urged one.

"You have your life insurance paid up?" joked another.

With the utmost caution, he approached the necroids. Though both physically and mentally strong, he was certainly spooked by these bugs. He felt as if the red glow was somehow boring down on his soul and sucking it straight out of him.

Todd knelt down on one knee and carefully extended his broom and bucket towards the nearest necroid. He did not breathe or blink, believing the slightest shudder could bring out an ill-fated response. The broom tediously made its way to the necroid. In what seemed like an eternity to Todd and his onlookers, he methodically pushed the bug into the bucket.

With a big sigh of relief, Todd cautiously began to stand with his captured prey. Moving as if he were in slow motion, he turned and started to walk back to his vehicle.

Before taking a full step, he could feel a searing burn run down his left calf. This pain was followed by another in his buttock and then in his back. Within seconds, he could no longer localize the burning sensations as they inundated his whole body.

Todd suddenly fell to the ground, paralyzed by the pain as a swarm of necroids began to devour him. They gnawed into his body and ripped with their protruding jaws big chucks of flesh right out of him.

It occurred so quickly that Todd's colleagues had no time to react. When they finally realized what was occurring, the necroids had completely covered the officer.

Todd tried to scream, but the pain became so severe that death enveloped him before he could utter a sound.

Shots rang out in the night as the police immediately began to open fire on the necroids. Bits and pieces of the bugs flung up into the air as bullets pulverized their bodies. Instead of attacking the officers, the remaining necroids decided to retreat. Sensing a large electrical source of power underground, they began to bore into the earth and dig. With their cadre of siblings already secure in the police and fire vehicles, they now sought out the only remaining power source left at Neurono-Tek: Samantha's bunker.

CHAPTER 21

THE PEOPLE IN THE MEGIDDO TOUR group began to scream and flee in terror. Most were a few pounds too heavy and their escape proved both slow and awkward. Some tripped over the rocks while others bumped haphazardly into each other.

The tour guide, Hillel, also sprinted away from the trouble. After witnessing Alex knock out one of the soldiers with a rock, he wasn't that curious to see their reaction. Unlike the others, he ran like an Olympic triathlon out of Megiddo and down the ramp. *Today was certainly not the day he would meet his maker.*

Amidst the commotion Jonathan threw a cherry-shaped object towards the soldiers. It exploded upon impact, and the air around it rippled like the surface of a pond struck by a pebble.

The soldiers fell to their knees, confused and momentarily dazed by the blast. Alex had passed these concussive mini-grenades out to everyone prior to their arrival at Megiddo, stating they may be useful in a time of crisis.

Alex immediately grabbed Marissa by the hand and yelled

to the others, "Let's go!"

Though not necessarily needing Alex's guidance, she did not shudder at letting him hold her hand.

Instead of running towards the ramp by which they had entered the city, Alex led them over to an area in Megiddo where the rocks and stones still piled over eight feet in height—tall enough whereby the soldiers could not get a straight shot at them.

Plus, Alex already noted in his contact's satellite view of the area that a few soldiers stood ready at the end of the ramp. They must have been hiding in the gift shop and got into position when the group entered the city.

Hillel had unfortunately already made their acquaintance. With a butt of a machine gun to his chest as a hello, he lay on the dirt path while being frisked by the other soldiers.

"Quick thinking, Jonathan," Alex commented. "You saved us back there."

"We're far from safety yet," he responded, pointing out their painfully obvious predicament. "And I have no other tricks up my sleeve."

SattAr and the other soldiers began to slowly regain their composure. While the seven returned to their feet, the one soldier still lay motionless on the ground. Barely breathing, he made a few gurgling sounds, letting everyone know death had not yet claimed him.

SattAr bent down and cracked in half a small fluorescent white cylinder. Taking one end of each half he placed them on both sides of the man's neck. As the white liquid disappeared from the cylinders the soldier's body became stiff and rigid. His core body temperature began to plummet and his lips and skin turned a discolored blue.

SattAr threw the empty cylinders on the ground. The soldier had been cryopreserved for later treatment. Time did not allow for immediate medical management, but he certainly was not going to let another man die under his command.

"They must have hidden amidst those stones over there," SattAr pointed.

Unlike Alex's satellite capabilities, he brandished no such technology. Because much of the UAA's spending for years was pilfered away in pork-barrel projects or wasteful government initiatives, the military forces had become grossly underequipped.

The large rocks SattAr pointed to ahead of him would obviously be the only safe place for Alex and the group to hide. Unless they were crouching behind some rubble, they had no other course of action but to proceed as he determined.

SattAr gestured to either side of the stone walls and signaled two of his men to flank the left side while another two took the right. The soldiers did as they were told and scampered into position while fully brandishing their weapons.

"Let them know we're here," SattAr said.

The soldier next to him understood his commander's orders. Taking a small pistol from his belt with a cone-shaped projectile at the tip, he pointed it at an opening between the rocks.

The pistol made a whooshing noise as it launched the projectile. Upon impact, it exploded with a thunderous boom and leveled the rocks around it into rubble. A large white dust cloud immediately plumed over the ruins, decreasing the visibility within the area.

What took years of excavation had been pulverized in a matter of seconds. It was an archeologist's nightmare. All the history was destroyed.

Megiddo was once again under siege.

SattAr hoped to flush out Alex and his companions from the rocks, not kill them. He assumed they would soon exit without further resistance.

"Hold your fire!" he announced to the soldiers as the dust cloud settled.

There was no response. SattAr and his men waited for Alex and his group to emerge, impatient to capture their prey.

During this time, the soldiers congregated at the base of Megiddo had rounded up the entire tour group and the men and women wearing the tie-dyed shirts. All yielded to their demands and knelt in the dirt at gunpoint.

Despite Hillel's initial welcome with the butt of a rifle, the soldiers released him once they confirmed his identity. With a few cracked ribs and a large bruise to the chest, he stumbled away from Megiddo, praising God for his release.

"We have waited long enough," SattAr said. "Load up the Ampere-Projectile."

He relayed his plans to the other soldiers who had flanked the remaining stone walls and gave them their new instructions.

Taking another cone-shaped shell from his belt, the soldier next to SattAr loaded his pistol once again and sent this projectile hurling into the center of the stony structure ahead of them.

Instead of an explosion, it set off a burst of electrical activity. Sparks scattered throughout the rocks and made a buzzing noise in its wake. After a few seconds, the electrical bursts stopped, leaving the area silent and smoldering in fumes.

Secured with the fact that this assault immobilized Alex and his group, SattAr and his cadre of soldiers slowly closed in on the stony ruins. With their guns poised, the assault commenced.

CHAPTER 22

THE EXPLOSION HAD KNOCKED ALEX and the group to the ground and rattled all of their nerves. Without any military training, they were dazed and frightened by their predicament.

William became so scared he couldn't talk, let alone turn on his soothing seventies music. Despite multiple attempts, his hands trembled too severely to manipulate the controls. Supertramp would have to wait… that is if they survived.

Marissa tended to Guri's breathing problems. The dust cloud created by the explosion had set off an asthma attack. His breathing had become labored. An audible wheeze could be heard even without a stethoscope.

She still carried her black emergency medical bag around her left shoulder. Equipped with everything from treating the common cold to tending to trauma victims, it provided a quick fix for a simple asthma attack.

Marissa grabbed a small syringe from the bag and administered a quick injection in the back of Guri's neck.

Within less than a minute his breathing normalized.

"Thank you," he gasped.

She placed her hand on his chest. The wheezing had ceased. "You'll be O.K. Just take a few more deep breaths."

Alex's mind was racing while he pieced together an escape route. He noted the UAA soldiers attempting to flank them from both sides while SattAr and the others stood their ground without any other evasive actions. His satellite view of the area revealed their position to be in a labyrinth of rock. The site made him feel like a rat caught in a maze.

Alex pointed at the others to get their attention. He did not want to utter a word as the UAA might be eavesdropping on their conversation. *Follow me*, he mouthed and turned his head towards an adjacent alley.

The others followed in a bent position in order to ensure their heads would not be visible along any of the lower outcroppings of rocks. Alex had seen a possible escape route. After studying the satellite picture and remembering the reconnaissance material he read about Megiddo before arriving, he believed a hidden tunnel might provide the only means for escape.

Two soldiers drew nearer to their position. In this area of the labyrinth, the rocks were thick and the walls tall. Despite their close proximity, Alex knew that unless the soldiers had another explosive charge or planned to scale the walls, they would be relatively safe.

Alex held up his hand to the others. The soldiers next to them had made a particularly odd maneuver. Instead of their continued reconnoitering, they had backed away from the rocks and placed a small metal spike into the ground. Attached to it was a thin wire with a long metal tip, which each soldier held into the air as they kneeled.

Electrical assault! He had read about this immobilizing weapon before but never expected it to be used on him. The words *pain*, *coma*, and *possible cardiac death* were the most pertinent things he could remember about it. The other details seemed to fall short at this moment.

How do I ground all of us in less than one minute?

Alex thought quickly of everything they had on them at that moment, down to the possible wiring in Marissa's bra. Taking an additional second to visualize her bra, he once again attempted to devise a plan.

Electrical attack, Alex mouthed to the others. Turning to Marissa, he gestured to have her medical bag, hoping to find what he needed.

Before he had a chance to look in it, Jonathan handed him a five-foot long piece of wire he had taken from Guri's apartment before they escaped.

Astonished, Alex asked, "Was this in the Bible code?"

Jonathan smiled. "No, but it was in my Boy Scout Manual. 'Always be prepared.'"

Alex grabbed the wire and with his teeth stripped the outer coating off one of its ends. He then wrapped that part a few times around his pocketeer and dug a hole in the dirt underneath him to bury the other end of the wire.

"Everyone, get down on one knee and grab my wrist," Alex whispered with a hushed tone. "And whatever you do, don't let go, no matter what."

"This does not look good," William blurted. "THIS… DOES… NOT… LOOK…

GOOD!"

While William continued to give his vote of confidence, Alex extended a long metal piece out from his pocketeer. Originally designed for soldering, Alex had a different intention for it at the moment.

He got down on both knees and held the pocketeer with the metal facing upward as high as he could reach. "Everyone hold on."

Alex could see the UAA soldier loading his pistol with a new shell and taking aim. Everyone around him grabbed his hand and knelt down just as he fired the projectile.

A burst of electricity instantly enveloped their position. Sparks flew all around them, but fortunately, the pocketeer's metal tip took the brunt of the attack. Like a lightning rod, it drew most of the electricity away from them and conducted it safely into the earth.

Their hair stood on end during the incident while only a fraction of the electrical charge ran through their bodies. Guri's teeth chattered while William mumbled that he hoped his dead body would be recognizable when someone found it.

After a few seconds, the last of the sparks crackled as a light, smoky film covered the air. No one was injured, just a little shaken up.

"Let's get going," Alex said. "They're moving in on our position."

Upon standing, they found their footing to be more unstable than they anticipated. The electrical shock must have slightly offset their equilibrium. They stumbled and veered to the sides at first but picked up more confidence the farther they walked.

Alex knew an escape route was close. Just ahead lay a 120-foot pit that attached to an underground tunnel, leading out of the city. Unfortunately, one of the UAA soldiers knelt directly in their path.

Taking another route would be too risky, Alex thought.

The UAA soldier stood after stowing away the metal spike and wire and then slowly began to walk towards their position. Only a stone wall separated them and if Alex continued moving in his current direction, he would be facing the wrong end of a rifle in about a second.

Alex reached his hand around the bend in the rocks and

lobbed one of his mini-grenades. Before the soldier had a chance to respond, it exploded, knocking him to the ground in the concussive blast.

"Move towards the pit!" Alex yelled as he pushed them in the correct direction.

Once they all passed, Alex set off at full pace. Bullets ricocheted all around him. He could feel the zip of at least two as they passed.

The soldier who fired was closer than Alex expected. Luckily, as he ran farther, a large stone blocked any further attempts at his life.

Alex reached the rest of the group at the edge of the pit. Originally in the ninth century B.C., it was an ancient means by which Megiddo's inhabitants could safely access the city's outside water supply in times of siege.

They all ran down the stairs along the sides of the pit without hesitation. Never had they traversed 183 steps with such quickness and dexterity in their lives. Even Guri made the decent without incident.

Upon reaching the bottom, a few more unfriendly volleys of gunfire greeted them. "Down the tunnel!" Alex shouted.

The 300-foot long tunnel at the bottom of the pit was well lit. Flanked by lights on either side and with a long wooden plank down its center, it definitely proved easier to traverse than in ancient times. Though admittedly, the ancient citizens of Megiddo weren't escaping UAA soldiers with machine guns.

"That was too close for me!" William said. "Too close."

The sound of their shoes hitting the wooden planks echoed throughout the tunnel. While the light-footed Marissa barely made a noise, William created a racket indistinguishable from an elephant stampeding.

Alex pushed Guri from the rear. He had no time to wait for any laggards. The soldiers were already descending into the pit while others ran to join them.

Jonathan reached the end of the tunnel first. Instead of daylight, the remnants of a dried-up old well greeted their approach. An earthen embankment above them buttressed by a wall of stone blocked their exit.

"Dead end," he turned to inform the group.

"What do you mean it's a dead end?" blurted William.

Jonathan looked down to see if there were any other exit points. Maybe an old stream could have carved out a natural tunnel, or maybe the ancient inhabitants could have created another offshoot tunnel. He found nothing.

Marissa jumped down from the wooden plank and into the well with her flashlight. Still, she found nothing. Only dirt and more dirt appeared in the flashlight's beam.

"We're trapped!" William announced upon Alex's arrival. "There's no place for us to go now except six feet under!"

Alex was not going to let that happen. He threw Jonathan his spare pocketeer and ran back down the tunnel without another word. Time did not allow for any discussion. New footsteps echoed towards their position and grew louder by the second.

Jonathan needed no instruction. He guessed what Alex was thinking and immediately began thumbing through the pocketeer's gadgets.

"William," he politely and calmly asked, "could you please give me a boost?"

"Hell," he sputtered, "I'd give you anything you asked for right about now."

William grabbed Jonathan's foot and lifted the man so that he stood on his shoulders. Fortunately, a good portion of William's size consisted of muscle. The other part, however, was comprised of Chinese take-outs, French fries and late night trips to the local diner.

"You O.K.?" William asked.

"Just keep it steady."

Marissa held onto William's waist to keep him from swaying. Without skipping a beat, he looked over to her and said, "They'll be time for that later."

"Please," she scoffed.

As gunshots echoed down the tunnel, he certainly did need the support. With each new volley he did his best not to flinch or throw Jonathan off his shoulders.

Although William's concentration was focused on not moving, his primary focus was on Alex. Marissa also shared his concern. She clenched onto William's waist a little stronger, both for his support and hers. With Alex alone and under gunfire, she feared for his safety and found herself thinking of little else but seeing him again.

"Let me down!" Jonathan requested.

William rapidly complied and almost threw the man to the ground.

"Quickly," Jonathan said, pointing slightly down the tunnel. "We need to get under those wooden planks."

The four of them expeditiously dashed down the tunnel and crammed under the wooden walkway. There was not much room underneath, but the gap proved adequate even for William's girth.

The earthen embankment where Jonathan had placed the pocketeer suddenly exploded, covering the area with dirt, rocks, and an impenetrable cloud of dust. A second loud explosion echoed down the tunnel.

The lights immediately went out, leaving them in complete darkness.

A lone voice rang out amongst the commotion. "Are we dead?" William asked.

Within a few seconds as the dust cloud began to settle, beams of sunlight started to filter into the tunnel. They were like little rays of hope, leading them out of danger.

"What are you doing lying around here?" Alex asked lightheartedly. "We need to get out."

"Alex!" Marissa greeted him with joy.

"You made it!" William added.

Alex took Guri and Marissa by the arms and helped them to their feet. William slowly got his footing while Jonathan stumbled to his feet.

"There's an archeological dig site next to us with a metal roof," Alex said. "I can hide us all there safely."

"What about the Stratoskimmer?" Marissa asked.

"It's too far away, and this place is bustling with UAA soldiers."

Alex led the way as he climbed the stone walls out of the ancient well and into the daylight. Gunfire began to erupt above them in the old city. Shouting in different languages accompanied the scuffle while screams of anguish signaled the mounting casualties.

Because of *The Disease*, the Israeli police were on high alert and had immediately swarmed the area once informed of the trouble. More reinforcements flew in while two attack helicopters hovered overhead.

The archeological site was not far away but, at the moment, its distance seemed insurmountable. They all ran in ducked positions as the gunfight continued relentlessly next to them.

One of the helicopters burst into flames and crashed adjacent to the ancient city as an all-too-familiar plane descended upon Megiddo. The same XR-2 that had attempted to bring down their Stratoskimmer now undertook a daring rescue operation to liberate the UAA soldiers.

More gunfire erupted but despite the Israeli's best attempts, the plane soared off into the distance. Isolated skirmishes continued as the Israelis subdued the last of the UAA militants. SattAr had escaped. *But would they?*

CHAPTER 23

SAMANTHA ATTEMPTED TO WORK in the bunker but could not help watching the events occurring aboveground. The large screens captured vividly the attack on the policeman and the subsequent firefight that ensued.

Since the skirmish, dozens of new fire, police, and military vehicles began to pour into Neurono-Tek. Though Samantha stopped counting at fifty, more continued to arrive.

"I told them," she would say aloud each time a new truck or car would arrive. "If they would have only listened to me in the first place, this might never have happened."

Not that she wanted to pat herself on the back, but she surely wished the proper authorities had taken her warnings more seriously.

Spotlights lit up Neurono-Tek brighter than if it were high noon on a clear day. Despite the distractions, Samantha continued to work on her experiments. She was like a machine. Running on almost no sleep and little food, she labored nonstop. In fact, it was the longest she had ever gone without sleep since pulling all-nighters in college.

The first experiment she performed after speaking with Guri Bergmann had been to duplicate his results. After taking brain, liver, and kidney cell lines from random specimens in the lab, she activated the bcl-xl gene in each of them. Surprisingly, none showed any evidence of immediate mitochondrial damage or cellular failure.

Tired of calling the protein *bcl-xl* the whole time, she appropriately named it the Bergmann protein and the gene that coded it, the Bergmann gene. It made things move a little more efficiently for her in the lab. Plus, if she didn't put her personal mark on the project, she wouldn't be Samantha Mancini.

After an exhaustive analysis of these tissue samples, she determined that the cellular damage must take either weeks or months to fully manifest itself. It was the only explanation of why these cells had not already died after being exposed to the Bergmann protein.

A clanking noise interrupted her work. It sounded as if someone had dropped a toolbox on the bunker's roof.

"Now what's going on around here?" Samantha yelled aloud while looking up at the ceiling. "If this place collapses, I'm going to file the biggest worker's compensation lawsuit ever! Neurono-Tek better give me overtime and hazard pay for this!"

The distraction was soon forgotten as she focused on the body in the glass room in front of her. Samantha sat at the computer console next to this encasement, diligently plotting her experiments while recording the ongoing results.

This Neurono-Tek bunker facility had been outfitted with the newest forensic accouterments. Most modern facilities in the world did not have such equipment, which was another reason why the NIH originally sought Alex's assistance.

The most avant-garde tool at her fingertips was the holographic replicator. It had the capability of holographically reproducing any cellular material or even an entire person so that experiments could be performed without destroying or using up the original sample.

Samantha utilized this tool to create a separate replication of the victim's body that was holographically positioned adjacent to it within the glass encasement. Unlike the original, it remained healthy and in its natural state before *The Disease* took its deadly toll.

"Now to see how this protein works on the whole body and not just a tissue sample," Samantha announced to no one but herself.

She then activated the Bergmann gene throughout the holographic victim's body.

While the experiment commenced, she watched the console's digital display to evaluate the ongoing results.

"Let's just speed things up a little and see what happens," she said to herself.

Another bang echoed from the ceiling, accompanied by a sizzling sound. Samantha had no idea what made such a racket. Because she was so entrenched in her work, she paid little attention to the distraction.

Maybe it was something that the bomb squad was undertaking on the surface or maybe it was just the natural sounds of the bunker. It really didn't matter. She felt secure in her hole in the ground and much safer than the men and woman on the surface.

The replicator accelerated the cellular processes on the holographic body by speeding up its biological time. It was a modern medical marvel. No longer did scientists have to wait years to see the results of their experiments on plants and animals. With this technology, what would take a lifetime of study could be accomplished in days or even hours.

Samantha watched in amazement for over an hour as the

results flowed into her console. What the medical community had been missing since *The Disease's* inception slowly displayed on the console, revealing the very nature of the condition.

But why did those people who were considered great generate the protein without any deleterious effect? She had pondered the question ever since Guri had told them of his original findings. It didn't make sense.

Samantha slowly sipped on a coffee mug nestled between her palms, hoping the nectar would bring her inspiration.

"Why, why, why?" she said aloud numerous times, as if someone would magically appear and offer her a solution.

"Unless… ?"

An idea suddenly came to her.

"It's the only thing that makes sense!"

Samantha began to frantically work at her console. Her body undulated as her fingers danced over the digital display. She moved so gracefully that one would have thought she were playing Beethoven's 5th Symphony rather than conducting a world-class experiment.

CLANK!

The noise jolted her from her seat.

This had not been a sound from the surface or any noise that should be heard from a bunker. Something definitely was not right.

Samantha stood and walked over the bunker's central console. She wanted to take care of the problem quickly so she could return to her experiment. She knew every extra minute that lapsed without a cure would mean additional fatalities.

The console showed no problem. All systems operated at maximum efficiency.

She turned her attention to the surface and watched one of the video displays in her bunker. Despite the previous excitement, the uniformed men and woman stood patiently on guard while the bomb squad sifted through the necroids' remains.

There were bits and pieces of the nasty bugs strewn all along the garden next to the main scientific building. Like handling nuclear waste, the squad meticulously placed each leg, eye, antennae, or unidentifiable bug piece into its own separate bag. The process appeared tedious and Samantha surmised it would take at least a day to accomplish.

"Huh?"

The clanging noises continued but without any obvious answer. As the sounds became louder and more frequent Samantha could not simply dismiss them. She didn't need to rely on any high-tech equipment to tell her something was amiss.

Samantha reached underneath the console and pulled out one of the emergency supply cases located throughout the facility. Sterilely sealed, she needed to place her hand on top of it to engage the unlocking mechanism.

Like opening up a bottle of soda, the case fizzed as Samantha raised the lid. Inside there was an assortment of survival needs, ranging from medical supplies to routine camping gear.

She took out the flashlight and walked over to where she thought the noise sounded the loudest. The epicenter seemed to emanate from a metal grate the bunker facility used to recirculate the air.

Samantha pulled over a chair and propped it against the wall. After taking off her high-heeled shoes, she steadied herself so she could get a better look through the grate's horizontal crevices.

"I hope it's only rats," she hesitantly complained, knowing all too well what might be creating the noise.

Taking her flashlight, she aimed it through the grating and down the shaft. Rats would have been a pleasant surprise, but instead she was met with rows of beady red eyes staring back at her.

She screamed at the top of her lungs. The necroids remained impervious to her superhuman vocal projection. In fact, they seemed to thrive upon it and began moving in a frenzied motion toward the source.

Climbing upon one another, they started to gnaw at the metal grating, attempting to make a hole large enough for them to enter the facility. Their protruding jaws full of razor sharp teeth had no problem overcoming this minor obstacle.

Samantha jumped off the chair, dropping the flashlight in the process.

"I should've called out sick this week!" she yelled.

While running back to the console in the center of the bunker, she surmised that the necroids must have tunneled their way through the earth and entered one of the bunker's ventilator shafts. In times of emergency they can be automatically sealed off. Samantha, however, never realized such a problem like this would arise and had kept them open.

She could almost kick herself at the thought. A simple press of a button could have prevented this mess. Now the whole project, and more importantly, her life, was in jeopardy.

A few necroids swarmed the flashlight she had dropped and began to devour it as the rest poured in through the vent. Samantha counted about sixteen in total, but in her haste she may have forgotten a few.

She looked into the supply crate under the console, hoping for some immediate answer to surface.

Nothing!

"Couldn't they have put at least one can of bug spray in here!" she yelled.The necroids approached her like a pack of hyenas closing in on its prey. Samantha wanted to call for help but knew none was available. She was trapped.

CHAPTER 24

"WE'LL HIDE IN HERE," Alex said while leading the group to a large open structure.

Because they had no other option, the others followed, most without even hearing what he had to say.

The deserted archeological site had been cordoned off to the public with yellow ribbons and signs saying *KEEP OUT* surrounding the area. With the progression of *The Disease*, the Israeli government had pulled most of its archeological funding and transferred it to emergency medical relief. Other countries also did the same, leaving this particular site dormant for over six months.

While everybody else either hurtled the yellow tape or ducked under it, William barreled through like a charging rhino.

Though the lights were not turned on, plenty of sunlight accommodated the area, providing them with ample visibility. Large metal poles surrounded the site's perimeter while a metal roof reminiscent of a circus tent covered it.

"This will do perfectly," Alex said while placing a cylindrical silver strip along one of the metal poles. Holding in place magnetically, it did not make a sound or signify in any way its functional status.

William looked at it as if it were some sort of joke. "I'm sorry Alex," he said while trying to catch his breath, "but what are you trying to prove by hanging that magnet?"

"Let's not take me away in a straitjacket just yet," Alex responded. "That magnet, as you call it, is an infrared disrupter. It's the same thing that the UAA utilized back at Crete to hide themselves. Now, I'm doing the same so the Israelis, or any other lingering UAA soldiers, don't spot us."

"But we're the good guys," William blurted. "The Israelis would let us go."

"Yea," Alex scoffed. "After the security verification, full body scan, and a long talk with the U.S. Embassy, we'd all be set free. But that could take days and time is not on our side."

William nodded his head in agreement as the body scan certainly did not pique his interest.

"This is interesting," Jonathan pointed out after they all had a minute's rest to catch their breath and regain their sanity. "This place is supposed to be the oldest Christian church ever excavated."

Continuing to read a wooden signpost attached to a stone base, Jonathan went on to say, "Archeologists believe this site dates back to the late third century."

"That's still when Christianity was outlawed by the Romans," Marissa said. "Believers had to pray secretly, most of the time sequestered in catacombs, until the religion was finally legalized in 313 A.D. by Emperor Constantine."

Feeling for the first time relatively safe, hidden by the infrared disrupter, they began to explore the area and breathe a slight sigh of relief. They were standing on top of a rectangular floor decorated by mosaics in different geometric patterns and colors. Walking around the site and reading the signposts on the floor let them mentally decompress from the ordeal they had just encountered. Plus, they had to stay there a little longer before they could safely board the Stratoskimmer without being spotted.

Jonathan said next what everybody had been thinking.

"I must admit. I was not able to find anything while in Megiddo that could help us on our journey. "

"I had a little trouble focusing up there," William said. "Call me odd, but when there are a bunch of lunatics trying to shoot or electrocute me, I find it difficult to concentrate. You know what I mean?"

No one had anything else to add. They all knew there was no way they would be able to investigate the surface of Megiddo today or even in a week due to the recent events. Their window of opportunity had closed too quickly and left them without an answer.

Alex ran through their recent experience in his head. After imagining Megiddo from an aerial view and reflecting upon all the different stones, walls, and pillars that encompassed the area, he was also left with nothing. He found no pattern or discernible clue that could be gleaned from this recent escapade.

Frustrated, Alex blurted, "So where to now?"

Jonathan tried to answer, but Marissa interrupted, "Wait. Before we go any further, I need to hear the end of this Bible code story."

"You're right," Jonathan agreed. "I have been the keeper of this information, but you all here have been the keeper of me. I must complete the story before we go any further."

"To begin with," Jonathan said, "what if I said something cryptic to you, like: take heed, every dizziness spell ends almost evenly. What would you think?"

"I'd think you had too much to drink," William responded

first, as if he were playing some word association game.

Alex interjected, "I'd say you were trying to tell me something about *The Disease*."

"That is correct!"

Marissa, William, and Guri all looked at Alex like he were a mind reader. It had certainly not been what any of them were thinking, and they were amazed he came to that conclusion so rapidly.

Alex quickly explained, "It's just a simple code. I used it with my friend all the time when I was a kid. All you need to do is take the first letter and skip the next three in that pattern to decipher it. **T**ake **H**eed, **E**very **D**izz**I**ness **S**pell **E**nds **A**lmo**S**t ev**E**nly. You see how *The Disease* is embedded within the sentence?"

"But the whole Bible code can't be that easy," Marissa quipped, skeptical the code could be uncovered with such a sophomoric trick.

"It isn't," Jonathan said. "Many have attempted, though, to decipher the Bible using such simple skip patterns. In the twentieth century, a rabbi discovered by using a skip pattern of 50 letters in the Old Testament's books of Genesis, Exodus, Numbers, and Deuteronomy he could spell out the word *Torah* in Hebrew. But the pattern led him no further."

He leaned back to stretch. The wince in his face and a slight groan gave a clue to his discomfort.

"All you alright?" Marissa asked, noting his obvious discomfort.

"Yes," he said through a forced smile. "My back just isn't what it used to be, nor am I as I young as I once was."

Marissa felt suspicious about the answer. It seemed to her as if it may be more than just a simple backache.

Jonathan continued, hoping not to draw any further attention. "Even Sir Isaac Newton, the man who first published the laws of gravity, learned Hebrew and spent most of his career attempting to decode the Old Testament. When they cleared out his desk at Cambridge after he retired, they found that most of the papers in it dealt with theoretic theology and not mathematics or astronomy."

"That's amazing," Alex said. "Such a brilliant mind. Did he find anything?"

"Not a thing. He used statistics, abstract mathematical equations, and even the movements of the planets and stars, but in the end, he was met with only failure and frustration. It was certainly not the way he expected to finish his illustrious career."

Helicopters flew over their tent and descended upon Megiddo. Soldiers began to jump out even before it landed. Donning thick black body armor, they scoured the city looking for any residual UAA combatants.

"Looks like we're stuck here for a while," William said, peering out of the tent at the continued commotion. "I hope someone brought something to eat. I'm famished!"

"Because of my hypoglycemia," Guri said, "I need to eat something, too, before I get lightheaded."

"You guys are like two little kids," Marissa said, pulling out a few medical supply bars from her black bag. "Here. Take one of these. I'm all out of lollipops."

"These wouldn't happen to be lactose free, would they?" Guri asked, taking one of the bars.

Marissa shook her head *no* while William devoured one of the treats. "Alex, Jonathan, would either of you care for one before they're all eaten?" she asked.

Though their recent adventures had made Jonathan appear slightly gaunt, neither he nor Alex accepted the food and graciously declined Marissa's offer.

"It wasn't that Sir Isaac Newton wasn't smart enough to

decipher the hidden Bible code," Jonathan continued through William's loud chewing. "It was that he lacked one major tool… a computer. You see, the code is time locked and human technology has to reach a certain level before uncovering its more complex secrets."

"So what would Newton have done if he had a computer?" William inquired as particles of food sputtered out of his full mouth.

"He possibly could have changed history as we know it. Events such as the rise of Adolph Hitler, the Holocaust, assassinations of presidents, and certain natural disasters have all been predicted within the Bible code."

"How does it work?" Alex asked.

"It all lies within the original words God gave to Moses on Mount Sinai almost 3,400 years ago. Christians recognize them as the first five books of the Old Testament and call it the Pentateuch while those of Jewish faith refer to it as the Torah."

Marissa commented, "I would've expected you to say the entire Bible. That just seems awfully short to contain such a large amount of information."

"Conceptually, yes, but mathematically, no. When viewed in its original Hebrew version, the Torah is a continuous strand of 304,805 letters without any spaces, just as it was first chiseled in stone many years ago."

Jonathan took his Bible out of his back pocket and placed it on the mosaic-decorated floor. Opening to its last page, he removed a quarter-size disc and held it in his open palm. Alex and the others watched intently while mentally drowning out all the noise surrounding them.

"Let's commence with something simple." He looked at his palm and said, "We'll begin our search with the word *Neurono-Tek.*"

A holographic grid of Hebrew letters appeared above the

disc with certain groups of letters circled, like a child's word search game. Below the grid, revealed the key to translate the code.

Alex and Marissa looked especially skeptical at the holograph before them. If they hadn't witnessed Jonathan's kindness, bravery, and intelligence firsthand, they would have immediately dismissed this code as some charade or hoax.

Jonathan sensed what they were thinking. "I can assure you that I'm not some run-of-the-mill nut or in some kind of cult. What you see before you is 99.9997% mathematically significant. If you take another work such as *War and Peace* or even the four books of the New Testament by the apostles, the results would not be the same."

He diffused the situation, but Alex remained skeptical. The whole idea of creating a word search still seemed sophomoric, if not ridiculous.

William twirled his finger next to his head when Jonathan wasn't looking to insinuate the man's loss of sanity.

Jonathan continued without hesitation, "The Hebrew translation of the word *Neurono-Tek* only occurs once in the whole string of 304,805 letters and immediately next to it *brain*, *Samantha Mancini*, *Alex Pella*, and *hospital* all appear. I can assure you this is no coincidence and is mathematically significant."

Alex could not disagree. In fact, after looking at it once again, it did begin to pique his interest. "So what does the computer do to create this matrix?"

"It begins by searching the Hebrew Torah for the word Neurono-Tek, starting at the first letter of the text. It then begins to look for every possible skip sequence up to a few thousand letters to form the word. If the computer cannot find the word, it goes to the second letter of the text and checks the skip sequences all the way until it reaches the last letter of the

Torah."

The grid slowly spun around its axis, giving them all a better view of the matrix.

"Because the skip pattern of Neurono-Tek is 3,245 letters, each row in the grid will subsequently be 3,245 letters while the amount of columns will be 94—which is simply 304,805 divided by 3,245. And what you see before you is just the essential portion of the grid. It's rather simple to create but fantastic to interpret."

"Call me stupid," William interjected with granola stuck between his teeth, "but I still don't understand how you made that grid."

"Here's a simpler example. If you had a text consisting of say 100 letters and were searching for a particular word with a skip pattern of twenty letters, each row subsequently would be twenty letters while there would be only five columns."

William nodded his head, feigning to accept the explanation. All the while he looked at Marissa's bag, hoping she had some kind of anti-psychotic medication to give Jonathan before they headed home.

"I'm not going to disagree with you that it is mathematically significant, nor can I contradict that the combination of letter grids that can be created is almost infinite," Alex interjected, "but I still am skeptical that this code can somehow predict the future."

"That's the art of reading it," Jonathan explained with a smile on his face. "And I can assure you, it's taken years of practice to learn how to properly interpret it."

"But why now?" Alex continued to ask. "What makes the year 2081 in the Bible code so special?"

"It's not 2081 that is encoded but the Hebrew year 5841, which runs from September 14, 2080 to October 3, 2081."

The holographic image faded away and multiple new grids

appeared in succession, each with different letters circled. It produced almost a hypnotizing-like effect to watch.

"When reading the Bible code," Jonathan explained, "one must search for patterns, words, or phrases that are repeated. The Hebrew year 5841 is just one of those precise instances. When looking at the grids here every time the number is present, it is crossed with words and phrases such as *Millions Will Die*, *The Earth Will Change Forever*, *It Will Confuse Many*, *death* and *The Disease*. The chance of seeing such combinations is about one in two trillion."

"I like those odds!" William said facetiously.

"Is this how you found me?" Alex asked.

"That's precisely correct," Jonathan responded. "Interestingly, your name was one of the most prolific in the entire code, with a total of 32 different hits. The nearest other word that came closest to that was twelve." He took a pause and looked Alex in the eye. "Most importantly, wherever *The Disease* was mentioned, so was your name. The two were inseparable."

Alex could not help but ruminate on what his parents once told him about being *genetically special*. What did that mean? And more importantly, did it have any bearing on their circumstances now?

"Is my name in there?" William asked, finally interested in the code. "If it is, I'm sure the words *handsome*, *good looking* and *Texas Longhorn* would not be far from it."

"All your names are," Jonathan explained, "and they are all associated, at some point, with *The Disease*."

"That's remarkable," Marissa commented.

"Let me show you the particular grid that led us here."

The holographic image quickly changed into a new word search pattern with different subsets of letters circled.

"There's Crete," Alex pointed out, "where we found Guri

and Megiddo where we are now, along with the year."

He looked at the grid and said aloud what everyone was thinking, "So next I guess we're off to the island of Patmos?"

"Anywhere is fine but this hell hole," William gasped. "I want nothing more to do with Armageddon or Megiddo or any other Biblical crap! I just hope this island of Patmos is full of alcohol and scantily-clad women."

Marissa smirked, knowing all too well the history of Patmos. "William," she said, "I have good news and bad news about Patmos. The good news is that it's a beautiful island with picturesque scenery. The bad news is that the island was evacuated six months ago because of its proximity to Astipalea. It's also where John wrote the Book of Revelation."

"You mean John Chimmerman, the famous author?" William asked. "I have a few of his books, but I've never heard of that one."

"No, John, the Roman citizen, exiled to Patmos because of his Christian beliefs in the first century A.D.," Marissa said.

William shook his head, still not understanding her point.

"There he had a vision from God about the last days on earth. It's where the number 666 originates and the four horseman of the Apocalypse was first written."

William summed up his feelings in four words, "Son of a bitch!"

He put his head down in disgust. On the mosaic floor where he was standing, he noticed a medallion pattern with two fish in its center. They appeared to be swimming in opposite directions with one above the other. It looked like the focal point to the room and because of their original haste, it had gone unnoticed.

Momentarily forgetting about Patmos, he said aloud, "What's up with the fish?"

Marissa walked over and examined them closer. "I read that

fish were the first symbol used in the early Christian church, hundreds of years before the adoption of the Constantine cross."

Jonathan added, "That's correct. Because the original Christians considered themselves fishers of men and due to the Gospel of John where he mentioned how Jesus fed a crowd of 5,000 from two fish, this symbol became the cornerstone of the early religion, much like the cross is now. Plus, many of the apostles were fishermen before following Jesus."

Alex looked on the mosaic floor at an inscription in Greek letters. "I wonder what this means?"

Guri said, "The God-loving woman named Akeptous has offered this table to God Jesus Christ as a memorial."

William looked shocked. "You read Greek?"

"I'm fluent in both ancient Greek and Latin," he responded while squinting. "You can say I'm a connoisseur of dead languages."

"What does this one say?" William then asked, pointing to an inscription next to him.

Guri squinted even harder. "You must remember Primillajand, Kyriake, and Dorothea and Chreste."

"What does that mean?" William asked.

"I don't think it's supposed to mean anything in particular. They're probably just four women who passed away before this church had been built and this is a small memorial."

Alex checked the infrared disrupter while the rest continued to examine the floor. It kept them all occupied as they bided their time before an escape to their Stratoskimmer became possible.

Alex checked his videre contact lens, examining the satellite view of the area. While the rest of the group kept themselves occupied, he watched for the perfect opportunity for their escape. Patmos was their next destination. Though this island potentially held the key to the world's salvation, it also possibly marked the site of their graves.

CHAPTER 25

THE SHEER VOLUME OF TECHNOLOGY and electrical machinery in the bunker overwhelmed the necroids and began to distract them from their intended prey, Samantha Mancini. Because the glass-enclosed autopsy room held the most energy-consuming machinery, a few of the necroids began to break off from the pack and scurry over to the glass encasement.

Samantha instantly recognized what these bugs wanted. As more of them became distracted, she continued rummaging through the crate, all the time still watching these little beasts out of one of her eyes.

A half dozen of the necroids continued marching towards her. It would only take one to cause a serious injury or even death.

"My epitaph will not read 'Eaten to Death by Necroids'!" Samantha said aloud. "It's either me or you that has to go. And I can tell you right now I'm not leaving!"

Samantha certainly was a fighter. Clawing her way out of nothing, she climbed to the top of all of her classes while financing her education entirely by herself. She despised laziness and vowed never to quit anything she started.

She viewed this attack by the necroids as more of a challenge than a threat. Although she had seen what occurred on the surface, it did not thwart her determination, nor did it invoke any sense of overwhelming fear.

"Ah ha!" she yelled at an octave below what would set the necroids off into another frenzied state. "Bite into this!"

A few high-powered cylindrical electrical cells placed within the crate caught Samantha's attention. Even though the bunker contained its own internal power source, a backup supply of electrical cells had been provided in case of an emergency.

Samantha slowly grabbed one of the gray cylinders, attempting not to make any sudden movements. She was familiar with this type of electrical cell and had utilized them in the past for a few of her experiments. One thing that stuck out about them was their instability and how they needed a specially-trained electrician to install them.

The six necroids continued to approach. Their beady red eyes glared up at Samantha while their teeth made a chomping noise in anticipation of another human meal.

The gray cylinder contained a black top that Samantha slowly unscrewed. At first difficult to turn, it quickly opened after a little extra pressure. Holding the top, she separated its inner components from the outer cylinder.

Attached to the top was an assortment of wiring, electrodes, and small orange disks that surrounded a long inner, green tube. Samantha slowly placed the gray cylinder back into the crate and looked closely at the electrical cell's inner mechanics.

Although she had no specially-trained electrician to activate it, Samantha believed that she knew enough about them to figure things out for herself.

Or so she hoped.

She then began to adjust the electrodes and wiring into proper alignment. With the conclusion of each step, the tube began to glow brighter until its luminosity became almost unbearable to the naked eye.

The last step would usually be to place the inner section back into the gray cylinder. However, Samantha had other intentions.

"I hope you're hungry," she announced with a smile.

Samantha edged out from behind the console and rolled the activated cell into the mix of the six approaching necroids.

"Watch out. It may give you a little indigestion."

The necroids instantly turned their attention to the glowing tube. The thought of devouring Samantha dissipated in the presence of such a large electrical generator. It was the necroid equivalent of the mother lode.

Instinctively, the creatures attacked the electrical cell without regard for one another. Chewing on the wires, gnawing at the tube, and climbing over each other, they acted as if they had not eaten for weeks.

Electrical sparks began to shoot out from the tube and the green glow began to waver with each new discharge. The necroids' eyes were aglow as the electricity filled their circuits and charged their bodies. Nothing stopped their voracious appetite.

Like a kernel of cooked corn, the first necroid exploded with a bang. Its remnants spread throughout the bunker, sparks still emanating from each of the pieces. In succession, the other bugs attached to the tube began to burst.

The last of the necroids would not relinquish its meal despite the fates of the others. The electrical power load started to overheat its circuits and, unlike the others, it began to catch fire. Through the flame, the necroid continued to feast. Undeterred by its melting body and failing circuitry, the bug dug its teeth deep in the tube until the green glow finally abated.

The necroid had conquered its meal. In doing so, its body had melted into the tube's wiring and the two were now permanently joined.

A single red eye still glowed ominously. The necroid survived but posed no further threat to Samantha or to any other electrical power supply. It had eaten its last meal.

"That's kind of creepy," Samantha said aloud.

The remaining necroids continued to scurry along the glass encasement to the autopsy room. Like flies on a lone light bulb, they would not leave the site.

Samantha cautiously walked towards them. Under her bare feet she could feel small bits of the destroyed necroids crunching while she walked. Some of the pieces were still hot to the touch. Samantha winced in pain and bit her lower lip, never letting out even a minor whimper.

Someone owes me a pedicure after this!

Samantha realized that tempting the remaining necroids with another electrical cell would not be possible. Nothing seemed to deter them from wanting to enter the autopsy room. They hadn't noticed at all when she rolled out the activated cylinder towards the other bugs.

Some of the necroids gnawed at the encasement. Flakes of glass and polymerized monofilaments, which created the clear façade, fell to the ground. It would not be long before one broke through the barrier and entered the room.

A large piece of necroid caught Samantha's eye just as she was about to step down upon it. Although mostly intact, it was slightly charred and still smoldering.

Samantha cautiously knelt down and began to examine it. She fanned her hand in the air to dissipate any potentially harmful fumes.

These things get uglier the closer you get.

Only the hindquarters of the necroid were still present; two legs and the end of its torso were all that was left. A gelatinous gray substance oozed out from its open cavity. Samantha nudged the bug with one of her long fingernails to get a better look inside it.

She was shocked by its contents. She found what appeared to be small internal organs and an array of circuitry wound together in a symbiotic relationship, each intermingling indistinguishably from one another.

Alex would love to see this!

A spark momentarily lit up the cavity, better exposing the internal contents. Unlike its exterior, the inside contained a mix of dark red and gray colors that contrasted to its stark, black exoskeleton.

"What's this thing supposed to be," Samantha whispered, "a machine or some sort of bug?"

Further analysis would have to wait. If the necroids entered the autopsy room, it would create such a major setback that further research on *The Disease* at Neurono-Tek might take another month to get restarted.

The sound of the necroids' teeth gnawing at the glass became louder and more annoying. It was as if a thousand people were running their fingernails across a blackboard at once. If these bugs didn't kill her, the sounds they made would quickly drive her insane.

I just want to smash those things against the glass!

A metal box labeled *Liquid Oxygen* next to the autopsy room suddenly caught her eye. Although the thought of taking one of those tanks and battering the necroids one by one crossed her mind, she realized such an endeavor would prove suicidal. They would attack her long before she could finish off one of them.

Before walking over to the central console, she looked back

at the liquid oxygen tanks once again. A grin slowly formed on her face, much like the Cheshire cat from *Alice in Wonderland*.

Without a second thought, she went over to the box and snapped open its padlock. She slowly opened up the lid, hoping it would not create any undue noises. Inside were four sleek, pale-blue tanks topped with silver nozzles.

Let's just hope this works!

While facing the autopsy room, Samantha took one of the tanks out of the box and unscrewed the top nozzle. A chilling blue liquid quickly shot out from the tank, evaporating into the air within seconds.

Like holding a fire hose, Samantha grabbed the cylinder with both hands and began to cover the entire glass wall of the autopsy room with the liquid oxygen. The necroids instantly froze as the spray covered their bodies, turning them a glistening blue.

Within seconds, the grinding sound ended as the devilish bugs fell from the glass and smashed into hundreds of pieces upon hitting the floor.

Just as the cylinder ran out of oxygen, the last necroid dropped to its death, creating a new pile of black debris for Samantha to avoid with her bare feet.

Samantha had secured the bunker. With the external ventilation shafts cordoned off and the internal threat finally neutralized, she could finally return to her work. She threw down the oxygen canister and walked over to the autopsy room's console, trying not to impale her sole on a frozen piece of necroid. With only a few minor scrapes, she began working once again. *Business as usual.*

Fortunately, the necroids created no breach in the autopsy room. The sterile atmosphere inside remained intact as did her experiment. The victim's body still lay in stasis under the sheer white blanket while two new holographic images of her body in a position reminiscent of da Vinci's *Vitruvian Man* flanked her sides.

One of the images appeared to be aging rapidly. As each minute passed, it grew another year older while the other holograph remained the same.

"This is unbelievable!" Samantha said, looking at the readouts on the console. "This explains everything!"

She examined the results closely once again, paying careful attention to every detail.

"I've got to tell Alex!"

CHAPTER 26

"DOES ANYONE WANT something to drink?" Alex asked while standing behind the bar.

William lounged on one of the Stratoskimmer's couches, pleased to finally be out of harm's way. They had been stuck at Megiddo for another four hours while the Israeli military reconnoitered the area. During that time, he had personally devoured the rest of Marissa's protein bars and a few items in her bag that she didn't think were even edible.

It had been a harrowing experience. While they hid in the old Christian church, soldiers scoured the area, shooting at anything that moved. It was fortunate that they decided not to surrender, as most likely they would all have received a bullet in the chest rather than a friendly handshake. Despite all the commotion, Alex's infrared disrupter hid them well.

William turned to Marissa, "Maybe you could hook me up with an IV and run the alcohol directly into my veins. It'll be quicker that way."

"I don't think that's sanitary," Guri replied.

"Try it anyway," William responded as if it might seriously

be a plausible idea.

"I just wish we found something at Megiddo," Jonathan interjected, still mentally browbeating himself for leaving the area empty-handed. He had barely been listening to the others since arriving in the Stratoskimmer as he continued to obsess about Megiddo. "I'm running out of time!"

While the others did not seem to notice, Alex detected something odd about Jonathan's last statement, *I'm running out of time*. The man was anything but impatient, and those words suggested that he might not be telling them everything he knew.

Alex studied Jonathan, like a physician would a patient. Since their departure from Neurono-Tek the wrinkles on the man's face did appear deeper and his overall appearance definitely looked gaunter than when they originally met. Though nothing struck him as being completely out of the norm, something seemed amiss.

"Is everything alright?" Alex asked in an open-ended fashion.

"Oh, yes," Jonathan quickly replied. "I guess I just got all wrapped up in the excitement. That's all." He continued by lightly saying, "Old guys like me are supposed to be on the golf course, not hunted down with machine guns."

Alex gave him a subtle glance, suggesting he did not completely buy the answer. Jonathan didn't offer any further information.

A faint red image of Samantha appeared in the middle of the Stratoskimmer's cabin. Lacking its usual crispness, the holograph looked faded and blurred. Unfortunately for all those aboard the ship, her shrill voice projected as loudly and clearly as usual.

"What's wrong with this telecommunicator?" she yelled. "Alex, are you trying to save money by purchasing junk?"

Before anyone could answer, she went on a tirade about

what had just occurred at Neurono-Tek. Meticulously informing them about the necroids, she finally ended the long story with, "And somebody owes me a pedicure."

"That was more exhausting than running away from those UAA guys with machine guns back at Megiddo," William jested under his breath.

Even Guri nodded in agreement.

Alex then quickly briefed Samantha on their recent escapades. He knew that no matter what he had to say, Samantha would find it paled in excitement to what she had just experienced. He could have told her they met God, discovered the lost city of Atlantis, and created a simple method for cold fusion and she still wouldn't have been impressed.

"Well, you're not going to believe what I discovered," Samantha then announced. "While I was single-handedly defeating the necroids, I had a few experiments running in the autopsy room. You remember the Bergmann, I mean bcl-xl gene that the nebbishy guy Guri was talking about?"

"I'm right here," Guri tried to say, speaking with a weak and cracking voice.

"Well, I ran the activated gene on a holographic copy of our victim here. And you know what happened?" she asked rhetorically. "All the tissue and organs in the virtual body deteriorated precisely as if it had been inflicted by *The Disease*."

"Did you use the lab's chronographer?" asked Alex.

Despite the poor quality of the image, they could all notice the annoyed look on her face. "No, I used my ass." There was a short pause. "Of course I used the chronographer. How else could I've made the holographic copy of this victim age so quickly?"

Alex took a swig of whisky and passed a similar bottle to Marissa. She welcomed the alcohol with open arms.

"The bcl-xl gene seems to be the cause for *The Disease*."

Samantha went on to say. "That's what's been killing everyone around the world. It seems this gene activates a cascade of events, which eventually destroys the body's mitochondria. And once they're damaged, the body has no way of turning food into energy—so it eventually dies."

"That Guri really did a good job by finding it," she then added sarcastically.

Guri was too frightened to rebut her.

"Not to burst your bubble," Alex commented, "but did you figure out how this thing spreads?"

"I'm not done yet!" she exclaimed. "Did you hear me stop talking yet?"

Samantha was on a roll. The recent experience with the necroids had sent her personality into overdrive. Combined with the lack of sleep, she had become more manic than Alex had ever seen her.

I definitely need to give her a long vacation after all this is over, Alex thought.

"I also used the chronographer on an embryonic sample of the patient's tissue," Samantha said, assuming everyone followed her train of thought.

"Embryonic sample?" Marissa politely questioned to disarm any fiery response.

Samantha stopped a second. She knew she got ahead of everyone else, but her mind kept on racing. "The autopsy lab here has a special instrument whereby we can create a virtual one cell embryonic sample from any person's tissue and run it through the chronographer. So it's like taking the fertilized egg after the moment of conception and watching the entire aging process from zero to a hundred years in a matter of a few hours."

Neurono-Tek's advanced technology certainly dwarfed that which Marissa had available at the NIH. She felt as if they had been using Stone Age technology the whole time in search of answers for *The Disease*. In fact, she had never even heard of a chronographer or a virtual embryonic cell maker. In one day, Neurono-Tek discovered more than the NIH could have ever accomplished in years.

"So I activated the bcl-xl gene from conception in the victim's embryonic sample and ran it to the age of 35 when she died," Samantha went on to explain. She looked down at her console readings just one more time to assure herself of the results. "And you're not going to believe what I discovered."

Out of all of them Guri was most especially interested in hearing the results. After spending over five years of his life discovering the bcl-xl gene and witnessing the scourge it had caused throughout the world, he wanted at least some conclusion to his work.

The New Reality had terminated his position the instant he delivered to them the gene. Legally banned from ever working on it again or divulging any of its information, he was left with many lingering questions.

"Instead of killing her," Samantha said, "it actually enhanced every part of her entire body. Just listen to this. Her muscle mass increased by 20%, her myocardial strength went up 18%, and the neural mass and supportive tissue in her brain increased by 24%. Do you know what this means?"

"She's still not as smart as you," Alex said sarcastically.

"That may be so," she responded, taking the comment more as a compliment than a joke. "But the early activation of the gene made her stronger, faster, and have more endurance. Plus, I estimated her IQ increased by at least 30 points."

She stopped talking for a second and then reiterated, "30 points! That's astounding!"

Guri felt an intense sense of vindication with his work, despite its deadly outcome. Though a hollow victory, he knew what he discovered could potentially evolve humanity thousands of years into the future. With the added mental and physical capacity, limitless possibilities for mankind could be achieved much quicker than natural selection would allow.

Food shortages, environmental changes, plagues, pestilence, and even war could become a thing of the past. Just as Alfred Nobel had been remembered for the Peace Prize, maybe one day Guri Bergmann would be memorialized as the person who helped humanity enter a golden age instead of the one who exterminated it.

"Those results are unprecedented!" Marissa said. "It seems the embryonic cells were primed at a very early stage and instead of the bcl-xl gene destroying them, it actually enhanced their overall maturation. I can understand now what made those people in Guri's research project be considered great. They were given a significant genetic advantage."

Marissa went on to think aloud, "I guess when an embryonic cell or a cell that has just been fertilized by a sperm has the bcl-xl gene activated, it is not toxic. Only when the cell matures does the bcl-xl gene and its protein become toxic. That's why the activated gene killed everyone who acquired *The Disease*."

"Not to beat a dead horse," Alex said cautiously, "or undermine the significance of your findings, but did you discover how this gene is transmitted or activated from one person to another?"

Samantha gave an unusually succinct answer, "No."

Their enthusiasm was tempered by this realization. Millions were dying and they still had no clue how to stop the spread of *The Disease*.

"Since we know the protein that's toxic to the cells," Marissa said, "I bet we can devise an infusion that could deactivate it or disrupt its transcription from DNA."

Samantha shook her head. "I wish that were so. It seems in

my experiment here that the toxic effects of the bcl-xl protein to the mitochondria are almost instantaneous. Even though it may take months to manifest its effects, the damage is done within the first day or two. By the time anyone is showing evidence of *The Disease,* it's too late."

"So where do we go from here?' Marissa asked. "Does anyone have any ideas?"

"It's a retrovirus," William said nonchalantly.

Marissa turned to him, "What did you say?"

"I said it's a retrovirus. It seems obvious that's the only answer."

"How do you know that?"

William gave her a wink as if to say, *I'm smarter than I look.*

CHAPTER 27

SAMANTHA STARED at William's holographic image. Like hers on the Stratoskimmer, it appeared red and fuzzy. Pieces of the necroids still smoldered throughout the bunker and the scratches on the autopsy room's glass were reminders of the recent assault.

"William?" Samantha encouraged.

Alex introduced the two of them when she joined Neurono-Tek. Since then, they had collaborated on a few successful research projects and obtained one of the last NIH sponsored grants. Despite his slovenly ways, Samantha always respected his insight and found him to be a good resource for various projects she had pursued.

"It's the only thing that makes sense," he reiterated. "When you think of different means of human to human transmission of a disease, a retrovirus similar to the HIV virus is the only possibility."

"Why so?" Samantha asked.

"First of all, how else could an activated bcl-xl gene get transmitted from one person to another? Second, it perfectly explains such a dramatic spread of *The Disease*."

"It's been a long time since I took virology in college," Guri interrupted with his nasal voice. Feeling responsible for the carnage created by his discovery, he did not want to miss any piece of information and hoped that by fully understanding the situation, he could help find a cure. "What exactly is a retrovirus?"

Usually annoyed with Guri's distractions, William instead seemed pleased to explain himself. Virology was his passion, and he enjoyed speaking as much on the subject as possible.

"As you are already well aware of," William said as if conducting class, "all of our genetic information is stored in what's called Deoxyribonucleic Acid or DNA for short. Just about every cell in our entire body has its own copy, and it's stored in a particular area called the nucleus. When a cell wants to make a protein, a designated portion of the DNA is copied into something called Ribonucleic acid, or RNA. The RNA is then transported out of the nucleus and is used by the cell as a blueprint to build a particular protein, such as the bcl-xl."

Guri nodded his head, acknowledging William's explanation.

"Instead of DNA, like in our cells," William said, "a retrovirus is composed of RNA. When it infects a human, this RNA is copied into DNA and then is incorporated into one of the cell's long strands of DNA in the nucleus. I've calculated that about 8% of our DNA originates from these viruses. Most of it is considered junk and unusable, but occasionally, these retroviruses have introduced something useful into the human genome.

"Finally," William said, "when the virus wants to reproduce, the DNA that was incorporated into the cell's genome is copied back to the original viral RNA form. And if the virus infects another host or a different cell, the process begins once again."

"So you believe that when the bcl-xl gene was turned on during the experimentation on Astipalea, a latent retrovirus was accidentally activated?" Guri concluded.

"Exactly!"

"Samantha," Alex said, "pull up a DNA profile of the victim and one of the control tissue samples there in the autopsy room. Let's see what's coded next to the bcl-xl gene in this DNA."

"Samantha, do this," she complained. "Samantha, do that. Hasn't your mother ever taught you words like please or thank you?"

"Could you *please* pull up the DNA profiles?" Alex said, half-heartedly.

"Now that's a little better!"

Samantha worked behind the console, scanning the DNA sequences from the two different samples. With the automated equipment in the autopsy room, the results returned almost instantaneously.

"There's no difference," she said. "They're both exactly the same."

Alex pulled a clear tablet from the wall and handed it to William. "Samantha, could you send over those DNA sequences to the Stratoskimmer on our secure line so we can have a closer look at it… please."

"Happy to oblige!"

What appeared to be random letters of A, T, G, and C immediately scrolled down the screen. The letters were side by side in two strands with the A and T, and the G and C always paired together.

"Thank you," Alex said.

Alex, Guri, and Marissa crowded around William. The letters meant nothing to them, but they all watched them scroll down the screen as if they understood.

The bcl-xl gene had been marked with a red color while the

rest of the letters were in black.

"You recognize anything?" Marissa asked.

William tilted the tablet and ran his fingers over the letters so that they would enlarge or change direction in the way they scrolled. Satisfied as to what he'd seen, he handed the tablet back to Alex.

"The bcl-xl gene," William said matter-of-factly, "is smack-dab in the center of a retrovirus."

"You can tell that quickly?" Samantha commented.

She did not want to appear condescending, but to make sense of the genetic code just by looking at a bunch of letters seemed impossible. It usually required a computer to decipher the letters into any meaningful data.

"One of my interests has always been latent retroviruses in the human DNA," he said. "As I mentioned before, 8% of our genetic code is comprised of these viruses. Through millions of years of evolution, their remnants have been mutated and spliced so many ways it's difficult to identify them. However, I wrote a paper a few years back about eight retroviruses in the human genome that could potentially be reactivated once again."

"I assume that what you're looking at right now is one of the eight?" Alex conjectured.

The transmission in Samantha's office suddenly flickered a few times and went dead.

"Alex! Are you there!"

"Yes," he responded. "We're all here. And screaming won't bring our holographic picture back any quicker."

"What happened?"

"Ever since we were hit by that magnetic blast our equipment has not been working completely right. We'll just have to finish this conversation like they did in the twentieth century—audio only."

"Alex, you're dead on," William interrupted, not noticing the absence of a visual feed. "The bcl-xl is directly within one of the eight viruses. I immediately recognized the site on chromosome 17."

"That's fantastic," Marissa commented.

"The bcl-xl gene," William went on to say, "has coding regions for enzymes such as proteases, integrases, and structural proteins adjacent to it on the chromosome. It's these exact enzymes that a virus needs to infect a cell and help it survive and reproduce. When the scientists on Astipalea went to turn on the bcl-xl gene they must have inadvertently activated the whole retrovirus."

Alex asked, "Samantha could you *please* run a simulation on the chronographer of the entire retrovirus's effect on the victim's non-infected body?"

"One step ahead of you, as usual," she responded.

CHAPTER 28

"I CAN'T GET ANYTHING by you," Alex said as he and the rest of the group exited the Stratoskimmer and began walking along a sandy beach next to the Aegean Sea. "You're on top of everything, aren't you?"

"Well, thank you," she responded as they all listened to her on the thin black mini-telecommunicators strapped to their wrists.

"You're welcome," he commented, smirking to the others.

As Samantha continued her monologue, the rest of them continued their stroll along the nicest beach the coastal city of Mavisehir, Turkey had to offer. Overlooking the Aegean, it had a wonderful view of some of the beautiful Greek islands and a cozy atmosphere that had drawn tourists to the area for many years.

Just like all the other Turkish coastal cities, this one had been evacuated because of *The Disease*, leaving the bustling markets vacant and the place totally deserted.

One would never know how much death the city had seen over the past year by looking at it. Just over two months ago the tourist hotels were converted into makeshift hospitals, while large piles of bonfire wood on the beach served as the local crematories. Most of the population had perished and those who survived fled the area, possibly spreading *The Disease* around the world.

Their stop here was not one of pleasure. Though the city did possess an overwhelming aesthetic allure, they had no time to enjoy it. Their minds were focused on finding a cure.

While trapped at Megiddo, the Stratoskimmer's pilot, Tom, made the best of his time by finishing some of the maintenance work not completed on Madeira. He had been displeased by how the ship had been flying even before their attack and wanted to reevaluate the entire system before their departure.

During his inspection, he made one startling discovery: the ship had been infested with necroids that somehow infiltrated its innermost circuitry. A few methodically moved around the motherboard, but most appeared to be fused with the wiring or other electrical mechanics.

Though not recognizing the significance of his finding, he cautiously showed the circuits to Alex in private, as to not create any panic. Alex immediately realized what had happened. While most of the necroids remained at Neurono-Tek, some must have boarded the Stratoskimmer before they left and had been revealing their location and relaying the ship's communications directly to the UAA. It made complete sense. He now understood how SattAr could have discovered him both on Crete and Megiddo.

Alex informed the rest of the group about the discovery and as usual concocted a plan to use it against the UAA. First, he encrypted all further communications with Samantha so that no one could eavesdrop on their conversations, regardless of the necroid moles deep inside the ship's circuitry. The grainy red transmission was thus a net result of this safeguard and not some computer glitch as Samantha assumed.

Secondly, this current pit stop on Mavisehir had been intended as a decoy to lure the UAA away from the Aegean. While Alex and the rest of the group planned on commandeering one of the abandoned boats in this western coastal city, Tom flew the Stratoskimmer out over the Pacific, hoping to lead the UAA on a wild goose chase.

"So, what was the retrovirus's effect on the victim's non-infected body?" Marissa then went on to ask.

"The experiment," she responded, "shows that just like when I activated the bcl-xl gene in the victim's body, infecting her with the entire retrovirus that included the bcl-xl gene inside of it produced the exact same results."

"Mystery solved," William confidently said.

"Not so fast," Samantha interrupted. "We still don't have a way to stop the retrovirus from spreading or a cure once the person is infected."

"In addition," Marissa added, "it doesn't explain how it's spread or why I never found this retrovirus on any autopsy."

Before she could make any further comments, she noted Jonathan lagging uncharacteristically behind them. The usual snap in his step was no longer present, and he walked along the sand as if he were trudging through three feet of snow. The others had been so involved discussing *The Disease* with Samantha that they did not notice his absence.

She ran back to him and placed her arm around his shoulder. "Are you O.K.?"

"Not to worry," he said, attempting to muster his most cheerful tone. "Your thoughts should be on finding a cure for *The Disease* and not on an old kook like myself. The world needs you right now. Send me out to pasture if you need to, but never forget our goal here."

Marissa held him closer and guided him through the sand.

"I'm not going to pull out the shotgun yet," she jested. "Come on. You probably picked up a cold along the way. I'll give you something when we're on the boat. You'll be fine."

Jonathan knew otherwise.

After looking at her experiment a little longer, Samantha exclaimed, "It seems as if the virus can only replicate in the body within a six hour time span, a week after its initial infection. After that, it totally stops reproducing. And ironically, the virus can only replicate in the inner lining of the lung, known as the endothelium."

"That explains why I never found anything!" Marissa quickly said. "If the virus can only replicate in the lungs, there would never be any evidence of its remnants in the blood or the tissue samples I examined. Also, because *The Disease* takes months to clinically manifest, the active virus is long gone by the time a person would go to autopsy.

"And more importantly," Marissa pondered aloud, "that means that the virus would only be contagious months before the person shows any signs of *The Disease* and for only six hours." She paused and then spoke into her telecommunicator. "How long do you propose the virus would remain alive outside the body?"

"I'm not sure? Maybe--"

"Less than a day," William interjected. "This virus has been out of commission for thousands, if not millions, of years. There have been too many mutations along the way for it to retain its longevity."

"The only problem," Alex concluded, "is that if it's produced in the lung's endothelium, it can spread extremely easily in an aerosolized form. All you would need to do is breath on someone else to infect them."

"Don't you love virology!" William said.

"So William," Samantha asked, "if you know so much about

viruses, how do we stop the spread?"

William was at a momentary loss for words. Though extremely interested in virology, he understood the answer to her question carried serious consequences. "We can't. Because of the mutation rate of such a virus and its high infectivity rate, we'd conceptually have to vaccinate the entire population of the world every two weeks for about four months to rid ourselves of *The Disease*."

"Plus, there's no way to stop the carnage caused by the bcl-xl gene once it's activated in the body," Alex added. "After it starts producing proteins, the damage is irrevocable throughout the body."

"This is the worst-case scenario we've always read about at the NIH," Marissa said. "The ultimate pandemic."

Jonathan whispered in a meek voice, "'The kings of the earth, the nobles, the military officers, the rich, the powerful, and every slave and free person hid themselves in caves and among mountain crags. They cried out to the mountains and the rocks, 'Fall on us and hide us from the face of the one who sits on the throne from the wrath of the Lamb, because the great day their wrath is come and who shall be able to withstand it?'"

"Revelation 6:15," Marissa quoted.

"I think hiding ourselves in a cave until this disease thing blows over sounds like a good idea right about now," William quickly commented.

Marissa added, "I better let the NIH know that it's time to activate the humanity disaster plan."

"This is only getting worse," William fretted aloud.

Marissa continued helping Jonathan as they boarded their boat. His skin felt cool and damp, as if he were trying to sweat off a fever that never occurred. The strong, eager eyes that once started the mission now looked hollow and lacked their usual spunk. She wanted to say something, but Jonathan gave her a small wink. "I'll be O.K.," he said as he slumped down on one of the deck's benches.

The sailboat was certainly a magnificent one. Trimmed entirely in white and with an expansive below-deck living quarters, this 40-foot vessel would definitely serve its purpose. The trip to Patmos would not be a far one and if they had to make the trek, why not procure the sleekest ship at the dock?

"Nice choice," William complimented while he and Alex began to pull up the sails. "Can you hotwire this thing to get it started?"

"If I can torch a whole building without a match in two minutes," Alex joked, "I don't think starting up this ship's engine will give me much trouble."

"But that was my home," Guri interjected.

"Just keep turning that winch," William directed. "There's no time to lament about your apartment. We could all be dead in a week anyway."

"Don't plan your funeral too early," Alex said. "We still have to finish up some business on Patmos and hopefully find that cure predicted in the Bible code. Isn't that right, Jonathan?"

He nodded his head and gave them each a smile.

"So where's the code say we go next after Patmos?" William asked, almost too afraid to hear the answer. "Hopefully somewhere warm and safe."

"Nowhere," he responded solemnly. "It all ends on Patmos."

CHAPTER 29

"WE SIMPLY CANNOT CONTINUE without further funding from The New Reality," Ari Lesmana insisted. "We are on the verge of independent economic prosperity."

Albert Rosenberg knew otherwise. He had been privy to their country's economic status for years and knew their creative accounting practices only created an illusion of prosperity. Though the unemployment numbers were declining, underemployment, food stamp usage, and the poverty index were at an all time high. The reality was they were plunging into an abyss of debt unheard of in the twenty-first century, condemning future generations to economic destitution.

"You must realize," Albert said, "my remarks at The League of World Leaders were certainly not intended for you or the UAA."

Ari gasped a sigh of relief as he eased himself back into his chair. Though he and Albert had come to a mutual understanding before the recent meeting with the League, Ari needed conformation that his country's sovereignty would not be in jeopardy.

"Your continued presence in the Middle East," Albert went on to say, "is vital for the economic and political stability of the region. I can assure you, there will be no interference with the UAA while you are in charge."

Despite the excellent quality of this communication, Albert's frail voice could barely be heard. Ari strained to hear every word and listened carefully so that he would not misinterpret a single syllable.

Albert's holograph in the center of Ari's office could not conceal his bedridden state. Ever since the last time they spoke he had taken a noticeable turn for the worse. Only his big blue eyes provided any vestige of his former self.

Masika glared down upon his image with pure disgust. The thought of partnering with any Westerner, let alone a successful capitalist entrepreneur, sickened her.

Out of site from Albert's vision, Masika's furrowed brow and contemptuous snarl kept Ari's attention throughout the whole conversation. It was as if the muscles she used for smiling had become atrophied and her scornful expression had become permanently etched in her face.

"I must assure you," Ari said in a rather boastful tone, "that the money loaned to the UAA is being utilized in a positive manner. Besides all the public sector jobs I've created, my mass stimulus packages, economic bailouts, and other generous programs have brought the UAA into a new era of economic prosperity. Only with my…"

Ari droned on ad nauseam. If Albert felt the slightest bit better, he would have curtailed this self-gratifying monologue from the very beginning. In reality, he knew that all these programs Ari spoke of were total failures and condemned the UAA to generations of economic disaster. Only an endless amount of loans could continue to pay for them all. Plus, they also created no real jobs and only hindered true economic growth.

"Do not pursue Alex Pella," Albert finally interrupted. "He has already thwarted you twice and his intensions are of no interest to you."

Ari suddenly went silent. Even Masika's chiseled expression changed. They both were stunned to realize that Albert knew about these plans.

"You must understand," Ari began to say in an attempt to circumvent the subject, "that this disease affects us all, and the well-being of this country, if not the world, is at stake. As leader of the UAA, I must not overlook any opportunity that presents itself to our great nation."

"Let me restate this simply," Albert again, "you must not pursue Alex Pella. He is a man among men and someone not to be toyed with."

Before Ari could make a rebuttal, the communication ended. He was left with only one parting caution from Albert. "Be careful of your actions."

Masika waltzed across the office. Through clenched teeth and an ever further furrowed brow, she blasted, "Albert thinks of you as a fool! You, not this Western-born Alex Pella, are a man among men! His eyes are clearly blinded by his greed, and he cannot see true greatness when it stands before him!"

She slammed her fist on his mahogany desk. "One day The New Reality, along with all of Western society, will bow down to you and the UAA!"

Ari had no doubt of the authenticity of Masika's words. Despite his horribly failing economic policies, he truly believed that he was the world's next savior.

The fire in Masika's eyes always excited Ari. Momentarily forgetting to think of only himself, he stared into her hypnotic gaze. Like a Greek siren, she could lure him into even the most dangerous of terrain.

He grabbed hold of her arm at once, wanting more.

"This is not the time!" she chastised.

Ari removed his hand but kept his eyes on hers the entire time. He felt no sense of disappointment. The true thrill with Masika was in the pursuit rather than the conquest.

"What is the latest status of our bunker?" she asked, without changing her expression.

Her domineering voice echoed off the office's ocean blue walls. Offset by a large bay window behind Ari's desk and cherry hardwood floors, the room created a relaxing atmosphere amidst the heated discussions that usually took place there. Pictures of Ari adorned all the walls; they were trophies of his conquests, windows into the perceived success he created for himself.

"'The mood in which we usually exist depends upon the mood in which we maintain our environment,'" Ari responded with a suave smile.

Masika became at ease. Her muscles went from their stiff and rigid state to a more relaxed position. Even the furrow between her brow became less conspicuous.

Ari had used this quote many times in the past. Taken straight out of

Nietzsche's *Daybreak*, it had a way of easing any tense situations between them. He had the book memorized and kept it close at hand for both inspiration and guidance.

"Our bunker is complete," Ari went on to say. "As *The Disease* ravishes humanity aboveground we, along with ten thousand of our chosen brethren, will be safe from its far-reaching deadly tentacles."

"You see, my wife," Ari went on to say with a swagger in his voice, "I will continue to pursue Alex Pella despite Albert Rosenberg's adamant warning."

The fire in Masika's eyes grew with her husband's every

word. Her pulse raced and pupils dilated.

"We," he went on to say, "define our lives and our country's destiny, not this man. We are the creators of our future, and no person shall stand in the way of my success—especially not a capitalist from the West."

Both emotionally and sensually excited by Ari's words, Masika grabbed her husband's arm, no longer resisting his advances.

"And if Alex Pella does not divulge to us the cure for *The Disease*," he continued, "then I will have him and his Western companions exterminated while we watch all of Western society and the world crumble in *The Disease's* wake. We will then rise and create a new world, a utopian world without boundaries or classes, completely controlled by me."

Before Ari could partake in Masika's advances, a holograph appeared in the center of the office. Upon its emergence Masika moved to the corner of the room so that she was once again out of sight.

"SattAr," Ari said in the most commanding voice he could muster. "May I help you?"

"Yes, Malik," he said with the proper greeting. "We have lost Alex Pella."

"You do not bring me good news. I was under the belief that our necroids were tracking him."

"They are," SattAr responded matter-of-factly, "but I now believe that his team discovered the necroids and have taken us on a protracted diversion over the past 24 hours."

"I need to see you at once," Ari said succinctly. Knowing his plan depended on Alex Pella and his companion's capture or demise, he had to addresses the situation immediately and delay personal pleasure for later.

CHAPTER 30

THE DAY SPENT SAILING across the Aegean provided Alex and his cohorts some needed relaxation. Without anyone trying to shoot or electrocute them, they used the time to catch up on lost sleep and mentally decompress.

William took the opportunity to fill up with as much food as possible in case they missed another meal while Guri could barely stomach any food due to continuous seasickness. Even Marissa's medical treatment could barely subdue his incessant nausea.

In the below-deck cabin, Jonathan spent most of the ride in bed fluctuating between fever-ridden sweats and rigorous chills with Marissa at his bedside tending to his needs. One moment she would have a damp cold rag upon his head and the next she would be bundling him in blankets.

Alex placed his hands on Marissa's shoulders as they watched Jonathan sleep. "How's he doing?"

"At times he becomes lucid and I think the infection has passed, but then he goes into the fever-chill cycle once again." She turned her head and looked up at him. "He really needs a hospital. There's not much more I can do for him here."

"There's a medical facility in the town of Skala on Patmos. We'll bring him there first. They may have something you'll need."

I hope.

"Isn't there anywhere better?" she pleaded. Knowing the island had been deserted months ago because of its proximity to Astipalea, she reasoned there would be no medical staff available to fully accommodate Jonathan's needs.

Alex knew he had limited options. The UAA would soon discover their ploy and would promptly be in pursuit once again. Plus, there were no other operational medical institutions for at least a thousand miles.

Before Alex could answer her question, Jonathan pushed himself up to a sitting position, discarding the blankets that once enveloped him. It was as if Lazarus once again rose from the dead. "Do not fuss over me," he said with a little spunk back to his voice. "I am not dead yet nor do I plan on dying. There will be no going out of the way on account of me."

He looked at both of them and extended an arm. "If you would, please."

Alex grabbed hold and brought him up to his feet. Before Jonathan could say another word, Marissa handed him a glass filled with a red liquid. There would be no argument as she pushed it up to his lips and watched him drink the entire thing.

With a little help from both Alex and Marissa, Jonathan slowly walked over to the stairs and grabbed hold of the railing, aiding his ascent up the steps.

"So nice of you to join us," William greeted them as they climbed up on deck.

The warm air and clear blue sky were medicine enough for Jonathan. It instantly lifted his spirits and made him feel alive once again.

"How are you doing?" Guri asked, still green with nausea.

Jonathan gave a friendly smile. "There's no time to stay sick."

William took one hand off the steering wheel and pointed ahead. "Welcome to Patmos everyone. Population currently at zero and percent chance of leaving the island alive I estimate to be the same."

I hope he doesn't speak at any motivational seminars, Marissa thought.

A medieval fortress buttressed by tall stone walls stood prominently on top of the island's tallest hill. The city of Skala stood at the foot of this hill while the city of Chora surrounded the castle. Both were comprised of white houses, narrow winding streets, and lush greenery.

William could not help dwelling on the last words Jonathan said before going below deck. *It all ends on Patmos.* He obsessed on it the whole ride and could no longer hold back asking, "What all ends on Patmos?"

Jonathan slowly walked over to Alex as everyone listened with anticipation.

"I have run the code over and over again searching for other clues but could find none. The code has taken us this far but will lead us no further. I neither know what fate has to offer nor what the future will bring. Only God knows what's in store for us after Patmos." The answer brought William no solace and only proved to increase his angst. Wanting to get as far away from this island as he could, he instead kept silent as he sailed into the coastal city of Skala. Like most cities they'd seen since leaving Neurono-Tek, this once bustling city had been deserted. The harbor was completely empty. Most of its inhabitants must have sailed away on anything they could find at *The Disease's* outbreak.

William adeptly steered the ship into the harbor. Passing

sandy beaches, hotels, and numerous resorts along the way, the boat slowly pulled up next to a long, wooden dock lined with metal moorings. Alex secured the ship on two of them but made sure not to tie the knots too tightly in case they needed to make an abrupt escape.

Guri hopped overboard and laid face-down on the beach. Though usually adverse to sand getting in his clothes or shoes, he was grateful just to get on land.

"My sailing wasn't that bad," William huffed after watching Guri's reaction.

Alex and Marissa both took one of Jonathan's arms and helped him onto the dock. Though he was still wobbly on his feet, he quickly started to regain his strength.

"So here is where John received the visions that he recorded in the last book of the New Testament," Jonathan said, admiring the entire island. He made sure not to mention the name of this last book, Revelation, as to not cause William further angst.

"Where to first?" Alex asked.

"To the cave where God spoke to John," Jonathan answered.

"Not so fast," interrupted Marissa. "We have to make a quick stop at the medical clinic here before we drag you any further on this expedition."

He attempted to argue, but Alex gave him a stern look, "Doctor's orders."

As Alex and Marissa helped Jonathan along Skala's narrow roads, William assisted Guri off the sand. "Get on your feet," he said. "This isn't the time to be playing in the sand. We have some work to do here."

"But I was not playing," Guri attempted to say before nausea interrupted any rebuttal.

With the return of some energy, Jonathan attempted to walk on his own. However, his leg muscles still proved too weak to carry him alone and he stumbled every time he attempted to free himself from Alex and Marissa.

"One step at a time," Marissa cautioned. "This isn't a race. Keep it slow."

A quaint white building with a red cross above its main door caught their attention. It was not far from the dock and they all assumed that the Greek letters on the sign must say medical clinic or something to that nature.

"This is the hospital?" William commented as they approached the front door. "It looks more like a beach bungalow than any medical facility I've ever seen. No wonder there's no one left on the island. They probably all died from lack of medical treatment."

The building's quaint appearance from the distance turned into a shabby décor the closer they approached. With white paint peeling off the walls, plants growing from its multiple cracks, and a crumbling roof it certainly appeared to be in ill-repair.

William shrugged his shoulders. "Any port in the storm, I guess."

"Alex," Marissa asked, "do you still have a pocketeer left to break into this place?"

"Used them both up at Megiddo. Maybe I can jimmy open one of the windows or climb on the roof to see if there's another entrance up there."

Without a word, William walked up to the front door and gave one strong kick. The flimsy wooden planks fell to the ground as its hinge broke upon impact.

"Pocketeer," William scoffed. "Climbing on the roof. Maybe we should dig a large hole and tunnel our way in?"

William led them inside, mumbling to himself the whole way. His first impression of the interior was that a bomb must have hit it. Papers were strewn all over the place. Chairs had been overturned and remnants of medical supplies and wrappers lay haphazardly across the floor.

"Looks like when *The Disease* hit," Alex commented, "people must have panicked and fled with everything in here that wasn't tied down.

"I hope there's something we can still use," Marissa said.

"I found something!" William shouted with glee. Bending over, he sifted through a few papers and grabbed a flat, rectangular object wrapped in black foil.

Marissa rushed over to inspect his discovery. Before she could get a good look, William ripped open the wrapper and began to eat it.

"It's a chocolate bar," William said with his mouth full. "It's my favorite candy. I can't believe I found it on the floor over here!"

Alex signaled everyone to the back of the building before Marissa had the opportunity to throw the candy on the ground. He and Jonathan walked around the small reception desk and entered one of the four adjoining examination rooms in the rear.

"It looks like the scavengers didn't take everything," he commented, pointing to a small glass cabinet stocked with medical supplies.

The rest of the room, however, appeared to be otherwise stripped fully clean. Empty drawers, bare shelves, and cleaned-out cabinets were all that remained. Even the pictures that once hung on the walls had been taken. Only squares where the sun had not bleached the walls remained.

"William," Alex said, "you and Guri search the other rooms while Marissa takes a look to see if there's anything usable here."

In good spirits after his unexpected snack, William took his favorite companion and set off to investigate the area.

"Locked," Marissa said, trying to open the glass case. "No wonder they didn't abscond with these supplies. They were probably too much in a hurry to find the key." She knocked on the hard glass. "Bulletproof."

"I guess they couldn't break it open either," Alex commented.

Marissa laid Jonathan down on the examination table in the center of the room. Despite some continued insistence, he finally capitulated to her wishes. His legs remained too weak to put up any resistance.

Alex took a small piece of plastic that he found in an open drawer, wedged it in the glass cabinet's lock and jiggled it until it clicked open.

"Thank God they used this old-fashioned lock here," he said, opening up the cabinet.

Marissa looked inside and began stocking her black bag with as many medication-filled glass vials, diagnostic tools, and other medical supplies as it could carry. "Jackpot!" she commented like a kid in a candy shop.

She then grabbed a clear bag of IV fluid and began pushing a few of the vials against the small, yellow plastic circle along its side. The contents of the vials immediately mixed into the fluid creating an orange-tinged solution.

"I feel fine," Jonathan insisted, knowing her concoction was meant for him. "You need not fuss over me."

Marissa pulled out the IV line from the bag and slapped the infusion patch attached to the end of it on his chest. "This will take about 30 minutes," she said while hanging the fluid on a nearby pole.

William and Guri returned from their expedition. While William entered the room empty-handed, Guri carried a stack of supplies, dropping a few on the way.

"I picked up some things I thought you may find useful," he said, laying the contents in his arms along the counter.

Marissa looked over and saw that most of the supplies

weren't even medical and those that were looked to be either trampled or gnawed on by a dog. "Thank you," she said appreciably, pleased they tried to help.

"Well, if you all are here on account of me," Jonathan said, "then I feel I must do something constructive with the time."

"You just rest," Marissa insisted.

Jonathan gave her a smile. Though he capitulated to the fluids, he certainly would not remain silent during the whole infusion.

"Patmos," he went on to say, "was once an old Roman penal colony. It seems difficult to believe now that such an apparent paradise could be considered a prison at any juncture but that is how the Romans used this island in their day."

"Was John in some type of prison while here?" Marissa asked.

"No. He had free reign of the whole island to do with as he pleased. He had been sentenced here around 95 A.D. because of his Christian beliefs and teachings."

"I thought they just summarily crucified all the Christians at that time," Alex commented.

"That is true. Thus, it is believed John must have been someone of wealth or power to receive this more lenient form of punishment. In fact, he was able to write while here on the island and have his messages sent to different parts of the Christian world without a problem."

"Sounds awfully lenient for the Romans," Marissa said.

"Fortunately, it was," Jonathan admitted. "In a cave about half way up the hill between the cities of Skala and Chora is where he is believed to have lived and written the last book of the New Testament."

"I guess that's our next stop," Alex surmised.

Jonathan nodded yes but before he could speak William blurted, "I thought we were heading up to the medieval-looking fortress, not some bat-infested cave."

"You mean the Monastery of St. John," Jonathan said.

"That castle's a monastery?" William said.

"Indeed it is. Commissioned in the year 1088 by Father Christodoulos, it was built over the previously destroyed Grand Royal Basilica that once also honored John. He also commissioned in the same year the Chapel of St. Anna, which now surrounds John's cave."

"I still think we should go to the castle," William huffed.

To pass the time, Jonathan went on to entertain them about the ancient history of the island when it was referred to as Letois after the goddess Artemis, daughter of Leto. Marissa seemed especially interested and listened intently as he explained how the Greeks believed this island had once sunk into the sea and was brought back to the surface by Zeus. He also went on to relay to them how the monastery was now believed to hold great ancient treasures, most of which have never been shown to the public.

Once the bag fully emptied, Jonathan sat up on the table and removed the infusion patch from his chest. The IV had definitely done its job as he jumped to the ground without the slightest bit of stumbling.

Before anyone could take his arm, he briskly walked out of the medical clinic. With a zip to his voice, he looked at the bunch of them and said, "I hope you weren't planning on standing there idle all day."

They all followed Jonathan's lead and left the dilapidated medical clinic to begin their journey up the winding, paved road to the cave. Along the way, Alex subconsciously placed his arm around Marissa's shoulder. Before he realized what he had done, he felt her arm reciprocate his affection.

No words needed to be spoken. There had been an unstated attraction between the two since they met and the gentle grasp each held around the other's side confirmed what they both had been feeling.

"Hey, hey!" William said, gawking from behind. "This isn't any love fest here. I thought we were trying to find a cure for *The Disease* on this trip, not a date."

Both seemed embarrassed that they let their emotions get the best of them. William was right. They needed to keep their senses sharp and put aside any personal distractions.

Alex removed his arm and looked back at his friend. "So you say that's the best way to do the Heimlich maneuver now?" he jested as if she were showing him some type of first-aid procedure.

"Guri," William pointed, "go help Alex with his Heimlich."

Because he felt so embarrassed by the situation, Guri did not know what to say. Instead, he made a few repetitive tics by squinting and pushing up his glasses. William only made the situation worse when he grabbed him by the side and said to Alex, "Is this how it works?"

Everyone but Guri seemed to get a chuckle out of the situation. Even Marissa, for once, found him amusing.

Despite his show of affection, Alex had remained attentive to their overall situation. Via one of the videre lenses he monitored the island from a satellite feed, checking visual, infrared, and ultraviolet emissions while on a small portion of the other contact lens he had a direct link to Tom in the Stratoskimmer.

Periodically since their departure, he had been receiving digital transmissions with an update of his progress. Tom communicated multiple times that the UAA continued to follow his ship. He had made a few stops in Guam and Hawaii to add to their confusion.

"This whole complex," Jonathan said as they reached their destination, "is now a convent full of chapels, gardens, and other sanctuaries built around John's cave. What started out as a single structure in 1088 has blossomed into this entire network of buildings."

The gate to the complex stood wide open revealing the beautiful whitewashed buildings inside. The exquisite shrubbery, flowers of all different colors, and an assortment of palm trees bordering the quaint cobblestone walkways made the area both serene and angelic.

As he entered, Alex eyed every crevice, alley, and chapel in the convent. He wanted no surprises this time. The satellite view showed the area to be deserted, but due to his previous experience on Crete, it only gave him a false sense of optimism.

Jonathan continued to lead the group through the maze of buildings and down a few flights of stairs until they reached the Chapel of St. Anna. Its entrance was surrounded by a white stone wall with a fresco of John receiving his visions from God above the door.

"As dreadful as this place is, it is nevertheless the house of God and this the Gate of Heaven," Guri said, reading the inscription on the wall.

"I can tell you all this right now," William said bluntly. "I am not ready to enter any gate of heaven yet."

"Don't worry," Alex countered, "the bowels of Hell already have a reservation waiting for you."

Jonathan led them down a few steps and through the doorway. Measuring about twenty by twenty feet, the room housed the small cave where John was believed to have written the Book of Revelation. Religious frescos, multiple crosses, oil lamps and other Christian icons decorated the cave's walls. A few benches had been placed in the center of the room for tourists to sit and hear a guide explain the history of this religious site.

Jonathan pointed to the crack in the cave's ceiling. "It is said

John heard the word of God through this crevice here." He then pointed to an indentation in the stone that had been lined with beaten silver. "It is also believed that is the place John used to lay his head while sleeping at night."

No matter what one's beliefs were, there was most certainly a sense of divine closeness in this small religious sanctuary.

"Jonathan," Alex asked, "any clue as to what we're trying to find here?"

"Again," he answered, "the code can only lead us in the right direction. The rest is up to us. Just as the Bible is a roadmap for mankind to follow, it is our free will whether we want to heed its guiding words or not."

"But can't there be another layer of this code you haven't explored yet?" Alex asked. "You showed us how the code progressed to this point. There has to be a next level. Sort of like the onion example you gave us."

"How about constructing the code in a three-dimensional fashion instead of a two-dimensional grid?" Marissa contemplated aloud.

"You are both right," Jonathan agreed. "I have looked into not only a three but also a four-dimensional layout with time being the extra dimension—both without success. I do not debate there is more to find, but how to find it is debatable."

William looked over towards him. "You know Jonathan, you're a great guy and all that, but sometimes this Bible code thing makes more sense to me than your answers."

Jonathan shrugged his shoulders and gave only a friendly grin in response. Without any direct guidance, they continued to search the area, examining every fresco, piece of art, and cross. William even hoisted Guri onto his shoulders to get a better look in the crack in the cave's ceiling.

"Put your hand into it," William implored. "See if you can pull anything out of it."

Guri tentatively did as directed, guided by the small flashlight given to him by Marissa. "What if there's a snake or a bug in there? I might be allergic to it."

"Don't worry!" William yelled up to him. "Alex knows the new Heimlich maneuver."

The crack yielded no treasures, and after a few minutes Guri had to be lowered to the ground. William's back could no longer take the extra weight.

"I know all these frescos and other pieces of art are beautiful," Alex commented, "but I think we should be searching for something that was around during John's time. Everything in here has been placed well over a thousand years after his death."

"I hate to say it," Marissa said, "but there's nothing else but rock. Unless we take down these frescos or start removing some of this art from the wall, there's not much more to see."

It almost seemed sacrilegious to touch anything in this area. Alex, along with everyone else, contemplated the moral repercussions of doing so.

"All I have to say," William insisted as he put his foot down, "is that we should be searching the fortress place on top of the hill. Don't get me wrong. I'm not in for another mile walk, but it looks like that's where we need to be."

"You're right!" Alex immediately agreed, thinking a few steps ahead of him. "You are completely right!"

William nodded in approval. "I'm just a guy trying to help out around here. No thanks is needed."

"William's right," Alex again reiterated, looking at everyone else. "Just like how Megiddo sits atop a hill, the monastery is located on top of the largest hill here on the island. It has to be more than a simple coincidence.

"But isn't that the case for every ancient city?" Marissa questioned. "Don't you think you may be drawing too quick of a conclusion?"

"Listen to Alex," William interrupted, "he's on to something here." It truly did not matter what Alex had to say at this point. As long as it began with *William is right*, he could have said just about anything after without any rebuttal from his friend.

"There's more to it," Alex added. "Jonathan, didn't you say the basilica was built on top of the hill where the monastery sits now?"

"The Grand Royal Basilica dedicated to John," he concurred.

"What if Father Christodoulos found something in those ruins and decided to build a new and better equipped fort around it? You also said there's great treasure housed within those stone walls. What if the greatest treasure to be found inside is knowledge, some knowledge that was imparted to John but never revealed?"

"What about this cave then?" Guri asked. "I thought this place was supposed to be where John lived and did all his writing."

"Maybe it wasn't," Alex said. "The Chapel of St. Anna and the monastery were both commissioned at the same time in 1088. What if the chapel here was just built as a decoy for the real treasure, which lies on top of the hill? Plus, if this cave had any true religious significance, why wasn't it commemorated back when the Grand Royal Basilica had been built before Father Christodoulos came to the island?"

He looked at Marissa. "You taught Sunday school. Is there anything in the Book of Revelation about a cave on this island?"

"Well," she responded. "No."

"Though I can't take away this place's beauty and religious allure," Alex concluded, "I just don't think we're going to find what we're looking for here."

No one refuted Alex's conclusion. His words resonated well with each of them and sounded logical. If they were to find a cure any time soon, ransacking this iconic religious sanctuary would not be the answer.

"Then we must make haste and be off to the monastery," Jonathan finally said, with only nods of agreement meeting his decision.

CHAPTER 31

LIKE HER COLLEAGUES, Samantha also utilized some of the last 24 hours to catch up on some needed sleep. Running only on fumes, she almost collapsed after last speaking with them. Her head rested upon the cold, hard console outside the autopsy room. She was so tired that she could have fallen asleep on a pile of bricks without a complaint.

During her slumber multiple experiments continued to run, most trying to ascertain some cure or a means to curtail the carnage propagated by *The Disease*. She had prepared them to run prior to falling asleep, hoping one would yield something tangible.

Drool ran down the side of her mouth and collected on the console. As she slowly lifted her head a long string formed, finally snapping down its center once she sat back into her chair.

"I feel like I've been hit by a bus!"

Samantha brushed her fingers through her hair and pushed a few strands behind her ear so she could see.

"What I would give to take a shower right about now." She looked around the bunker. "A billion dollar facility and it doesn't even have a place to wash your hair. Who designed this place?"

Though she complained about the accommodations, there were self-cleaning bathing blankets that she could wrap around her whole body to wash herself. Griping about the situation, however, seemed much more satisfying.

She examined the progress of her experiments on the console. *Nothing.* Uniformly, they all produced no meaningful results. It seemed that if the Bergmann gene became activated in anything other than embryonic tissue, it would prove to be a death sentence.

Samantha switched a few parameters on one of the experiments and tried a different biochemical technique on another. After these initial results, her expectations were low. Never had she seen an illness both so unique and lethal. The longer her testing continued, the less confident she became about finding a cure.

Even with all her scientific knowledge and belief that she could accomplish anything, Samantha was left with the conclusion that this disease might wipe out all of humanity after all. Unless she found something soon, this possibility seemed an imminent reality.

The world would quickly forget our presence. Humanity would just be a tiny, yet interesting, blip on earth's four billion-year timeline, quickly forgotten in the vastness of the universe.

A lump formed in her throat as she contemplated the enormity of these consequences. All the problems that plagued her before this began seemed suddenly infinitesimal. With a philosophical air she thought about what she would write if given an opportunity to scribe humanity's epitaph.

"They tried to play God and now are with Him"? "Tinkering with the genetic code is like playing Russian Roulette"?

She threw up her hands and laughed. "I got it," she said

aloud. "'They were just a bunch of dumb-asses who thought they knew everything.'"

Laughing was her way to deal with any stressful situation. Before she could mentally amuse herself anymore, a loud crash caught her attention.

She looked around the bunker to see if any more necroids had somehow invaded the facility. Another crash brought her to her feet. This time she realized the noise originated above ground.

Samantha looked at the screens and saw two of the police vehicles had crashed into one another. Cops scurried around the scene and turned their large spotlight onto the accident site.

Two cars bellowed smoke from their hoods as green liquid spewed from underneath them. Interestingly, they were both vacant. It was as if they had been possessed.

Samantha walked up to one of the screens and shook her head. "This is no poltergeist!" she screeched. "It's those damn necroids! They got into the cars."

It quickly became obvious that more than just the cars had been affected. A fire truck that originally seemed to be heading to the scene of the accident began to pick up speed as it haphazardly drove down Neurono-Tek's main street.

The sleek, red vehicle was vaguely reminiscent of its 20th century predecessors. Shaped more like a bullet, the truck still had multiple hoses attached to its side along with the traditional red flashing lights and sirens along its top.

Samantha watched in horror as the truck barreled into the two smashed cars, throwing them up into the air and down on the crowd of emergency personnel. The fire engine continued its rampage, smashing into other cars, knocking over street signs, and running over bystanders until it crashed into the front of a tall building at the end of the road.

The front half of the vehicle became embedded into the

building. Its lights and sirens still blared while white soapy foam trickled out from its sides. Screams of agony lay in its wake. The injured were scattered along the streets while overturned cars trapped a few of the emergency personnel. Neurono-Tek had become a war zone.

The bomb squad immediately descended onto the area. Dressed in padded black uniforms and transparent helmets, they surrounded the fire truck and began to disassemble its inner electrical circuitry. They also searched for any surreptitiously placed contraband.

Everyone on the scene assumed Neurono-Tek had come under some type of terrorist attack. Within minutes, the bomb squad had most of the truck's inner electrical circuitry disemboweled and placed alongside of it. This vehicle would pose no further threat.

"Stay calm," a voice bellowed from each of their uniform's lapel microphones, "and stay vigilant. Report to central command anything strange the instant you see it."

Samantha heard the warning and could not help but laugh. "Thanks for the heads-up, buddy!"

"Get me whoever is in charge out there," she then blurted as she activated her console's emergency line. The signal immediately went out to the central dispatcher's office and forwarded to the official directing the scene aboveground at Neurono-Tek.

"Commander Gorman here," a loud, gruff voice responded within a few seconds of her request.

Samantha looked up to one of the screens and saw the man responding to her call.

"Gorman here!" he reiterated before giving her a chance to speak.

"Yes," Samantha said, trying to sound both pleasant and calm at the same time. "This is Dr. Mancini and I..."

"I don't care who you are lady," he abruptly interrupted. "I'm in the midst of a major incident right now and don't have time for any house calls. How did you get dispatched to me in the first place!"

Samantha watched him on the screen as he finished his tirade. The man looked like a high school bully. With a short crew cut, chiseled jaw, and muscles so big they bulged out of his uniform, he seemed as if after this incident were all over, he would take everybody's lunch money.

Samantha cleared her throat. "Excuse me?" she said. "This is Dr. Mancini, one of Neurono-Tek's top executives."

"Lady," he countered, "I don't care if you're the Queen of Sheba. I don't like any interruptions when I'm in a critical situation."

Samantha's tolerance immediately came to an end. The disrespectful tone was one thing, but getting called *lady* twice crossed the line.

"Listen here Commander Gorman! I'm positioned right underneath you here in Neurono-Tek's secure bunker and can see everything that's going on around you. If you would stop being a bonehead and listen to me for a second, I can tell you what's happening up there!"

The shrill of her voice left the hulk of a man speechless. With his mouth agape, he stood there stunned as if he had been verbally manhandled.

"Remember those ugly bugs that killed one of your men yesterday?" she continued in the same tone. "They're called necroids, and somehow they must have gotten into a few of your vehicles and taken control of them."

"I don't care what they're called," he finally said. "I just want to know how we can stop them before they destroy this whole damn place and the men and women sent here to secure it."

Despite his gruff exterior the question was valid, and

Samantha had no answer. All of her experiments had been on *The Disease* and none had been dedicated to procuring any information about the necroids. She had used liquid oxygen to dispose of them, but this method would certainly not be feasible under these different circumstances.

Before Samantha had a chance to answer, one of the bomb squad's large black trucks slammed into a parked police car behind the commander. The impact jolted him to the ground, instantly ending their heated communication.

"Commander Gorman!" Samantha shouted. "Are you alright?"

She received no response but continued to ask the same question until she saw him slowly pull himself back to a standing position. A few of his colleagues were not as lucky. A car pinned down two of them while another three laid motionless on the ground with blood trickling from their ears.

The whole area erupted to life as other vehicles began to drive erratically and collide with buildings, people, or other cars. Many of the emergency medical personnel found it impossible to tend to all the injured. Those that attempted to do so became instant casualties themselves.

"Evacuate by foot!" Commander Gorman yelled. "Leave all vehicles behind. This is a direct order! Evacuate Neurono-Tek at once!"

CHAPTER 32

SATTAR ENTERED ARI'S OFFICE only to be accosted by his wife's unwelcome snarl and a myriad of self-gratifying pictures of the Malik along the walls. The silence and lack of emotional response by either Ari or Masika made him feel as if he were at a funeral.

"Malik," SattAr greeted with the proper bow and saluted with the O above his head. "You have requested my presence."

"Yes I have," Ari responded as if speaking to a group of a hundred or more.-

Ari arose from behind his desk and casually strolled over to where SattAr stood. Masika remained in the corner of the room and silently watched. With every second her animosity towards SattAr brewed more intense.

"Do you know why I called for you?" Ari asked.

SattAr shook his head side-to-side. "No I do not, Malik."

"I grow despondent," he continued, "that Alex Pella and the rest of his cronies will soon discover a cure for *The Disease*." He paused a second. "And do you know why I am concerned about this?"

"No, Malik," SattAr answered.

"You see," Ari explained, "I have come to the conclusion that the true success of the UAA relies on the West not obtaining a cure for *The Disease* before we do."

"The West will hold the cure over our heads," Masika chimed in through clenched teeth, "and make us slaves to their capitalist ideology."

SattAr felt as if the two fed off of one another's paranoia. Any sane person would realize that in the global economy the only way to truly rid the world of *The Disease* would be to treat everyone. He found the notion clearly nearsighted.

"In fact," Ari explained, "I would rather the cure never be found than the West have it in their hands."

"The Malik needs the cure!" Masika insisted.

SattAr felt bombarded by the two and almost wished he were struck down by *The Disease* instead of remaining in this office any longer. He did not need to be reminded of his orders. Surprisingly, Alex Pella had proved to be a much more formidable foe than he expected. No civilian, or even trained military professional, he had ever encountered showed such cunning, intelligence, and overall ingenuity than this man. Despite his inability to capture him, he had an unspoken admiration for Alex.

"If I were to have the cure," Ari went on to say in a boisterous tone, "then there will be nothing the West can do to stop the spread of the UAA's world influence. Not even The New Reality will be able to stand in my way!"

"Then I come with good news," SattAr said. "One of my special operatives on Patmos has recently reported unusual activity on the island."

"Patmos?" Ari questioned.

"It's an island off the western coast of Turkey, not far from Astipalea, where *The Disease* is thought to have begun."

Masika slowly walked over to the both of them. No longer content in the shadows, she felt her role was best served next to her husband. As she approached, SattAr paid her little attention and continued to speak with Ari eye to eye.

"What did this operative see?" Ari then asked.

They both used the word *operative* loosely. These men were actually looters who had been given military clearance to pillage abandoned Greek islands such as Patmos for their wealth. The operatives knew the risk in what they were doing but were paid extremely well by the UAA. In fact, Ari had thousands of them deployed throughout the Aegean looting the area and bringing back the wealth to their country.

"Other than the few monks who remained at the monastery," SattAr said, "the island has been utterly deserted until this morning when a boat occupied by five Westerners sailed into port."

He reached into his baggy pocket and took out a quarter-sized, clear circular disk. As he held it in his hand, the circular disc projected a clear holographic image.

The picture was indisputable. Alex Pella and his cronies were on Patmos. Their subterfuge had been discovered.

"Did you call off our pursuit on their Stratoskimmer?" Ari asked.

"No. I don't want them to get the impression that we were onto their ruse. The only way to capture Alex and the rest of them will be by surprise. He has proven his ingenuity before, and I cannot risk losing any upper hand that I have now. Plus, I have made arrangements with my operative on the island to help with my plans."

"Capture Alex Pella alive," Ari commented. "I don't care what you do with the rest of them. Kill them, torture them, or even let them go after a thorough interrogation. They are of no concern to me at this point."

Masika slapped his hand, like a mother disciplining a child. Her lips pursed and eyes glowered with rage. "They are all enemies of the UAA. Do not be a fool, Ari. They must all die!"

Her abrupt outburst took both Ari and SattAr off-guard. No one touched the Malik in such a way without meeting immediate execution. It was a crime beyond sacrilege.

They all remained silent. Though the slap was not intended to cause pain, the impact had severely bruised his ego. No one told the Malik his business, let alone his wife or any other woman. Even the most powerful people in the country barely raised their voice to him. There were certain rules, and Masika's display of dissent broke them all.

Almost too embarrassed to speak, Ari finally mustered up enough pride to say, "What do you think you are doing?"

"No! What do you think you are doing?" she reiterated, finally not afraid to openly show her true role within the marriage. "We cannot show them any mercy!" Spit spewed from her mouth. "They are all enemies to the state and have no place in the UAA's future!"

SattAr swore loyalty first to his country and second to the Malik. Ari's wife did not fit into the pecking order nor did he want her to. He waited to see how Ari would handle the situation.

"We will talk of this later," Ari said, trying to save a little face.

He could not meet his wife's gaze. Too intimidated to defend himself any further, he failed to raise his voice.

"So what are your orders, Malik?" SattAr said in an attempt to make him directly confront the situation.

A strong leader would not yield to mere threats. He may bend to reason but never falter in the face of confrontation. SattAr had always suspected Ari to be a weak leader who led only through his charisma and not from any inner strength or wisdom. He would not leave until he saw whether his suspicion about the man was accurate.

"You heard your orders," Ari finally said. "I want Alex brought back alive and if his cronies give you any trouble, kill them.

"Yes, Malik!" SattAr responded as if nothing unusual had just transpired.

SattAr knew the success of the UAA did not rely on being the first to find the cure for *The Disease*. It was the people living in their country who made it a success, not the Malik or any of his grandiose projects. Ari had forgotten that he was serving the people and they were not serving him. Many kings and dictators had lost their heads over this same mistake.

Upon exiting, SattAr left behind any respect or confidence he ever had for the man. He would not forget what he had seen today, nor would he place any further trust in this façade of a man.

CHAPTER 33

THE CLIMB UP THE SMALL, winding road to the Monastery of St. John was more arduous than expected. Because of the circuitous route, it took longer than anticipated.

Between William's moaning and Guri's long-winded explanation of his sinus problems, the trek became almost insufferable. Even Jonathan began to falter near the end of it. After initially leading them up the hill, he had slowed down his pace. Whether it was from exhaustion or pure insanity after hearing about Guri's ethmoid sinusitis ad nauseam, he began to stagger a few steps behind the group.

The monastery's walls were taller and more impressive than they appeared at the bottom of the island. It would have taken a concerted effort by an ancient enemy to attempt scaling them. No wonder this medieval fortress still remained intact after over a millennium of weathering.

Fortunately, the main gate to the monastery had been left open, negating the need to find some means of forcing their way into the building.

"You see that?" Marissa asked before they walked through

the towering gate.

A small, black funnel of smoke bellowed out from the monastery. Because of the wind, it was almost imperceptible as it dissipated soon after hitting the atmosphere.

"Good eye," Alex said. "Maybe there's still a monk inside who stayed behind to guard the place from any possible intruders."

"You mean we're not alone?" William quickly asked.

"I do see on the satellite's infrared scan what looks like a single person inside the monastery."

"Or maybe it's someone from the UAA sending smoke signals to the rest of them on the island to attack us," William randomly expressed. "Or maybe it's a madman burning all incriminating evidence from a heinous crime he just committed."

"Or maybe it's just cold up here," Jonathan said. "The temperature must have dropped at least forty degrees since we reached the top of this mountain."

They all looked at each other, confusion filling their faces. The temperature remained a sweltering 85 degrees Fahrenheit. The hill they traversed was tall but not massive enough to cause any significant temperature change.

"Are you feeling alright, Jonathan?" Marissa asked.

"As I said before, there is no need to worry about me. Your medical treatment has brought me back to my former self and this chill will not dispel any of your good work."

She eyed him from head to toe, visually examining every part of his body down to his fingernails. Marissa slowly walked over to him while continuing her inspection.

"Is that a rash?" she muttered aloud. "You seem all red. Do you itch?"

"I feel no itch, scratch, burn, or other ailment," Jonathan said, still smiling. "It's probably the sun. I probably got a little too much exposure at Megiddo."

Marissa touched the side of his face with her finger. The rash did not feel warm or raised and failed to blotch upon impression. Instead of further inspection, she immediately embraced him.

"We'll find the cure," she finally said, trying not to let her emotions get the best of her. "We will. We'll find the cure."

Marissa did not have to announce her diagnosis. They were all intelligent and knew what she wanted to say. *Jonathan had The Disease.*

Again Jonathan's words echoed through William's head. *It all ends on Patmos.* Though distraught over his colleague's fate, he could not help but contemplate: *Who will be next?*

"Do not cry for me," Jonathan said. "I am not dead yet, so mourning now will just be a waste of tears."

"Did you know?" she asked.

He held her by the shoulders in a kind and gentle manner. "*The Disease* takes no favorites. Just like death, it is the great equalizer. Though I naively believed it would spare me, I see now my fate has been determined."

"Should we get him back down to the medical clinic?" William asked.

Marissa shook her head no. There was nothing left at the bottom of the hill that could treat *The Disease* in this final stage of the illness. Though she wanted to help, she could do nothing now but pray.

Jonathan attempted to allay their fears by turning from them and walking through the hulking medieval gates as if there was nothing wrong. Though plagued by aching muscles and quickly dwindling energy, he would not allow himself to reveal to the others how badly he truly felt.

The inner courtyard of the monastery sharply contrasted with its outer, uninviting walls. It was as if they had exited a dungeon and entered the Garden of Eden.

Beautiful white stone walls adorned all the buildings in the monastery. Boasting an exquisite array of chapels, overhanging arcades, interconnecting courtyards, and Byzantine-era frescos, it paralleled John's cave in both magnificence and holiness.

"Now where's that guy you saw?" William asked, frantically searching the inner courtyard for any signs of movement. Like a spy, he crouched alongside the walls and darted his head out to look around the corner each time he came to a building's edge.

"What do you think you're doing?" Alex finally asked as he looked on with amusement. The comical diversion was just what they needed.

William put his finger up to his lips. "Shh! They'll be able to hear us."

Alex gestured to the building next to them. "Whoever the person is, I can see his infrared signal in the building right in front of us.

"It's most likely one of the monastery's monks," Jonathan said. "I think we should introduce ourselves before we go dillydallying around this place searching for a clue John might have left us."

"I agree," Alex said while walking alongside Jonathan to the building.

Guri and Marissa followed without the least bit of trepidation. Only William stayed outside in the courtyard, waiting for the worst to befall them.

"I'll guard the door out here," he stated as the others entered the building, "and make sure no one sneaks up on you."

Large arched walkways, marbled floors, and glass-encased parchments met them upon entering. Beautiful religious paintings and frescos decorated the walls while shelves of books and reading tables had been assembled throughout the room.

"The famous library of St. John's Monastery," Jonathan

uttered while soaking in the history. "It is said to house ancient documents signed by Byzantine emperors, an original copy of the book of Job, and seventh-century manuscripts from St. Gregory the Theologues' sermons."

"You are correct," echoed a voice from one of the halls. "This library also boasts more than 900 ancient manuscripts, many written on parchment, 2,000 books and 13,000 copies of different documents."

A thin man with a prematurely graying beard down to his chest welcomed them with open arms. He appeared to be one of the monastery's monks as he wore a purple robe known as a cassock, a wooden cross hanging from his neck, and small, rounded glasses at the bridge of his nose.

Though the man appeared innocent and friendly, Alex shared at least some of William's paranoia and would not yet fully embrace him as a friend. He stood back and inspected him for any type of flaw while the others shook his hand.

"My name is Father Kritikos," he said, "and I am the sole curator here at the monastery. The others either left or perished at the hands of *The Disease*. God rest their souls."

Alex listened intently to the man. His accent sounded Greek, but a hint of something else resonated in it. Maybe it was a dialect of the island, or maybe Greek was not the man's first language.

"What brings you all to Patmos?" the priest asked. "I have not seen a single person here since the evacuation."

Alex spoke up before anyone had a chance to answer. "We're on a field expedition to retrace the footsteps of John, the writer of the Book of Revelation."

"Odd time for such a project," the priest said inquisitively.

Alex knew that whatever he may answer, it would sound suspicious. No one would be on any scholarly trips to this part of the word, at least not without wearing a level five decontamination suit.

Instead of any further circuitous answers, Alex decided to respond to him in a straightforward manner. He didn't know how much time Jonathan had left and didn't want to waste any of it trying to fool this priest.

"We believe it may provide us the answers we need to find a cure for *The Disease*," he went on to say.

"How may I help?" Father Kritikos asked without hesitation.

"What is the oldest section of this monastery?" Jonathan inquired.

"There are actually two," the priest said. "The first one you passed in the courtyard before entering the library." Then he added with a smile, "Follow me."

The man took a long metal cane from behind his back and hobbled past them to the door. Alex watched him walk and tried to determine the reason for such an odd gait. It didn't look like there was any pain in his back or hips nor were there any signs of muscular problems. He could not put his finger on it but knew something seemed slightly awry.

William, while still hugging the side of the library with his back, watched Father Kritikos enter the courtyard. He dared not say a word, hoping the man in robes had not seen him upon exiting.

"You see these pillars?" the father said. "They are the remnants of the original pagan temple of Artemis which used to stand on this spot before any Christian building was erected."

Three weathered, brownish-white pillars stood side by side in the center of the courtyard. A rectangular-stone block, most likely the vestige of an ancient roof support, lay atop them. Two bells, much like America's Liberty Bell, hung between the three pillars.

Marissa tried to imagine what this grand temple must have looked like in its prime. Beautiful stone carvings, multiple statues dedicated to Artemis, and a triangular pediment adorning its roof must have made this building the jewel of the island.

Alex walked over to the pillars and began to closely examine them. Jonathan did the same, hoping to find any clues on these ancient stones. They ran their hands alongside of them, trying to identify any ancient markings. They also inspected the pillars from different angles, hoping an alternative view would uncover something that they had missed.

Alex took out a monocle and held it up to his right eye. He walked around the pillars twice before saying, "Nothing."

"I agree," Jonathan answered. "If there were any clues left on these old stones, time washed them away years ago."

"Where was that other spot you mentioned?" Alex asked, clearly giving up any hope that the pillars would help them.

"In the monastery's main church," he explained. "It was the first structure erected here in 1088 when Father Christodoulos came to this island. Let me take you to it."

Upon hobbling out from this portion of the courtyard, the priest turned to William and asked, "Are you also coming with us young man? The church is one of the most magnificent buildings here in the monastery. You surely don't want to miss it."

My cover is blown!

Alex laughed. "Who would have ever thought he would've seen you? Dressed in that bright red shirt up against the white wall, you were like a chameleon."

William kept quiet and begrudgingly walked behind them from a distance as the priest led them through arched walkways and into a connecting courtyard full of potted plants and hanging flowers.

A plethora of Byzantine artwork and frescos greeted them as they walked. The monastery was like an undiscovered art museum with riches abounding at every corner.

An older building with a domed roof stood before them. Unlike the stark white walls and archways around the entire monastery, this structure appeared to be built from a different stone similar to the three pillars in the adjoining courtyard.

Alex recognized the similarity in stone between this building and the pillars and surmised that it must be the church. It all made sense.

While admiring the monastery as he walked, Alex still kept a keen eye on the satellite and continued to watch for any surreptitious activity.

The priest pushed open the church's wooden door and held it as everyone, including William, walked inside. Candles burned and a fresh smell of incense filled the air.

"This is magnificent," Marissa uttered.

The church certainly did have a striking ambience. With a golden chandelier hanging from the top of the dome, red curtains along the walls, and a gold-colored altar with religious frescos painted along its sides, its décor seemed straight out of the Middle Ages.

Instead of a crucifix, which usually hung behind most altars, an ornately painted fresco of Jesus on the cross stood in its place.

"The church is off limits to all visitors," Father Kritikos said. "Because of its highly religious significance, only the most elder of priests here in this monastery are allowed to enter."

Alex walked over to the altar and inspected its artwork. He thought there might be some hidden clue embedded in these ancient frescos. Jonathan and Marissa joined him in his search while William and Guri watched from afar, knowing they probably couldn't help even if they wanted to.

As Jonathan walked behind the altar, he could not help but notice a large stone around which it had been built.

Before he could comment, Father Kritikos said, "That's an original stone found at this site in 1088. It was believed to originate from somewhere in Artemis's temple."

Alex knelt down and began to inspect it. Looking around its edges and laying his hands along its top, he tried to glean any information it had to offer. He could not help but think if there was any clue back at Megiddo that might help him now find what he was looking for in this church. He ran through the experience there but could not garner any tangible clues from it.

Getting frustrated, he turned to Jonathan and asked, "Was there anything else in the code which could help us here? I feel like I'm trying to find a needle in a haystack."

Marissa nodded her head in agreement.

"Could you check that original code you showed us where *The Disease* and Megiddo came together?" he asked. "Is there anything you could have missed?"

Jonathan took out the silver coin-shaped object from his Bible and placed it in his hand. The ancient Hebrew grid of letters appeared above it in the same configuration as he last showed them.

Alex asked, "Does it say anything about a certain stone, passageway, or symbol?"

Jonathan took a deep breath and began to scour the code for any other discernible clues. He searched a few minutes, but only gave Alex a look of consternation in response.

"Or maybe..." Marissa added, brainstorming aloud, "does it mention that old church we hid in while the Israelis and UAA soldiers fought?"

Jonathan's eyes immediately widened as if hit by an epiphany. What was so difficult to see for all these years now seemed all too obvious.

Almost too ecstatic to speak, he finally said, "Marissa is a genius! I never noticed that these Hebrew letters crossed with the word Megiddo." With a glint of boyhood excitement in his eye he explained to everyone in the room, "We were in the right spot at Megiddo the whole time! We weren't supposed to be searching in the old stony ruins of the ancient city. The church was our true destination. The word translates into church— Megiddo's church!"

"So what did we see there?" Marissa frantically asked.

"There's one thing that really sticks out in my mind," Alex quickly responded. "Unlike post-Constantine churches where an altar and crucifix are the center of attention, the first Christian churches at Megiddo boasted a communal table reminiscent of the Last Supper and a picture of two fish as their focal point."

Alex, Marissa, and Jonathan immediately began looking around the room for any of these features. Almost immediately, their eyes fell upon the same object. It was an old circular, wooden table, which William currently used as a seat.

"William, what are you sitting on?" Alex asked curtly.

"My ass. What else?" he responded.

They all scurried over to the corner of the room and looked at the table. In the midst of priceless artwork and gold it seemed oddly out of place. It was old but certainly nowhere near the age of the church.

"I bet this is a copy of the original table that once stood here in the Basilica," Marissa said. "And probably every two hundred years or so another table has to be remade to replace the prior one."

"I bet you're right," Alex responded. "But after having William sit on this one it'll probably need replacement in a day or two." He gazed at his friend as if to say, *please get off the table.*

"We'll need to move it," Jonathan said as William begrudgingly arose.

Marissa looked underneath the table and saw that its large base had been bolted down to the stone floor. "Don't try to move it yet," she said. "This thing's not going to budge."

Getting on her knees, she bent over and took a small surgical knife from her bag. The device looked like a pen with a red light at its tip. Taking the device, Marissa slowly sliced off the top of each of the four bolts. A trickle of smoke and a small spark accompanied her actions.

Finished.

Marissa stood back up and looked over to Alex, Guri, and William. "We'll need to lift the table first before repositioning it. I removed each of the bolt's heads, but their necks are still tethered to the floor through the table's base."

The priest watched in silence with just as much enthusiasm as the rest of them. It was as if he was also learning of the church's hidden secret for the first time.

They all grabbed hold of the table. Before lifting, Jonathan came over and grabbed an edge.

"I don't think so," Marissa admonished.

Jonathan backed away with his usual smile. Unwilling to make a fuss, he obeyed the good doctor without an argument.

"One, two, three, lift," Alex said as they raised the table about a foot off the ground and slowly moved it onto the red carpet in the center of the church.

"The two fish," Jonathan quickly said, pointing to the floor that the base of the table had covered. "Just like the ones we first saw at Megiddo's church."

Other than the four threaded bolts sticking up from its center, it appeared to be an exact replica. The two fish were situated on top of one another and swimming in an opposite direction.

"I would bet that this part of the floor dates back to the original Basilica," Jonathan commented.

Alex instinctively walked over to the fish and grabbed two of the bolts. After straining his back, he turned to William. "How about a little help over here big guy?"

With the aid of his friend, they pulled up on the bolts and lifted. A square portion of the stone floor where they were attached came with them. The two slowly moved the stone over to the red rug and lowered it next to the wooden table.

Marissa took a flashlight out from her bag and looked through the hole left in the floor. "There's an entire cave underneath here," she said while illuminating different parts of the hidden sanctuary. Her eyes widened with excitement and she could not help but let out a little yelp.

Marissa raised her head in amazement. After collecting her thoughts, she said, "You're not going to believe what's down there!"

CHAPTER 34

GREEN-COLORED AIRCRAFT with the UAA falcon painted on their sides began to arrive, quickly surrounding the old monastery. The assault on the old fortress had begun and this time SattAr amassed an entire unit of 200 elite soldiers for the task. It would all end here and now on Patmos.

"Secure the perimeter," SattAr commanded. "We must make sure there are no means of escape."

The soldiers knew their orders and had special assignments for such a rapid military attack. Usually a mission of this type would last at least ten hours. However, SattAr made an ambitious push for the entire operation to be no more than 30 minutes.

He knew that giving Alex any more time than that would mean failure. After being thwarted twice before, he would take no chances this time.

Every ten to twenty feet around the monastery's outer wall a soldier pushed a long silver pipe into the ground. As soon as it hit the earth, the pole came alive with lights along its sides and a glaring red glow at its top. Four metal appendages snapped out from its lower portion, lifted the pole into the air and then slammed it back down into the ground, securing the pole tightly into position.

Within five minutes over fifty of these poles had been efficiently placed around the perimeter.

One of the soldiers bearing two stars on his lapel approached SattAr. "Organic gate secure and activated, sir."

"Very good," SattAr responded while staring at a holographic blueprint of the monastery next to him. "Once the gate is up to full power, we'll commence with the air drop inside the walls."

"Yes, sir!" the soldier said and left after giving him a curt salute.

SattAr examined the hologram. Usually he had hours to decide where to deploy his men for such an assault. Today he would make an exception. Alex was too formidable a foe to squander any time. Even without an army or weapons, the man proved more dangerous than an entire squad of Special Forces.

He placed his finger on different places along the hologram. Small red dots formed wherever he touched. These spots would be the landing points for his men.

The organic gate began to emit a low humming noise as the space between the poles began to blur and distort, creating a psychedelic effect along the monastery's perimeter. The soldiers backed away as the gate began to pick up full charge. Hairs along their skin stood on end while a nauseated feeling cramped their stomachs. The closer they stood to the poles, the more the feeling intensified.

The gate was intended to cause such an effect. Programmed to repel any organic matter, it created a biological energy field that would make even the strongest man drop to his knees in agony. The closest anyone could get to it without severe nausea and the loss of all bodily functions was about ten feet. Any closer and it would put a healthy person into immediate cardiac arrest.

The field it generated also permeated fifty feet belowground, making an underground exit, like the one Alex and his colleagues pulled off at Megiddo, impossible. Most soldiers detested erecting this field because of its side effects. Even standing at a safe distance created enough discomfort to make them feel queasy for at least a day after the mission's conclusion.

SattAr made final adjustments on the holographic schematic of the monastery and sent the coordinates to his men in the air. The assault planes would arrive in ten minutes and drop off the soldiers at the designated spots.

Despite all his planning, he could not but help contemplating: *Am I doing the right thing?*

Was he betraying his beloved country by following the Malik's orders? Though he was not near the organic gate, his stomach churned with uncertainty.

CHAPTER 35

MARISSA WAS THE FIRST to enter the cave. She used a wooden ladder that had been left under the opening in the floor. Alex followed next until one-by-one they all descended under the church. The ladder creaked and sounded as if it were about to give way at any second. Even so, the old wooden structure withstood the weight as they all slowly descended its rungs.

Only Marissa held a flashlight. The rest procured one of the church's candles to help illuminate the subterranean area.

The cave offered nothing spectacular. Unlike the one they visited lower down the hill, this one had not been decorated with priceless works of art or adorned with any religious icons.

Its rocky walls, however, were not bare. Etched carvings covered their surface in a mosaic of scenes that seemed to tell a story long forgotten.

"I wonder if John did all of this?" Marissa said, pondering aloud. "Do you think this is the true cave of the apocalypse?"

Alex wondered the same thing. "Father Kritikos," he asked, "have you ever been down here before or even heard of this cave?"

The priest's expression said it all. He appeared just as mesmerized as the rest of them and clearly had never set foot below the church. He seemed to stumble upon his words as if trying not to say the wrong thing. "John's mysteries still abound. Even after 2,000 years."

"It seems clear now why the original Christians built the Grand Royal Basilica on this particular spot," Jonathan commented through chattering teeth. "It was not for any military or strategic purposes but instead meant to preserve one of the greatest Christian relics ever found—the carvings of John."

"Are you alright?" Alex quickly asked.

With all of their eyes on the cave's wall, they failed to notice Jonathan's worsening medical condition. His skin had turned bright red while his whole body trembled rigorously.

Marissa rushed to his side and put her arms around him. She wondered how he had the stamina to stand, let alone climb down the ladder unassisted. Upon her embrace he seemed to crumble down to the ground.

Embarrassed, Jonathan said, "Do not waste your time on an old man such as me. My life has been full, and I cannot wish for anything else. You are all here to find a cure for *The Disease*. I have taken you far enough. What happens to me at this point is inconsequential."

Ignoring Jonathan's request, William slowly moved him so his back rested comfortably against the wall.

"What happens to you… ," Alex began to say but suddenly curtailed his train of thought as his contact lens alerted him to activity outside the monastery. Ships bearing the UAA's emblem began flying in so rapidly that it reminded him of a flock of geese landing in an open field. They had been discovered. Though he wondered how the ruse had been uncovered, his greater concern now was to decipher John's carvings on the wall and escape with the information.

Marissa directed her comment towards Jonathan, "Former President Andrew Jackson used to say: 'One man with courage makes a majority.' Your health is just as important to me as everybody else's."

She knelt down and pushed the end of a syringe of medication into the side of Jonathan's neck. The effect proved immediate as his tremors rapidly decreased. Feeling better, he then attempted to rise to his feet.

Marissa placed a loving hand on his shoulder. "Sit," she ordered. "If you want to help, you can do it from where you are right now."

He smiled and dared not put up an argument. Though far away from his family, he felt suddenly right at home.

William gave Alex a quick shove to garner his attention. "What's going on?" he quietly asked.

"Oh, nothing. Just looking around the cave."

"Don't give me that bull!" he said in a hushed tone, not to draw attention. "The only time you don't complete a sentence is when you're preoccupied. You see anything on that videre lens of yours that you haven't told us about?"

William had called Alex's bluff.

"Let's just say, it's all under control."

"Don't tell me it's the UAA," he quickly, yet quietly said.

Alex watched as the troops assembled outside the monastery and created a secure barrier. They had been surrounded. The only means of escape now was through the air and unfortunately, their Stratoskimmer would be shot down immediately if it flew within a mile of the monastery.

"I just contacted Tom," Alex explained. "He's sending three of my aero-bikes under stealth that I had on close stand-by in case of an emergency to land right outside the church. They'll be here in five minutes. Let's use the time to figure out what's carved here on the walls before we get everyone in a panic."

William tried not to hyperventilate. Because his music player had short-circuited in the electrical blast back at Megiddo, he had nothing to comfort his nerves. Hugging Guri was out of the question while sucking his thumb would look a little juvenile.

Before he could ruminate any longer about the impending danger, Alex grabbed his shoulder. "I need you right now to keep a cool head. We don't have much time to figure this thing out."

"Figure what out?" Marissa asked, only hearing the final part of the conversation.

"Oh," Alex said, surprised he had been talking too loudly. "Figure out what all these carvings on the wall mean. Presumably John must have placed them there for some reason."

"I agree," she said.

Guri and Father Kritikos also had been scouring the walls for clues since their entrance. Oblivious to anyone else's conversation, they had their candles held at eye level to better examine the engravings.

Jonathan continued to rest against the cave's wall. Despite his sedentary position, he had enough light from the candles and flashlight to visually inspect the area.

Pictures had been chiseled into the rocky walls all along the cave. No words accompanied them, and none appeared at all uplifting. Uniformly, they all depicted different catastrophic events that could possibly end all life on earth.

"'When he broke open the seventh seal,'" Jonathan quoted from memory, "'there was silence in heaven for about half an hour. And I saw the seven angles who stood there before God were given seven trumpets.'"

"Is he beginning to hallucinate?" William asked. "Because he's starting to talk a little weird right about now."

"'The seven angels who were holding the seven trumpets began to blow them,'" Jonathan continued to say with eyes wide open and scanning the carvings around him.

"It's the Book of Revelation," Marissa said. "He's quoting straight out of the New Testament."

"It's all here," Jonathan said with his eyes wide open in awe. "He carved out all of his visions."

Never had he seen something before that brought him so close to God. Though his body was dying, his soul felt more alive than ever.

"What do you mean?" Alex asked.

"Don't you see?" Jonathan answered. "The Book of Revelation written by John is not about a single cataclysmic event, like most believed, but is instead a vision of both past and future apocalyptic events."

Jonathan tried to rise, but Marissa's kind hand kept him seated. Without enough strength to defy the doctor's request, he remained on the floor.

He pointed to a carving not far from his position. Marissa illuminated the area better for all to see.

"'When the second angel blew his trumpet, something like a burning mountain was hurled into the sea,'" Jonathan again quoted, "'a third of the sea turned to blood, a third of the creatures living in the sea died, and a third of the ships were wrecked.'"

The crude carving showed a large rock impacting the ocean. Along the beaches, bodies in the form of stick figures laid on their sides with their eyes closed. Fish depicted as a sideways number eight were dispersed in between them.

"Do you think what John saw was an asteroid impact?" Alex asked.

"I am neither a prophet nor a soothsayer," Jonathan said, "but I must agree it seems he saw some type of cataclysmic impact."

"So why doesn't he just say that?" William asked. "Instead of writing about trumpets and angels, why doesn't he just say that a big rock hit the earth and a lot of people died?"

"That's not how they wrote," Marissa interjected. "If you wanted to communicate an apocalyptic event in the first century A.D., you would have to use symbolic and allegorical language of the day, taken directly from the Old Testament books of Daniel, Ezekiel and Zechariah. It's how a person told a story back then."

"Then I'm glad I was born in the twenty-first century," William grumbled.

"Did you hear Grecco stole three bases last night in the baseball game?" Alex asked slyly.

"He did!" William said. "That's a record!"

Alex shook his head. "I lied. But what I wanted to show you is how we just did the same thing. *Stole a base* is symbolic language."

William understood Alex's point but still felt disappointed that Grecco had not stolen three bases. He loved baseball and knew all the players and their statistics down to the decimal. You could joke with him about almost anything—but baseball was off limits.

"'I heard a loud voice speaking from the temple to the seven angels,'" Jonathan again began to quote from memory. "'Go and pour out the seven bowls of God's fury upon the earth.'"

He pointed to a carving with a large crack down its center. To both of its sides people lay on their backs while the buildings around them stood in ruins. Rain and lightning also filled the apocalyptic scene. "'Then there were lightning flashes, rumblings, and peals of thunder, and a great earthquake. It was such a violent earthquake that there has never been one since the human race began on earth.'"

Alex walked over and looked closer at the carving, hoping to find some similarity with the world's current plague. The picture clearly had no relationship with *The Disease,* nor did it give any warning when this event would occur. "Again, another catastrophic event," he said aloud, "but it certainly doesn't look like what's occurring now." He contemplated a second and said, "Probably represents some cataclysmic tectonic plate movement."

As much as Alex enjoyed admiring all of these carvings, he knew their time was limited. Plus, every twenty seconds William would give him a stare as if to say: *Is it time to get out of here yet?*

"Jonathan," Alex asked while trying not to sound too rushed in his cadence, "is there a carving here that seems to pertain to *The Disease*? I bet the answer is hidden in here somewhere. We just have to find it."

Jonathan looked around the cave with the sole intention of finding something that correlated to their current situation. Marissa did the same, hoping to unlock the 2,000-year-old mystery.

Father Kritikos stood at the side of the cave, patiently keeping his thoughts to himself. Alex was not sure if he simply didn't want to interfere or had a different agenda all together. Did he not want to commit sacrilege by walking around the cave? Was he left speechless because of their momentous discovery? Whatever the reason, Alex knew he needed to keep an eye on him.

"I've been looking at this carving here," Guri said with his usual weak intonation, "and it does bear a resemblance to the events of today."

They all walked over to the drawing while leaving enough space for Jonathan to see from his seated position. It appeared that mankind had succumbed to a dynamic solar event. The sun, depicted with long, undulating beams seemed to consume the earth and lay waste to her inhabitants. The few people touched by one of the beams remained standing while the rest lay on their sides, dead from whatever cosmic event had occurred.

"I don't know Guri," Marissa admitted. "It looks more like what would happen if the world lost its entire ozone layer or it could possibly represent the outcome of a massive solar storm."

"Marissa may be right," Alex agreed. "There have been many theories of how a flurry of emissions from the sun could cause devastation to the earth."

Guri pointed at Jonathan. "I hate to say this," he acknowledged, "but if you looked at Jonathan without knowing anything about him, what would you think?"

They all stood quietly, trying to understand Guri's point.

"That he had a really bad sunburn," Alex said as if hit by an epiphany. "I see what you mean Guri! John probably had a vision of mankind succumbing to some unknown event and because they all died with reddened skin, he must have surmised the cause was somehow from our sun."

Jonathan quoted, "'The fourth angel poured his bowl into the sun. It was given the power to burn people with fire. People were burned by the scorching heat and blasphemed the name of God who had power over these plagues, but they did not repent or give him glory.'"

"It's been in the New Testament all along," Marissa said, "but we failed to see it."

"Just like the Bible code," Jonathan concurred. "There are many layers to it; you just have to know where and how to look."

William was not impressed. Though John may have predicted *The Disease* 2,000 years ago, how did it help them now? The plague continued to spread and this carving only proved to reiterate the world's current plight.

"Where's the cure?" William finally said in frustration. "I didn't risk my life to find some hidden carving, even if it is 2,000 years old."

"There's one more thing," Guri interrupted. "Take a look at the sun's beams a little closer. What does it look like it represents?

"Oh my God," Marissa blurted. "From the distance I didn't notice it!"

"It's a double helix," Alex said. "These beams of light look like small strands of DNA. That's amazing!"

Even William seemed impressed. Despite all his complaints he knew this carving was the archeological find of the millennium and may in fact be the answer they had all been seeking.

"But is the carving supposed to tell us *The Disease* originated from our own DNA or are we to hypothesize something else?" Marissa asked.

Guri responded, "No, I think he's trying to infer that the cure lies within our DNA. Just think of it," he continued to say while pushing up his glasses, "there must have been something that genetically protected ancient man from this retrovirus. If there weren't, humanity would have gone extinct eons ago. Also, look at the double-stranded beams of light. Only those people touched by one of them live while the rest have already perished."

"Guri's right," Alex concurred. "It's almost like the sickle cell gene. Where malaria is endemic it helps protect people from this disease. And I concur with Guri. There must be something in our own DNA that can cure *The Disease*."

Always the curmudgeon of the group, William asked, "But where is it?"

"I think we can figure this out a little later," Alex said with alarm . He turned to look at everyone in the cave. "Listen. While we've been down here the UAA has surrounded the monastery and are about to assault our position any minute."

William gasped as if he had just heard the news for the first time. Marissa and Jonathan too appeared astonished by Alex's revelation. This moment was certainly not the time to be running for their lives once again, especially when the cure seemed so close.

"I have three aero-bikes right outside this church under stealth," Alex went on to say. "They just arrived and we can all safely escape before those UAA soldiers close in on us." He looked over to Marissa. "Why don't you take Jonathan and get a head start while William, Guri, and I digitally catalog the entire cave. Tom's already set the bike's autopilot to fly us to an undisclosed location. Just get on the aero-bike and let it do the rest."

Alex grabbed Jonathan's arm and with Marissa's aid helped him up the ladder. Luckily, he had regained some of his strength after the last injection and did most of the climbing himself.

"Take care of yourself," Marissa said, looking down from the hole in the church's floor. She blew Alex a kiss and quickly went out of sight.

"We only have a minute to do this," Alex said while handing the other three a small pen-like device. He then directed each of them where to stand in the cave. "When I say *go*, I want each of you to snap the digitizer into the wall at eye level and walk to the center of the cave. It'll only take a second and we'll get out of here. Father, I want you to come with us, too."

Before Alex had a chance to look at the priest, he saw William collapse to the ground and jerk upon impact. Guri followed a second later. Their digitizers both fell to the rocky floor with a clang.

What's going on?

"Father!" Alex began to say until the words seemed to

freeze in his mouth. His whole body became instantly numb and his lungs felt like they were about to collapse under the weight of gravity.

As he fell to the ground, Alex's last sight was of Father Kritikos standing over him. The priest had his cane extended and its tip was aglow with a red light.

CHAPTER 36

POLICE AND FIRE VEHICLES still ran amuck within the Neurono-Tek complex. It almost appeared reminiscent of a demolition derby. The cars and trucks caused significant damage not only to the buildings but also to themselves. This loss of so many public vehicles seemed insurmountable. Financially, both the state and local governments would be unable to recoup the losses.

Despite the future economic fallout of this event, the real problem still remained: the necroids. They continued to infest Neurono-Tek and their numbers were possibly growing, threatening to spread outside the complex and into neighboring areas.

"Alex," Samantha repeated again on her tele-communicator. "Alex."

She had been trying to contact him for over an hour but without any success. It was uncharacteristic of him to fail to respond to her call, even in the most inopportune moments.

Dear God, I hope nothing happened to him.

Whatever the reason, it preoccupied more of her thoughts

than the chaos above. The entire complex had been evacuated. All emergency personnel ran off by foot, leaving the place deserted except for her down in the bunker. She watched on her video screens as the chaos continued above without any intimation of stopping.

She shook her head in disgust. Since the dawn of time humanity has been at war with itself, and now in the twenty-first century, it remained the same. The only difference currently was that humanity had become more creative in the ways to wreak havoc and lay waste to one another. The necroids proved to be the latest in a never-ending list of self-destruction.

Samantha sat behind the console and evaluated the data emerging from her experiments on the necroid remnants. After taking a few relatively intact pieces, she had vacuumed them into the sterile autopsy room for further analysis.

The results took her by surprise. Her instruments at first had trouble identifying if it were more mechanical or biological in nature. Robotics and flesh seemed to merge synchronously as one in this creature.

A computer chip made completely out of cellular material, wiring created from endothelial tissue, and a cerebral matrix produced from a combination of neurons and fiber optics encompassed just part of this creature's unique design.

Samantha could not help ponder the philosophical consequences of what she had witnessed over the past few days. Between discovering that *The Disease* had been inadvertently cast upon man through their tinkering with the genetic code and now with these necroids, she wondered how long it would be before humanity wiped itself from the planet.

Not today. Not under my watch!

Samantha evaluated the streams of data pouring out of the instrument panel. The more she read, the more she realized the true revolutionary nature of these necroids. The science behind them had such potential for good, but sadly it had been used only for this macabre creation. It was a shame to see such brilliance wasted on a machine meant for destruction.

"Who would have thought?" Samantha said. "These things aren't bugs, they're snails?"

A schematic of the necroids' DNA appeared holographically before her. In the shape of a circle, the strand of DNA had multiple colors along its length, representing individual genes.

Samantha tried to contact Alex once more but without success. She had discovered something truly amazing about the necroids and needed to speak with him immediately about her findings. Since he seemed to know significantly more about these creatures than she, Samantha wanted his input on these results.

I guess it's up to me.

Two more circular strands of DNA appeared above the console. These looked slightly smaller than the first but again had multicolored genes throughout the ring.

Mollusks?

The data returned with the same results. The necroids' DNA was largely taken from a mollusk, not unlike the common garden snail. Though other creatures such as an oyster, octopus, and a mussel fell into this category of creatures, the DNA had an 80% match rate with that of a common snail.

"I'll never look at another snail the same way! I just wish we had a bunch of birds out there to eat them all."

She did not understand why a snail's DNA proved so compatible in making such a vicious beast. These docile, slow-moving organisms seemed to be the last creatures anyone would think to use in creating this machine-hybrid combination. There must be something in the other 20% of the necroid's DNA that turned it into such a vicious beast.

"I got it", Samantha said aloud as a possible solution came

to mind.

"If it's good enough to kill a snail," she thought while setting up a new experiment on the console, "it should be good enough to get rid of a necroid."

A single necroid replaced the hologram of the three circular DNA strands. Numbers and symbols surrounded the creature while a small digital clock was positioned underneath it.

"Here we go," she said.

The clock began to run, and the numbers and symbols within the hologram changed rapidly. As the digital display read two minutes the necroid's outer shell began to whither and turn a dull shade of gray.

At the three-minute mark the experiment ended. Most of the numbers above the console reached zero and the creature now appeared more reminiscent of a raisin than of its former self.

Samantha immediately hit the console's emergency line. "Get me Commander Gorman!"

Within a minute the man greeted her with the same unfriendly welcome as before. Charm was obviously not one of his better points. He again sounded impatient, but after their last verbal altercation, he seemed more apt to directly confront a horde of necroids than a single Samantha Mancini.

"Commander Gorman, I know how to stop the necroids."

"Well, so do I," he countered gruffly.

The response surprised Samantha as she hadn't expected him to find a solution that quickly. For a moment she had regained at least a little faith in the man.

"That's wonderful," she said. "I'm delighted to hear the news. Did you also discover these necroids are susceptible to molluscicides or have you and your team reached a different conclusion?"

"I don't know what you just asked me, but in exactly five

hours the U.S. military will launch an air attack on Neurono-Tek, leaving a crater where the entire complex once stood. Bye-bye necroids!"

Samantha could not believe what she heard. The man was clearly insane and his lunacy appeared to be spreading. Only a madman would order an air strike to solve a simple problem.

"Let's think this through," Samantha tried to respond calmly. "Blowing something up isn't always the right thing to do."

She felt as if she were speaking with a toddler. And she attempted to use the same tactics that had worked on her own kids when they were that age.

"I know it may seem like the next logical step," she slowly continued to say, "but I found something a little less violent that won't cause billions of dollars worth of damage."

"Unless you can tell me there's a thermonuclear warhead sequestered down there in that bunker, I'm not interested. We're at war with these necroids and if they spread, the damage would be in the trillions. I must act now to stop the spread of these damn bugs."

"Mollusks," she corrected.

"I don't give a damn what you call them. Hell, they could be walking pieces of shit for all I care. All I know is that they caused twenty casualties at Neurono-Tek with eight being fatal. I don't like those numbers at all!"

Before Samantha could respond, he added, "And I suggest you get out of that bunker down there before the bombing begins or you'll be fatality number nine. Commander Gorman out!"

As if this day could get any worse!

CHAPTER 37

AFTER TURNING OFF THE AUTOPILOT, Marissa flew the aero-bike with ease. Fearing the UAA would give chase, she had wanted complete control over the vehicle in case of any unwelcome incident. Though this particular model boasted the latest advancements, it still handled like any of the other bikes she had flown in the past. Jonathan sat behind her on the seat with his arms wrapped around her waist. Both donned a self-contained air helmet that allowed them to reach higher altitudes without the fear of anoxia.

Their escape from Patmos had gone extremely well. The stealth mode Alex installed on the aero-bike allowed them to fly right out of the monastery without being detected at all. Even the oncoming UAA assault ships flew by without the slightest inkling of their presence.

Marissa only hoped now that Alex and the others made it out of the monastery just as safely. She wanted to call them, but the stealth mode prohibited such communications.

The autopilot on the aero-bike directed her to a small island in the western section of the Aegean Sea. She could only assume that Alex had arranged for a Stratoskimmer to rendezvous with them and fly them back to the States. Hopefully there, Jonathan could receive the proper medical attention needed until they finally unraveled the cure for *The Disease*.

The answer felt so close. What seemed like an impossibility a few days ago was now becoming a reality. If they could just determine what John's message meant about the DNA strains, millions—if not billions—of people could be saved.

Marissa turned her head and gave Jonathan a thumbs up gesture to check on his condition. Because his grip around her waist was slowly weakening, she was growing more concerned over his condition.

He did not respond. She gently nudged him with her elbow, but again she received no reaction.

"Jonathan!" Marissa screamed futilely. In stealth even the communication system within their own helmets had been deactivated.

She knew something must have happened to him. They were so close to the cure. She just needed to keep him alive a little longer.

I have to land this thing. Jonathan needs immediate medical attention!

The Aegean contained numerous unmanned, tiny islands. She took the bike down, hoping to find one. Many were even too small to appear on the aero-bike's satellite map.

Ahead, she could see a small outcropping of such islands. Mostly of rock and sand, one would suffice for a quick landing.

Marissa flew onto a pebbly shore and set down under a small patch of palm trees. The meager shade they provided would certainly be better than full exposure to the mid-day sun. She threw off her helmet and gently lowered Jonathan down from the bike to the edge of a tree. His body felt like Jell-O and went limp in her arms.

"Jonathan," she said, removing his helmet.

He jerked violently and began foaming at the mouth. He let out a loud groan as his body contorted in a seizure.

Marissa grabbed a few vials from her medical bag and injected two of them in the side of his neck. Within a few seconds the movements abruptly ended, leaving Jonathan in a pool of his own sweat and saliva.

"You're going to be O.K.," Marissa said in a reassuring voice. "It's all over now."

Jonathan slowly awakened. At first confused, he eventually regained his coherence.

"I hope I haven't inconvenienced you," he said with a groggy tone to his voice. "What happened?"

Marissa knelt down next to him. "Nothing that a little modern medicine can't fix. How are you feeling now?"

Jonathan would be lying if he said he was feeling anything other than horrible. His entire body hurt, and he felt as if his guts had been torn right out from his belly.

"I've had better days."

It was certainly an understatement. He could barely keep his eyes open and wanted nothing more than to scream out in pain. It took immense mental discipline not to go mad.

Marissa dabbed his brow with a wet wipe.

As he lay under the palm tree his vision began to fade. The only thing left clearly within his sight were the few rays of light that trickled through the branches above. It reminded him of the carving he had seen back at Patmos of the sun. It seemed all too surreal at this moment.

With the little strength he had left, Jonathan sat up and took out his Bible. Marissa attempted to keep him supine, but he lightly fought off her efforts.

"Jonathan," she said, "I insist. You must rest a little longer."

He wished a little rest would suffice. However, he had

witnessed the final stages of *The Disease* with his own eyes and knew there was little time left. Despite all she had done for him his body could not go on much longer. He needed to remain alert, if just long enough, to do one last thing.

Jonathan pulled out the circular coin-shaped object from his Bible and placed it onto his palm. The beams of light had given him a vision. Whether divine in nature or a hallucination from a dying brain, it seemed like everything at that moment made sense.

"I finally understand," he said. His breath was shallow and words seemed to be more mouthed than vocalized. "The cure for *The Disease* has been with us the whole time. We just didn't know where to look."

"Really?" Marissa responded, skeptical of his admission. Because confusion commonly follows a seizure, she wondered if Jonathan was truly coherent at this point. It could be minutes or hours before someone in his condition would regain normal cognizance.

"You just take it easy," she said. "Save your energy for later. We still have a long flight ahead of us."

Marissa went to inject Jonathan with another vial, but he quickly grabbed her wrist before she could administer any further medication.

"Please," he pleaded. "Give me just a moment."

Unfortunately, he knew a moment might be all that he had left.

Marissa placed the vial back into her bag and patted his head with the wipe. "Go on," she said, hoping he might tire himself and fall asleep if he continued talking.

Above the coin Hebrew letters appeared.

"Do you know what it means?" Jonathan asked. He brought up a hard cough and cleared his throat.

Marissa shrugged her shoulders.

"It's been in every one of the matrices that the code created," he continued to say. "Whenever I place your name or any of our other companions' names into the code, these letters cross them. Also, wherever *The Disease* or the places afflicted by it are mentioned, the same seven Hebrew letters always appear."

Multiple code matrices began to flash before them, one after the next. Important words and phrases were always circled, and in each new checkerboard pattern the same Hebrew letters always appeared.

Marissa could no longer believe Jonathan spoke out of delirium. Despite his raspy, weak voice, he seemed more coherent now than he had for some time. "What does it mean?" she finally asked.

"Alex Pella."

"What do you mean Alex Pella?" she responded in disbelief.

"Alex Pella is the answer," he reiterated. "The mathematical chance of finding his name in all of these matrices is basically zero, with odds being less than one in a hundred trillion."

"How can he be the answer?"

Jonathan mustered a smile. "He isn't, but his DNA is. John of Patmos saw Alex's DNA over 2,000 years ago and carved it onto the cave. He must have thought it represented beams of light." He looked at her intently, "We must now let those beams shine down upon mother earth and save us from extinction."

Marissa tried to speak, but he silenced her with a finger to her lips. The holographic projection began to spin a few rotations until a large three-dimensional matrix emerged. Different Hebrew letters ran its width, length, and height, creating a box-like shape.

The disc began to glow as Jonathan mentally reprogrammed the device. His eyes fluttered while his cheeks reddened. The man had merged with the machine. All the Hebrew letters in the hologram started to change multiple times a second, running the gambit of the whole alphabet.

The hologram then began to elongate and rotate on a central axis until finally it stopped moving and the letters remained constant.

"There it is," Jonathan finally said. The words almost seemed ephemeral and they were spoken with little breath behind them. Marissa, however, could understand him completely.

Within the center of the hologram different letters tuned red, green, white, blue, orange, or yellow and created a perfect double-helix pattern. Along the edges on both sides red and green alternated its entire length while the other colors matched in a reproducible fashion forming a ladder bridge between them.

"You found the next layer to the code!" Marissa commented wide-eyed.

Jonathan could only answer with, "Beams of light."

Marissa looked closely and saw that the same two letters formed the sugar-phosphate backbone of the DNA while another four letters made the matching base pairs that connected the two halves.

Jonathan took a deep breath and leaned his head on the tree. His eyes closed slowly while his mouth remained smiling.

"I have to get these results to Alex right away!" Marissa said. "We have to find out what this means at once. The world needs to know..."

Before Marissa could finish her sentence, she noticed Jonathan's lifeless body. His breath was gone and his cool, pulseless wrist told her that he had crossed over. No more suffering. She knew no medicine at this time could reverse the will of God. Jonathan had passed.

Marissa leaned down on his shoulders and let out a tear. Death had taken another friend, and she could do nothing about it. Though it was the inevitable ending to all living things, death never proved easy to face.

After mourning a little longer, Marissa placed the disc on her palm. As soon as it touched her skin, the double-helical DNA holographically appeared once again.

Wiping off her face, Marissa grabbed Jonathan's Bible and stood. She had remembered a moving passage in Luke about death and felt as if she needed to read it aloud.

Marissa leafed through the Bible until she found the appropriate page. As she read, a few loose pieces of paper fell out of the book and floated gently to the ground.

She did not notice them at first.

After reading the passage, Marissa couldn't help but wonder why she survived while so many other good people didn't. Was it luck, chance, or divine purpose? Whatever the reason, she felt undeserving.

A refreshing, cool breeze swept across the tiny island, causing the branches on the palm trees to sway with its gentle touch. The salty air brought Marissa back to her senses. There was no time to wallow in self-pity while billions were at risk of succumbing to *The Disease's* ruthless grip.

Marissa got on her knees and began to cover Jonathan's body with the small pebbles on the beach. She hoped to protect his body so that later someone could return and retrieve it for a proper burial.

As she gathered some stones, her hands accidentally came across the papers that had fallen from the Bible. At first, she thought they were litter and was about to ignore them. However, a familiar smile on one of them caught her attention, and she knew this was not trash.

The man appeared much younger, but she immediately recognized his identity. The soft facial features, thick hair, and unmistakable grin could be none other than Jonathan Maloney's.

She inspected the picture along with the other two that she had found next to it on the beach. Jonathan could be found in all three. In each he dressed in a long black robe and wore a bright white clerical collar.

He never told us, Marissa thought.

The man was a priest.

In the first picture, what looked to be his biological family surrounded him. It appeared as if a celebration had commenced, maybe a wedding or some other joyous occasion, as smiles filled their faces.

Marissa smiled as she looked at the other two photos. Though taken more recently, Jonathan still retained his charming and joyful appearance. His smile seemed contagious as all around him were aglow with happiness. He had a way of bringing out the best in others. She only wished she had more time to spend with him.

Father Maloney.

Marissa placed the pictures back into the Bible. Time to determine what the strand of DNA in the code meant.

CHAPTER 38

A SHARP, STABBING PAIN in his neck suddenly brought Alex back to consciousness. Though his body wanted to continue sleeping, he willed his heavy eyelids to stay open. Alex blinked a few times to adapt to his new surroundings. At first, he saw only dark shadows gliding across a field of blurred light. He tried to squinting in order to bring his vision into better focus.

"Wake up all of them!" a voice bellowed next to him. "They may also be of some use to us."

Where am I?

As Alex's vision began to return, he quickly realized only that he had been surrounded by an array of military personnel all dressed in green with the UAA falcon on their shoulders. William and Guri sat motionless to either side of him with their heads down.

Alex tried to stand but felt as if he weighed two tons. He was only a few inches off the seat but the staggering pressure on his body caused him to immediately collapse and gasp for air. He tried to push himself up but his arms felt equally heavy.

Gravity accelerators!

Alex knew fighting would be futile and that any further attempts to get off the seat would only prove counterproductive. The gravity accelerator had him pinned to the chair. The weight of his own body would crush him to death if he again tried to stand.

A familiar-appearing soldier went over to Guri and William and injected a syringe into both their necks. Alex recognized the man's eyes and nose but could not place where he had seen him before. Was it someone that he encountered at Megiddo or Crete? He could not tell.

Guri and William slowly began to awaken. Like Alex, they soon learned of the gravity dampeners and quickly stopped all resistance.

With effort, William turned to Alex and gave him a look as if to say, *I told you so.*

Alex had to admit, William's seemingly unjustifiable paranoia back at Patmos seemed painfully justifiable at this moment. He had let his guard down, and they had been captured as a result. They were lucky the UAA hadn't killed them on the spot.

Alex wondered why Father Kritikos worked with the UAA. It seemed like such an unholy alliance.

He thought another moment and then looked straight at the soldier with the syringe. He met the man's eyes with a glaring stare. "Father Kritikos!" he exclaimed. Alex knew he recognized this man.

The soldier smiled smugly.

"You're no man of the cloth," Alex said, realizing this imposter's true identity. "What did you do with the priests back at the monastery?"

"Let's just say," he responded with a familiar voice, "that I wasn't burning wood when you arrived on Patmos."

Alex felt sickened by the man's remorseless confession. Had

he any dignity or sense of honor? Killing the innocent was an act of cowardice. He wanted to wring the man's neck for what he had done.

"I see we have already made friends here," a voice resounded from behind a line of soldiers.

Alex knew immediately from whom it came. The pompous cadence and the self-serving intonation made the man's identity undeniable.

To no surprise, Ari Lesmana waltzed out from behind the soldiers. Dressed in ceremonial Arab garb, he held his head high and approached his guests.

"Is this guy for real?" William mumbled.

Guri began to tremble in his seat. For a comic book loving hermit, the situation became too overwhelming. Sweat poured down his brow, and his face looked like a ripe tomato.

"Breathe slowly," Alex whispered. "Don't show him you're scared."

Alex's comforting words did nothing to expunge Guri's anxiety. He felt as if he were about to have a nervous breakdown. Plus, the weight of the gravity accelerators on his body only proved to exacerbate the suffocating feeling that had overtaken him.

"Stop whimpering!" Masika said as she accompanied her husband through the line of soldiers. "You disgust me! You all do!"

She spit on the floor as if to tell them they were no better than the ground that she walked on.

"Charming isn't she?" William muttered just softly enough for only Alex to hear.

Masika's reputation preceded her. Though the UAA attempted to minimize her role within the government, many understood her influence on Ari. Therefore, Alex did not seem surprised to see her by his side at this moment.

"Dr. Alex Pella," Ari said. "How nice of you and your friends to join us here at my palatial estate in Tabas."

So that's where they took us, Alex contemplated. This place did look more elegant than a regular governmental building. The room around them seemed like something that would be used for entertaining or maybe even a ballroom dance. High ceilings, crystal chandeliers, and golden-framed works of art along the walls made this place a spectacular sight.

Masika walked over to Guri and squeezed his cheeks together with one hand. "Why do you speak to these sniveling cowards as equals?" She pushed his head back while releasing her grip. "I despise even looking at them."

Guri could not help but break out in sobs. He sounded like a wounded dog. William didn't know if he should feel bad for the man or burst out in laughter at the sound he made.

Alex felt a hand squeeze his shoulder. Though it caused no real pain, it did make him twitch in surprise. "This is no way to conduct a civilized interrogation," scolded the interloper standing behind him.

Masika glowered at him in response.

"Good work SattAr," Ari commended.

As the man walked from behind them, they instantly recognized his face. The person who had been hunting them down since this excursion began stood right before them, and they could do nothing but sit helplessly on their chairs and watch.

"Crap!" William sputtered. "Just when I thought this day couldn't get any worse."

"And Albert Rosenberg once said we should not underestimate you," Ari commented, more to exalt himself than to belittle Alex. "I think it is obvious that it is you who should not have underestimated the UAA."

Like it was a fair fight, Alex thought. An elite Special Ops team versus an unarmed bunch of civilians without any military training.

Just then Alex realized the name Ari had uttered. *Albert Rosenberg.* At first he thought he misunderstood. "Did you say Albert Rosenberg?"

"That I did," Ari responded nonchalantly.

Alex instantly knew the collaboration between the two meant trouble. Albert was one of the most brilliant men he had ever met. His recent political and economic successes represented just the pinnacle of a long and triumphant career. There must be a reason why he would associate with a megalomaniac fascist such as Ari Lesmana.

Obviously, Albert had been using Ari as some sort of pawn in his overall bid for world domination. There would be no other logical reason for him to conspire with the man. Ari's ego obviously blinded him from the truth, and Albert most likely played him like a marionette.

"It has come to my understanding that you have found the cure for *The Disease,*" Ari went on to say.

"Sure," scoffed William sarcastically. "And we also found the fountain of youth and the lost city of Atlantis along the way."

He received a quick response with the backhand of Masika's fist across the face. Blood oozed out from the side of his lip but despite wanting to cower in fear, William would not give her or any of them the pleasure of seeing him flinch.

Guri's moaning began to pick up momentum at the sight of William being struck. The wailing reached a new level in annoyance and pitch. Between the moans, he would cry or mumble incoherently.

"I said stop it!" Masika insisted.

Her command only proved to exacerbate his wailing. If they didn't administer a tranquilizer soon, he would be headed for a nervous breakdown.

"He doesn't know anything," Alex implored. "Let him go." He looked at William. "Let them both go. I'll tell you everything you need to know. Just give Guri something to calm his nerves before he gives himself a heart attack."

William whipped his neck to the side and looked directly at Alex. He knew his friend didn't have the cure and was bluffing. Though admirable, he couldn't let Alex take the fall by himself. "The truth is," he loudly exclaimed, "Alex only knows part of the cure. I know the rest."

Alex kept a blank stare, trying not to show any emotion. Though he wanted to contradict William at this moment, he knew it would now be futile. He admired his friend's bravery but also wished he would keep his mouth shut. Alex had gotten William into this predicament and felt like he should be the one to take all the responsibility. He did not need to endanger either William or Guri anymore at this point.

"Regardless of who knows what," Ari said, "You are all invited to stay here at my estate until I have a full and total disclosure of the cure."

It was an invitation that they could not refuse.

Alex saw through Ari's cordial façade. Just like he patronized the citizens of the UAA with feigned interest in their well-being, he did the same for them. He also knew whether they provided him with the cure or not, they would all meet the same fate: execution.

Instead of provoking him, Alex decided to play along with his game. "Other than these gravity accelerators restraining us to the chairs," he said, "I couldn't have asked to stay at a more beautiful place than here at Tabas."

Ari prided himself in the opulence that he created. Alex's words only proved to stroke his growing ego.

Guri turned his head side-to-side and began to panic. "I don't want to stay!" he moaned through the tears. "I don't want to stay. Let me go!"

"I cannot take this any longer!" Masika shouted. In a rage of anger, she grabbed Guri by the mouth and shoved a small, black pill into it. He attempted to spit it out but Masika's tight grip upon his jaw would not allow for such an action.

Guri's eyes suddenly went blank as his body began to tremble.

"What did you give him?!" William shouted.

Guri's entire body suddenly turned a sullen color of gray while his hair fell from his head in one clump.

"Why?" Ari asked. Masika had obviously overstepped her authority and taken a unilateral and rash action.

Before Ari could scold Masika further, Guri turned completely black. Both eyeballs fell to his lap, accompanied soon by bits of skin and muscle. Within a minute all that was left of Guri had been gravitationally plastered against the chair. The sight of a smoldering pile of black flesh, bones, and clothes proved too much for William to handle.

"You monster!" he shouted. "You killed Guri!" He tuned to Alex. "She killed Guri!"

Alex kept a stoic face, not giving any of them the satisfaction of an emotional response. Though surprised, he had no delusion both he and William may soon meet the same fate.

"Take them away," Ari shouted. "Now!" He turned to Masika in anger. She seemed invigorated by the whole incident and did not care about her husband's disapproval. This was the fate she wished for every Westerner and capitalist.

"They killed Guri!" William continued shouting as he and Alex were briskly escorted out of the room. "Those sons of bitches!" his faint voice echoed from afar.

SattAr stared at Ari in disbelief that his wife killed one of the men who possibly could have provided them with the cure. How naive it was to believe that Alex, alone, held the answer.

Before SattAr could comment, Ari looked him in the eye and with a boisterous voice bellowed, "You have a problem soldier?"

SattAr's expression did not change. He didn't fear the Malik.

"This is war," Ari smugly continued, "and if you cannot stomach the casualties, you are in the wrong profession."

As Ari and his wife began to exit the room, he turned back to SattAr who remained motionless and said, "I'll give them exactly 24 hours, and if Alex doesn't provide us with the cure, I want him and his friend immediately terminated."

CHAPTER 39

SAMANTHA STILL COULD NOT BELIEVE Commander Gorman had ordered an air raid on Neurono-Tek. It seemed like such a ludicrous action. Although she did sympathize with him about the casualties, razing her company to the ground was obviously not a viable option.

The entire state relied on Neurono-Tek's hospital, and their country—if not the world—depended on their cutting-edge research. Only a few institutions like theirs remained in the United States. A country that once boasted a few hundred of such facilities now only had a meager three to continue vital research. Losing one of them now would not be an acceptable option.

Samantha attempted to contact Commander Gorman a few more times to plead her case. Only his assistant responded to her requests and proved just as stubborn as his superior.

"All you need to do is spray the entire area with metaldehyde," she pleaded with them. "It's lethal to the bugs and harmless to humans."

She soon realized she could give Commander Gorman the

solution to world peace and the meaning of life but he would still insist on an air strike.

Samantha slammed her hands against the console. Frustration mounted. Stuck alone in the bunker, attempting to find the cure for *The Disease,* and now trying to avoid annihilation overwhelmed her. She could multitask, but this was ridiculous.

She also grew worried that Alex had not returned her communications. She knew something must be wrong, and she felt helpless to do anything about it.

A loud siren began to blow around Neurono-Tek's perimeter. Samantha didn't even need to listen to the audio on the video screens to hear the earsplitting noise.

Though she could not view them, she knew the military had surrounded Neurono-Tek with a five-mile *DO NOT ENTER* perimeter. The area had been cordoned off for the air strike and now the siren indicated its imminent commencement.

Samantha knew staying would be suicide, but like a captain of a sinking ship she refused to vacate the premises. She would rather die a martyr than a quitter.

Experiments still ran in the autopsy room. She intended to work until the final minute, hoping her last effort might bring them closer to a cure. All her results streamed directly to the NIH. Hopefully they could pursue the research further despite their meager scientific capabilities.

The NIH, Samantha thought. That may be the answer!

She suddenly realized that despite losing most of its once coveted research capacity, the governmental organization still remained politically influential. If she could somehow obtain their help, maybe the entire air strike could be averted.

"Get me Dr. Howard at the NIH immediately," she shouted in the tele-communicator on her console.

It did not matter that it was now 2:00 A.M. At this point,

she'd wake up the President of the United States if she needed to.

An audio-only response sounded from the console. No visual image accompanied this communication.

"Hello?" said the half-asleep voice.

"Yes," Samantha said matter-of-factly over the siren's annoying blare in the background. "This is Dr. Samantha Mancini with Neurono-Tek, and I need your help immediately."

Dr. Howard's voice instantly became clearer. "How can I help?"

He had been well aware of the circumstances at Neurono-Tek. Though the media had withheld part of the information, he knew the complex had been locked down due to a possible terrorist-type attack.

Samantha quickly briefed him of the circumstances. If this communication were not coming from a secure line with confirmation of its destination, he would have thought the whole thing a joke. He was not laughing.

The consequences of destroying Neurono-Tek at this juncture of *The Disease*, along with the present problems caused by the vastly depleted medical system, would be catastrophic.

Dr. Howard ran the scenario over in his head multiple times, deliberating over any option he had available.

"I can call the congressmen I know on Capitol Hill right away," he finally said, "but it could take hours if not days to stop an air strike. And you obviously don't have that kind of time."

"Don't remind me," Samantha responded.

"The only way I could possibly stop an attack on Neurono-Tek on a more immediate basis is if there were a potential biohazard that would be released into the environment as a result of the air strike," he went on to think aloud. "But from what you tell me there isn't."

"Did I mention that I have isolated the pathogen behind

The Disease and that an air strike could disseminate it over a hundred mile radius?"

"You should have said that in the first place!" he responded almost in a panicked tone.

She would have, but she had just made it up when Dr. Howard told her what he needed to hear. She had not isolated the pathogen and even if she did, it would be instantly vaporized in the bombing. Though not a poker player, she was betting the house on a pair of twos.

"This would be catastrophic!" Dr. Howard went on to say. "I have to stop this strike if it means intercepting the planes myself!"

She could hear him shuffling papers in the background and awakening his wife from sleep. "I'm getting on this right away. You have my word, Dr. Mancini. I will do everything I can for you!"

The communication ended.

I hope this works.

Samantha cautiously watched the screens, hoping no bombs or missiles would suddenly reign down upon the complex. She had no idea how soon the attack would begin but had a bad feeling it must be coming soon. Commander Gorman did not seem to be a patient man. If it were entirely up to him, Neurono-Tek would have been turned to rubble an hour ago.

CHAPTER 40

"I CAN'T BELIEVE SHE KILLED GURI," William reiterated ad nauseam while pacing the room. He turned to Alex. "Did you see that? His body… it just turned to black mush. Have you ever seen such a crazy thing?"

Unfortunately for Alex, he'd had the misfortune of witnessing it twice in just over a week.

He tried to ignore both William and his remorse over Guri's demise as he searched the room for some means of escape. Though they were given a meager 24 hours to produce the cure, he had no intentions of complying.

While being escorted from their interrogation, he assumed they were headed for a dark and Spartan confinement. Instead, their accommodations turned out to be as luxurious as the grand ballroom where they had just been.

The opulence of the entire palace, including this room, was not lost on either Alex or William. They had never before seen such lavish décor. It made King Louis XIV's Palace of Versailles look like a pauper's cottage. Obviously no expense had been spared in the construction. If only the citizens of the UAA knew where their hard-earned money had been spent, they would be disgusted.

"Why'd they put us here anyway?" William went on to ask in the midst of his lamenting. "I thought they would just torture us on the spot to get all the information they wanted."

Like William, he didn't understand why they didn't just finish their interrogation back in the ballroom or why Ari Lesmana granted them a full day to produce the cure. Was there something more urgent or pertinent at the present time that made the cure a second thought?

William momentarily suspended his rant after discovering a well-stocked refrigerator filled with food and an assortment of beverages. After taking out a few sandwiches, an entire chocolate cake, and a two-liter bottle of soda, he mumbled, "I just need a little something to calm my nerves."

Alex further searched the room, looking for any way out. He knew a breakout would prove difficult as most likely the entire place had been bugged. With surveillance equipment now the size of a pinhead, a hidden camera could be located anywhere.

We have to find a way to get out of here!

Alex bent down and pulled an infrared disrupter out from the side of his shoe. Though stripped of all his gadgets, the UAA had overlooked both his sneakers and contact lenses as a source of any suspicious contraband. Their carelessness could prove to be his salvation.

William's eyes widened with anticipation. He knew Alex must have concocted some plan for their escape and wanted to draw attention from the obvious surveillance back to himself instead of his friend. "They killed Guri," he continued to moan almost theatrically with a mouth full of cake.

Alex surreptitiously then began to reconfigure the infrared disrupter while pantomiming that he had been simply tying his shoes. He looked cautiously at the door, almost expecting a few UAA guards to storm in and beat him into submission.

Luckily, his actions produced no such response as William's lamenting most likely gleaned all their attention. Alex stood and stretched his back as if nothing had occurred. "Let's make our escape," he said aloud.

"But," William sputtered as bits of food shot out of his mouth as if originating from a Gatling gun. "But... but I thought we were supposed to keep quiet."

"We're fine for now. I set the infrared disrupter to scramble all sound communications. The UAA will think there's a glitch in their surveillance system, and by the time they determine the truth, hopefully we'll be gone. "So what's the plan?" William asked enthusiastically while shoveling even more food into his mouth.

"That's as far as I got."

William stopped chewing. His cheeks were out like that of a chipmunk and the optimistic smile on his face turned into a look of despair.

Alex held up his hand. "Hold on there, big guy. It's not like I don't have any ideas. First, let's assess what we know about this room."

"O.K.," William quickly responded, trying to help. "It has a well-stocked refrigerator and the toilet doesn't appear to clog easily."

"In addition to that," Alex went on to say, "this room appears to be designed for the safety of the individuals inside of it and not as a holding cell of any sort." He pointed to the windows. "They're bulletproof. I inspected them carefully and if you look at them at an angle, the glass is layered between polycarbonate, thermoplastic sheets. And the ornate wooden door holding us in here is obviously a façade. Did you notice how it moved on rollers? I bet it has a solid iron interior."

He turned and looked around the room. "I would also suspect this whole room is lined with a few inches worth of iron."

"I don't know about you," William countered, "but it doesn't make me feel too safe right about now. How are we going to break through solid iron? That magnet thing of yours surely isn't going to do the trick, and they took all of your other gadgets."

"Except my contacts," Alex slyly responded.

William chewed his food slowly, trying his best not to look too unimpressed. "O.K. then," he added sarcastically. "I guess we'll use your 20/20 vision to rocket us out of here."

"That's Plan B," Alex jested. "What I'm trying to say is that I've been able to access the entire specs of this palace and am looking at the architectural layout of this specific room right now."

"But how'd you do that? Shouldn't the specs be classified or something? What did you have to break into to get that?"

Alex shrugged his shoulders. "Nothing. The layout is public knowledge."

"That doesn't make sense."

"It should," Alex scoffed. "Did you think a megalomaniac like Ari Lesmana would keep the design of this architectural masterpiece a secret? No," he said, answering his own question, "of course not. He wants the world to know all about his magnificent creation, even if it compromises this palace's security."

"Thank God that moron let those top secret specs get posted or we'd be in even more trouble."

Alex walked around the room, acting as if he were simply admiring the artwork along the walls. He needed to keep the ruse going so that the UAA security would not grow suspicious.

There were a few ways to escape, but as Alex ran through

the room's design he determined that each would be a major undertaking and raise suspicion almost immediately. Plus, they didn't have the tools for such projects, nor did they have the privacy to accomplish anything unnoticed.

Stumped!

"I'm going to the bathroom," Alex said.

"Don't forget about the courtesy flushes," William responded. "I'll have to also use it again pretty soon."

"You got it," he said, not wanting to waste any time explaining. Alex desired not to relieve himself but to instead look for a way to escape.

Something about the bathroom's architectural design had caught his attention. It appeared as if it were not originally meant to be attached to the main room and had been added almost as an afterthought.

The décor of the bathroom immediately struck Alex as being out of place. With a marbled floor, a large Jacuzzi, and sauna, it seemed as if this room had been originally part of an indoor spa and was converted to a bathroom.

There was also a slight step down when entering the room. It would not have seemed unusual unless one were looking for nuances of incongruity.

Now this is a throne room.

Alex went over to a white marble-lined sink and washed his face. After turning off the gold-plated faucet, he dried off with one of the towels embroidered with the UAA falcon. He looked into the mirror as if examining a mole or an unsightly hair. However, this ruse was meant only to provide him with a further opportunity to highlight the specs of this room on his contact lens.

Unfortunately, the entire bathroom also boasted solid iron walls beneath its elegant outer façade. It would take a high-powered laser or small explosion to even make a dent in them.

Alcatraz seemed less impenetrable at this point.

Alex took one final look around the area and began to exit. Upon leaving, he noted a small closet that appeared to lie just between the two rooms. Because the bathroom and main room were adjoined at an angle, there was a small, triangular space between the two where a closet stood.

It appeared the architect didn't want to waste any space and used this extra room to create this closet.

That's it, Alex thought. That's how we're going to get out!

"William!" Alex yelled. "Stop eating and come into the bathroom."

Unfortunately, that was like telling a herd of cattle to stop charging.

William downed the rest of the sandwich and he walked nonchalantly over to meet his friend.

"I found a way to get out of here," Alex said with his hand over his mouth as if wiping his face—just in case the UAA guards could read lips. "Follow me."

Alex led them over to the sauna. It was a large glass-encased room with wooden benches surrounding a central pit filled with heated rocks. He opened the door. "After you."

"Don't I get a towel or something?"

"Just act natural," Alex responded. He thought a second, knowing what natural meant to William. "Just act normal and sit over there on one of the benches."

Alex went over to the heated rock pit in the center of the room and set the control panel to steam. Its bottom began glowing red and heat instantly started to exude from the rocks. He then sat on a bench in the exact opposite corner of the room and leaned back as if relaxing.

William did the same without asking any questions.

Alex slowly laid the infrared disrupter next to him on the bench. There could be no miscalculations now as the window of opportunity would last only a few minutes.

William quickly opened his eyes after feeling someone shove his shoulders. No one was there and Alex appeared asleep on the bench. *What was going on?*

He again felt the same shove and heard someone say, "Let's go!"

Is this place haunted?

William jumped up, afraid the sauna had some sort of poltergeist. "Alex," he quickly said, "I think there's a ghost in here!"

He suddenly felt someone grab his shoulders but again no one was there. He began to tremble in his shoes. Nothing at all scared him as much as ghosts, and he certainly didn't want to stick around and see what they had in store for him.

Before he could run out of the sauna, he turned and saw his body still laying on one of the benches. He must be dead and had turned into a ghost! The sauna must have been a death trap.

"Get a grip," Alex said. "I can guess what you're thinking. No, we're not dead. I just set the infrared disrupter on a light-freeze mode. It'll only last five minutes before the whole thing overheats and melts down. Let's move."

What a relief! William sighed.

Alex grabbed him by the arm and escorted him out of the sauna and into the adjacent closet. The door opened but to their eyes nothing moved. It was a surreal feeling to push and move objects without seeing anything change. In essence they were ghosts, moving unperturbed throughout the bathroom without being seen.

"On the count of three," Alex said, "we're both going to slam against this back wall here until it breaks."

Fortunately, the closet had shelves only at eye level and nothing stood underneath except a long bar meant for hangers.

"One, two… three," Alex counted. The thinly plastered back

wall collapsed under their weight as they vaulted themselves into a cramped and dark passage.

William and Alex got to their feet. Blackness enveloped them like an impenetrable dark cloud. From seeing nothing move, to now seeing nothing at all, sent their senses into a frenzy. The whole ordeal, at first, seemed disorienting, but after a few seconds Alex again grabbed William by the arm and led him down the passageway.

"I have the layout memorized from the architectural specs," Alex said. "When we reach the wall ahead of us in about twenty feet, we'll make a sharp right and continue walking straight for almost a quarter of a mile. That'll lead us directly to the hangar. Hopefully, there'll be something I can fly to get us out of here."

William offered no complaints. The plan appeared sound. Now if they could only execute it without getting killed.

They continued walking in the dark until Alex's hand hit a wall in front of him. "Time to turn right and the exit will be straight down this way," he whispered.

Alex's voice brought William some relief. Between the pitch black and the utter silence of this passageway, it created a sensory deprivation-type chamber that slowly drove him mad.

They scurried down the passage until Alex's hand came across another wall. Fortunately, upon hitting it a hollow sound echoed back, indicating that only a thin piece of whitewall separated them from the hanger.

Plus, time must have run out. It definitely had been over five minutes since their escape and the infrared disrupter must have melted down by now. The UAA guards watching them should have noticed their absence and probably already set off a silent alarm.

Alex dug his fingernails into the wall and slowly prodded at it until he created a small hole. Their eyes welcomed the refreshing beam of light as it entered the dark passageway.

Alex's retina needed to adjust a second before he could look through the hole.

"What do you see?" William asked.

Alex's eyes finally came into focus only to notice the enclosed hangar had been essentially vacated except for a few planes. The place could easily hold at least a hundred airships but only a couple remained. Where had they all gone?

Right now it didn't matter.

What did matter were the two UAA soldiers who were on guard about a hundred feet from their position.

What to do? Sneaking up on them through a wide-open hanger would be impossible while simply charging their position would prove suicidal.

"What do you see?" William asked again.

"A hanger with a few airships," Alex whispered. "You remember how you were once an all-state lineman?"

Puffing out his chest he responded, "What do you mean once? Once an all-state lineman, always an all-state lineman."

"Good. In order to get out of here we have to take out two UAA soldiers guarding the nearest Stratoskimmer."

The revelation unfortunately blew some of the steam out of William's response. However, at this point he would do whatever was necessary to escape. The thought of meeting the same gruesome demise as Guri provided him all the courage he needed. "Let's do it," he said, mustering his confidence.

Alex tilted his head back and grabbed the videre lens out of his right eye. With no others option available, this would have to suffice. Placing it on his hand, he inverted the lens from its natural convex shape to a concave configuration. Upon doing so, a realistic holographic image of Ari Lesmana giving one of his longwinded speeches projected from it. Albeit without audio, the visual would hopefully be sufficient.

Before William could make a comment, Alex said, "Make

a small hole in the wall along the floor. I want to slide this projection out so that it can catch the guard's attention."

William complied, understanding full well where this plan was headed.

Alex bent down and slid the videre lens along the floor and into the hanger after William made the hole. He then looked out through the hole that he made and saw the holograph was in perfect position about a foot from the wall.

Doing his best Malik impression, Alex shouted through the small hole in the wall, "Excuse me. Yes, excuse me soldiers."

The two guards immediately turned towards their position. Surprised, they both pointed theirs guns at the holographic image. However, upon realizing their mistake, they shouldered their weapons and marched over to greet the Malik.

"I believe they bought it," Alex whispered. "It appears they think that they are receiving a transmission from Ari." He waited a few moments as he watched the soldiers approach their position.

William positioned himself next to Alex in a three-point football stance, waiting to spring into action. He knew this flimsy, plaster wall in front of him would certainly collapse with little effort. He held his breath as he visualized his next move. There was no time to be scared nor was there any time to second-guess Alex's plan. What he did in the next minute would determine not only their fate but the fate of the entire planet.

The two soldiers greeted the holographic image of the Malik with the proper gesture and awaited his next command. However, when they saw his mouth moving without sound, Alex immediately perceived the suspicion in their eyes.

Before the soldiers had a chance to react, he immediately nudged William's shoulder and said, "Hike!"

William instantaneously leapt to his feet and with a roar

barreled through the wall as if it were paper mâché. In the same motion, he tackled both soldiers with the skill of an all-pro lineman. The two UAA guards were taken totally by surprise and had absolutely no time to react. Before they could mount a response, William slammed both their heads into the floor, knocking them unconscious.

Alex grabbed both the soldiers' weapons as William got to his feet. They then instinctively began to run straight to the nearest Stratoskimmer, almost expecting either to be shot or at least have a gun pointed at them along the way. Neither occurred and they scurried up the ship's steps without further interruption.

"We made it," William gasped.

Unlike the eloquent décor of Alex's Stratoskimmer, this one was Spartan by comparison. Apparently utilized for troop transportation, the hull contained only cold, metal benches along its walls.

Alex ran up to the cockpit and took the pilot's seat. William followed, huffing and sweating as he sat in the chair adjacent to him.

"Nice work," Alex commented. "Now let's get out of here!"

All out of any other tricks or gadgets, Alex gave a sigh of relief as he safely flew the Stratoskimmer out of the hanger and up into the stratosphere.

CHAPTER 41

THE ROAR OF ENGINES and the magnetic tug of low flying air ships instantly gave Samantha goose bumps. Not that she feared dying, but all of a sudden death seemed so final. Plus, she wished she had at least said goodbye to some family and friends. She also wished she could have told certain people to go shove it, but now it was too late.

She knew communicating with Dr. Howard at this point would be futile. He had failed to curtail the attack. Hopefully, he and the NIH would have better luck finding the cure.

Samantha sat back in her chair and watched the screens around the bunker waiting to see explosions, smoke, and bright flashes of light. Commander Gorman had done it. He must be smiling ear to ear right about now, gleaming at the fact that he got a chance to blow something up.

She wondered what type of upbringing could forge such an adult. Had he been beaten as a child? Did his father never show him any affection? Was he teased by his classmates? At this point it didn't matter. Commander Gorman was about to destroy Neurono-Tek and possibly the only means to finding a cure for *The Disease*.

"Dr. Samantha Mancini!" a familiar voice resounded from her central console. "I convinced the Chairman of The Joint Chiefs of Staff, Admiral Fine, to personally call off the air strike!"

As air ships continued to fly above the Neurono-Tek complex, the words brought her little solace. Had they not gotten the message, or had Commander Gorman overridden the chairman's authority?

Samantha did not say a word, expecting the first bomb to drop any second.

"Dr. Mancini," Dr. Howard reiterated, after waiting a few seconds without a response, "are you still there?"

The blare of the sirens and roar of the engines ceased almost at once. Never had quietness sounded so refreshing. Never did she think anyone could convince such a boneheaded man as Commander Gordon to change his mind. She would live another day.

Dr. Howard had saved not only Neurono-Tek but also millions of other innocent people afflicted by *The Disease*. Samantha felt a great sense of relief and let out a large sigh, exhaling all her inner angst in one breath. It was as if her whole body instantly went limp with exhaustion and could no longer hold up its own weight.

You know what, she thought, I am going to tell all those people I can't stand to shove it anyway, even if I'm not going to die any time soon.

"Dr. Howard," Samantha finally said after a long breath, "I owe you my deepest gratitude. I cannot thank you enough for what you've done."

"Who knew an old goat like me still had a little power left on Capitol Hill?" Dr. Howard joked. "Now you have to do me one favor."

"Anything."

"Find that cure."

"Yes, sir," Samantha answered, ending their communication.

CHAPTER 42

ONCE THEY WERE SAFELY FLYING above the Atlantic Ocean, Alex took one of the silver, secure transmission pads from the Stratoskimmer's console and placed it on his lap. Ever since escaping all he could think of was Marissa and Jonathan. Had they escaped? Were they captured? Were they still alive? The weight of these questions bore down upon him as he reconfigured the transmission pad to assure its security.

William sat back in the copilot seat, exasperated by their recent experience. With his adrenaline rush long gone, he too wondered what happened to both Marissa and Jonathan and respected Alex's ability to remain calm and continue working even after all that had just occurred. Though not saying it, he marveled at his friend's mental fortitude and overall physical endurance.

"Marissa," Alex said, talking into the square transmission pad. "Marisa," he repeated.

"Alex!" a voice immediately responded, though her image did not appear on the screen. "Thank God it's you! Are you, William, and Guri alright?" she asked. "I've been so worried

300

about you guys! I didn't know what happened to you and have been waiting here at the rendezvous point for almost twelve hours."

Alex knew that this would not be the best time to discuss their recent escape nor the details of Guri's death. Instead, he simply responded, "We're safe and I have sent Tom in a different Stratoskimmer to come pick you up. How are you and Jonathan?"

Marissa then went on to explain how Jonathan had succumbed to *The Disease*. Putting all emotion aside, she continued, "Before he passed, he found something very interesting. Taking into account the sun beams that looked like strands of DNA in John's cave at Patmos, Jonathan seems to have discovered the next layer to the code. Let me send it to you."

A three-dimensional double helix appeared on Alex's transmission pad. "It's definitely DNA," he commented, eye-balling the image, "but I can already tell you that it's way too short to code for any type of protein."

"I assume you have a sample of your own DNA on file at Neurono-Tek?" Marissa asked.

"I have over a billion samples of DNA on file," Alex responded, "including everyone who works at Neurono-Tek."

"Good," Marissa said with some relief. "Based upon Jonathan's last interpretation of the Bible code, I believe this strand of DNA has something to do with you and the cure for *The Disease*. Let's see what we can find if you cross-reference it with your genome."

"Sure," Alex acknowledged, accessing Neurono-Tek's secure genetic files. *Such a small piece of DNA. What could it mean, and what could it have to do with me?*

Alex again thought about what his parents told him about being genetically unique as he accessed Neurono-Tek's central database and cross-referenced the DNA with both his and a sample of a random thousand people.

A cursory examination provided him with no indication of its significance. Because the entire human genome possessed over 250 million base pairs that formed the interlocking steps of the double-stranded helix, this sample containing only a hundred seemed almost inconsequential.

"O.K.," Alex commented. "It appears the genomic sample you provided me can be found somewhere within everyone's 46 chromosomes. In fact, the hundred base pair combination is located on average about ten different times in any given individual's DNA."

"That doesn't make sense," Marissa acknowledged. "But the Bible code made it seem like we'd find the answer right away."

She could hear William grumble a few derogatory things about the Bible code and how their efforts had all been for naught.

"Let me rethink this whole thing," Alex said while running a few different options on his transmission pad.

Multiple color-coded strands of DNA then appeared on the pad with the areas of interest highlighted red. He enjoyed viewing them this way as it enabled him to visualize different possibilities all at once.

"If this DNA doesn't code for anything," Alex said aloud, "let's at least see what other things can be found near it."

He then manually began inputting commands into the transmission pad. Ten different strands of DNA appeared. Again they had been color-coded, but now the words *intron, exon, coding, noncoding, telomere,* and *junk* appeared above specific sections.

The DNA spun along its axis like a top while Alex watched in a hypnotic trance, waiting for an epiphany.

"I bet what I'm looking at is supposed to be a promoter

region," he finally said after concentrating on the image. Alex then pressed the screen and it displayed a whole new strand of DNA. Following a cursory review, he went on to examine another sample.

After looking at a dozen more images, he was convinced that the DNA strand of interest given to him by Marissa always stood conspicuously close to a section of DNA that coded for a protein. Though the protein was always different, its position wasn't.

It has to be a promoter. But what makes this sample so special? There still doesn't seem to be anything so unique about it.

"I wonder where this DNA strand of interest is located in my DNA?"

The entire screen went blank except for a single segment of DNA. Alex nearly jumped up from his seat with excitement. All the worry, angst, frustration, and exhaustion immediately left as a rush of adrenaline zipped through his body like a shock of electricity.

"That's it!" he announced.

"You found something?" Marissa eagerly asked.

"Let me just analyze the adjacent DNA found next to it to see what gene it activates," Alex anxiously answered. "And once I find the gene, I can see what it codes."

The DNA image on the screen was immediately replaced by that of a three-dimensional protein. Reminiscent of a haphazardly built Tinker Toy model, the protein's building blocks known as amino acids were represented by differently colored spheres, which were attached to one another by thin black lines. The structure spun on its axis as Alex watched in awe.

"What is that?" William asked as he nudged his body next to Alex's.

"The cure!"

CHAPTER 43

SITTING ATOP A MOUNTAINOUS RIDGE in the south of Yemen, a grand resort house overlooked a breathtaking view of the Arabian Sea. Once owned by a wealthy entrepreneur, the vacation home had become the possession of the UAA when he was deemed to be a political dissident by Ari's internal military police.

The former tenant ended up in a pauper's prison after he spoke out against the Malik's failing economic policies. However, the truth of his words was suppressed by the government-controlled media, and he was summarily incarcerated because of his political insurrection.

Ari stood at the balcony and gazed out in the distance towards the Arabian Sea. Along a vast, sandy plateau next to the water, he watched as a parade of heavy machinery emerged from his bunker located underneath it. The enormity of this project made it seem as if all of the UAA's resources had been devoted solely to its completion.

Ari turned to all those in attendance. The enormous balcony could hold over 2,000 people comfortably. At the moment it appeared to be at capacity, filled with the highest ranking UAA dignitaries and their spouses.

Masika accompanied Ari and wore a long, red robe-like dress with a black belt under her bosom. The color of the garment made her also standout in the crowd, creating a stir among the audience.

Ari stepped up on a small platform placed on the balcony so he could address the crowd. Upon the sight everyone present, except his wife, hushed and placed their hands atop their heads in an O shape. The Malik was about to speak.

"You all are probably wondering why I summoned you here today," he began.

They all placed their hands down once he began to speak. No one dared interrupt the Malik. Instead they stood, awaiting his next comment.

Despite their feigned loyalty, most had grown tired of his failed economic policies, rising inflation, and broken promises. They were all high-ranking government officers and had witnessed firsthand the economic ruin of their country by this man and the growing dependence on foreign currency for its continuation. However, no one dared speak out against him in fear of both the downfall of their political career and possibly the termination of their life.

"What you see before you," Ari went on to say, "is the greatest government project ever undertaken!"

He paused, awaiting his just adulation. The crowd did not disappoint him and applauded on cue. Everyone smiled as if the happiness had been surgically sewn onto their faces.

"It represents our salvation and emergence as a world power!"

The crowd continued their applause. Usually much louder, it remained tepid at best.

An artificial lake slowly grew larger behind him along the

plateau above his bunker. Occasionally some water would spout up, creating a fountain-like effect for a few seconds and then subside. Many stared at the plateau, wondering what this all meant. No matter what idea came to mind, nothing seemed to explain what they saw before them.

Ari went on to further grandstand about himself and the economic success he had brought to the UAA. He also touted at length the beneficial effects of his stimulus plans. Most understood by now that the only thing the plan did was stimulate the country's further economic dependence on foreign money and raise their national debt to unfathomable levels.

This rhetoric that once sounded promising now lost its luster. After a few more self-ingratiating remarks to the growing crowd's disinterest, Ari said, "This brings us to the final stage in my economic stimulus plan."

Many had long tuned him out, turning their attention to the lake along the plateau. However, his last statement caught all of their attention.

"I have promised the people of the UAA both prosperity and that one day our country will become a world power," he continued, emphasizing his statement by slamming his fist into his palm. "And what you see behind me is the answer to this promise.

The crowd again applauded, weary of his statements. Instead of excitement, they braced themselves about hearing the cost of such a huge endeavor. They could only imagine how much of the UAA's hard-earned money had been thrown away on this project.

Ari went on to explain that under the plateau was a massive bunker. Built to withstand a nuclear war, the bunker was created to immediately sequester them along with another eight thousand of his most ardent supporters until either a cure for

The Disease became available or the plague ended on its own volition. He touted its benefits and spoke in a grandiose fashion about the revolutionary nature of the project.

"We will rise like a phoenix from the earth's ashes," Ari boasted, "creating a new world founded on our ideals, our principles!"

The applause immediately dwindled as a low mumble of concern began to rise among the attendees. The words *immediately* and *sequester* resonated poorly with each one of them. Panic-stricken and wanting to leave, most began thinking of the best way to escape.

Those in the back of the balcony began to flee towards the elevators while those in the front slowly eased their way backwards. They would not be taken willingly and be forced to leave all their family and friends behind. The plan sounded both illogical and amoral.

"Stand your ground!" Masika shouted with a shrill to her voice. "Show the Malik respect! Don't you see that he's attempting to single-handedly salvage this pitiful country of ours and again make it great!"

She stood up on the platform next to him, her red dress standing out like a beacon against the blue sky's backdrop.

"We all were nothing before Ari Lesmana took control of the UAA," she went on to say in a less-harsh tone. "He is the one who has given us hope. He is the one who has given us direction. He is the Malik! Who does the country turn to when it needs food, shelter, or the necessities of daily living? Not God, not his family, not anyone else but the Malik. He is both our spiritual and political leader. His word should not be doubted."

Her words spoke volumes about Ari's tenure as the Malik and how he saw his role in that position. Many surmised he felt that way, but Masika's comments only solidified their suspicions.

The crowd's mumbling only grew louder. Her lecture did not do anything to settle their nerves. In fact, her condescending diatribe only began to provoke panic amongst the attendees. Some began to turn and flee while others knocked each other down just to get off the balcony.

"Cowards!" Masika shouted, disappointed in these people she called countrymen. "You are all cowards!"

"Enough!" SattAr announced from the back of the balcony. Surrounded by fifty of his elite and fully-armed military personnel, he and his entourage blocked everyone's means of escape.

Like parting the Red Sea, he walked unhindered through the crowd as they moved away from him.

"SattAr," Ari said with his usual smirk. "I was wondering when you would join us."

CHAPTER 44

MASIKA REFUSED TO STEP DOWN from the platform. She would not let SattAr intimidate her. Her position in the UAA was solid. She was the wife of the esteemed Malik. No politician or military personnel had any authority over her.

The chaos of the mass exodus ended, and most of those who attempted escape had been escorted back onto the balcony. The armed soldiers blocked the exits. With machine guns strapped to their shoulders, they deterred any further retreat.

SattAr's arrival proved to be an auspicious one. Ari appreciated how his men wrangled up the crowd like a bunch of cowboys would a wayward herd of cows. The security at the estate certainly had not been trained or expected to perform such a feat.

Contrary to his wife, Ari did not get offended by the crowd's reaction. Instead, he shook his head at the time and thought, Simple people. This is why I am the Malik and you all are my subjects.

He assumed they were not intelligent or enlightened enough to see the brilliance of his plan. Only a true genius, like himself, could realize the potential of his plan and understand the prosperity it would bring to the UAA.

Ari stepped down from the platform and awkwardly bowed to SattAr. It was a perplexing gesture as his subordinate should have been the one showing respect to him.

Masika snarled at the gesture and even SattAr did not know how to react to such a display. He attempted to make the *O* sign above his head but resorted to just keeping his hands to his side and let Ari finish with the bow. If the Malik went down any further his nose would have touched the ground.

"You have come just in time," Ari finally said, putting his arm atop SattAr's shoulder. "We are about to escort all these people here and another eight thousand men and woman into my bunker."

He brought SattAr to the edge of the balcony and looked out at the growing lake along the plateau. Ari gazed upon it, believing his own words. The thought of Alex Pella and *The Disease* had been momentarily forgotten. One triumph at a time—he could deal with the potential cure in the morning. And if none were produced, he would be safe in his bunker, awaiting the right time to emerge triumphantly.

"Can you understand all that I have done?" he proudly asked.

SattAr certainly did. He fully understood how Albert Rosenberg and The New Reality continued to loan money to the UAA without any expectation that it could ever be repaid. The fact was Albert wanted Ari to continue his reliance on foreign economic support until ultimately the UAA bankrupted itself. It would be easy then for The New Reality to take over the entire country, just as they recently did with Iceland, Greece and France.

"I hope you all remember this day." Ari turned to the frightened crowd and boasted as he stepped back up on the platform. "You all can tell your descendents that you were there with the Malik as we all entered the bunker. I assure you all that this will not be a day you will ever forget!"

The crowd gazed upon the Malik with trepidation. Why had he forsaken the rest of his country? Why were they not personally informed previously about this plan? There were no answers. Only one fact prominently remained. They would be forced to accept yet another direct order from the Malik and have it shoved down all their throats without a chance to discuss alternative options.

Jeers started being thrown by the crowd. Many came from the Malik's personal cabinet members while others were from some of his closest friends. They were tired of his failed plans, broken promises, and of the economic crater he had created for the UAA. With another huge economic failure standing in front of them, they wanted no more of the Malik.

SattAr listened to the crowd and fully understood their fears and concerns. He, too, had come to the same, unfortunate conclusion that something needed to be done. The people have spoken, he thought as he hopped up on the platform next to the Malik.

Masika scowled at him. "Get down," she glowered. "Mind your place."

Ari still tried to appease the crowd. Never before had he received such a strong, negative response. While unsuccessfully attempting to win the crowd's support, he hadn't noticed SattAr's presence nor heard his wife's ongoing admonishments.

Ari had no time to react. Before he made another attempt to rally the crowd in his favor, he suddenly felt a sharp, piercing pain in his left side. It felt like a bolt of lightning had just struck his chest and immediately took away his breath.

He looked down only to find a silver dagger, with the UAA emblem etched on its ivory handle, embedded in his ribs.

SattAr held the weapon. Before he could utter any final words, he fell to the ground. Death had overtaken him before his head hit the platform.

The crowd momentarily shuttered at the sight of Ari's assassination. There was no cheering, applause, or laughter. Instead, they all stood somberly in place. Some murmured a prayer while others kept quiet. A dark era in their country's history had ended, and now a time for a new rebirth had begun. Despite the threat of *The Disease* still lingering, they believed better days were ahead of them.

Masika physically lamented at the sight of her husband's death. Her hands clenched and her whole body shook in rage. She tried to claw out SattAr's eyes but he grabbed her by the wrist and pushed her to the side.

"How can you do this to me!" she shouted. "What am I supposed to do now?"

Masika fell to her knees and began to cry. The tears she wept were for herself and not her husband. His dead body lay sprawled across the platform in a growing pool of blood. She did not care. He only reminded her of her own fall from grace.

The hollow feeling inside her had grown to unfathomable levels. She could see no further point of continuing this meaninglessness life. Her existential existence all of a sudden had no purpose, and she was left with an insurmountable sense of hopelessness.

Masika took out a small pill from her dress and placed it into her mouth. Within a few moments she met the same ignominious fate that she had unjustly thrust upon Guri Bergmann. Death came quickly as her necrotic corpse fell to the platform and turned to ash.-

CHAPTER 45

DESPITE THE FACT THAT GURI spent most of his life in isolation, his funeral had been well attended. Neurono-Tek's chapel brimmed with over 300 people, well over its allowed 200 limit. After what had transpired on the premises lately, the fire marshal deemed it the least of his worries.

Rabbi Rudinsky had just given his final prayers, concluding the funeral. Both sadness and laughter marked the ceremony. The rabbi asked everyone not only to remember Guri's death but also all the others who had been taken by *The Disease*.

Because the details of Guri's demise had been kept secret, the official word was that he succumbed to the ravages of *The Disease* and had been cremated prior to transport. Few knew the truth, and those who did swore they would take the secret to their grave.

Alex stood up and said a few words during the ceremony. He tried to capture Guri's personality as most in the room had never met the man. Those who attended only knew that he helped discover the cure for *The Disease* and died in the process. Alex told the congregation about Guri's love for comics and of his funny quirks. Most let out a little laugh but in the end felt as if they got to know this secluded man and wished they had an opportunity to meet him before his death.

William knelt in the front pew and cried like a baby throughout the ceremony. Though he tormented Guri most of the time, he felt a deep sense of remorse with his loss. Marissa patted him on the shoulder, surprised by his emotional outburst. She never fathomed he had a soft side and was refreshed to see it after all this time.

The chapel began to empty after Rabbi Rudinsky thanked everyone for their attendance and wished them all a happy and healthy life. His words left everyone with a heightened sense of religious vigor and a positive outlook after such tumultuous events of the recent weeks.

Marissa grasped Alex's hand as the two rose together from the pew. Much had happened since Patmos over a week ago. Because she was the NIH's representative sent to Neurono-Tek, she helped Alex and Samantha manufacture the protein coded by the gene discovered within Alex's DNA. Ultimately, it did prove to be the cure for *The Disease*, and Neurono-Tek began mass producing it for global dispersion.

Despite Marissa's long hours of work, she spent all of her spare time with Alex. Late-night dinners, long talks, and an occasional walk around Neurono-Tek made their connection even stronger. For the first time in his life, Alex actually found someone he wanted to settle down with. He had no doubts that she was going to be with him for a long time.

"I'll see you this Friday after I return from Greece," Marissa said as she kissed him on the cheek.

The two parted ways upon exiting the chapel. Though her trip to Greece would be short, she was personally needed to oversee the proper dispersion of the cure to the country. She had a car waiting to drive her to the airport. Alex insisted that she use his personal Stratoskimmer, but after their recent troubles with the ship, she said she wanted to fly commercial.

Alex gave her a final wink before she entered the car.

"I see we made a new friend," Samantha said sarcastically and loud enough for anyone within a mile to hear. "And you told me your trip overseas was a dangerous one: electrocution, getting shot at, necrotic pills. I can see now what danger you really encountered."

William walked between the two of them. "You think Marissa has a sister or maybe a friend or something," he asked, still wiping tears from his eyes.

"Is that all guys think about?" Samantha commented. "I mean, come on, there has got to be something else going through your heads during the day."

Alex and William looked at each other and said in unison, "Nope."

"And that's why women should run the world," Samantha responded, sighing in disgust.

"I'll remember to tell that to Albert Rosenberg when I meet with him later today," Alex jested. "I'm sure he'll be waiting with bated breath to hear what you have to recommend."

"I wish those necroids killed me in the bunker," Samantha joked. "We have how many more years working here together?'

"I thought I heard her say she had a sister," William interrupted with only one thought in his mind.

Alex turned to his friend. "You know we're going to Father Jonathan Maloney's funeral this Friday. It's not a place where you need to take a date."

"I just thought it might liven up a somber time," he said, shrugging his shoulders. "You know, between the death of Guri here and Jonathan, it kind of gets to you."

"O.K. I'll ask Marissa," Alex said, "as long as you stay on your best behavior."

He did feel as if he owed his friend something. After almost getting him killed numerous times, he did want to show his sense of appreciation. Marissa recently commented about one friend she thought William would find particularly attractive. Maybe he could persuade her to bring her to the funeral in Vermont.

Alex also felt the same way as William. The deaths of Guri and Jonathan had both been an emotional blow. He ran the circumstances surrounding Guri's murder through his mind over and over. Was there anything he could have done to prevent it? Was there something he could have said at the time to diffuse the situation?

"Then I'll see you next week," William said, interrupting Alex's train of thought. "I'm just going to stop off at the employee cafeteria before I leave here. The funeral made me a little hungry." He waved to them both and walked within the cordoned-off area towards one of the buildings at the other end of the complex. "Don't forget about my date!" William shouted from a distance.

Alex took a deep breath and thought about the funeral in Vermont. Though Jonathan's death had not been completely unexpected, he did feel a great sense of loss with his passing. Alex was also amazed at how much Jonathan accomplished while on their expedition while being so sick. His physical and mental stamina must have been staggering.

He recalled Jonathan's quiet, unassuming demeanor. Because of the man's modesty, he would have never surmised that he graduated from M.I.T with an electrical engineering degree and had been a successful entrepreneur before entering the priesthood. Jonathan had given up his fortune before being ordained and vowed to live a life of sacrifice and spiritual devotion. He preached in Vermont for over twenty years and spent most of his time tending to the sick and needy.

The diocese had to rent out a huge hall in St. Albans, Vermont to accommodate the over 3,000 people they expected to attend the funeral. He had touched so many in the local community that his death impacted its residents significantly.

"Does this mean I'll have to stay here and clean up this mess while you're away?" Samantha chimed in.

"I certainly didn't make it," Alex countered. "I see a broom over there that has your name on it. Why wait until I'm gone? You can get started now."

"Let me tell you where I'm going to stick that broom!"

The two walked within the designated area sectioned-off by the police. Between having to spray the entire complex three different times with metaldehyde to kill off the remaining necroids and all the construction, Neurono-Tek was nowhere near back to normal yet. Fully-armed police and members of the bomb squad patrolled the area 24 hours a day. Fire engines were at every corner and the National Guard guarded the complex's entire perimeter.

A sizable amount of the reconstruction had been accomplished over the last week; the foreman of the operation promised Alex that Neurono-Tek would be at 100% operating capacity within twenty days. *That is, if nothing else occurred.*

"All joking aside," Alex said, "I have to admit that I'm very impressed about how you fended off the necroids and a full-scale military attack on Neurono-Tek all by yourself and helped find the cure for *The Disease* in the process."

"Let's just say I'll be waiting for my Nobel Peace Prize in the mail any day now," Samantha scoffed, trying her best to be modest. She knew what she accomplished at Neurono-Tek had been an enormous feat. Still, she could not fathom how she survived her entire ordeal without losing her sanity.

"No, I really mean it," Alex reiterated. "You did a fantastic job."

"I suppose after years of therapy I can look back on it and say the same," she said. Despite her jovial manner, the incident had been extremely traumatic. Every night for the last week Samantha had awakened in a cold sweat. Hopefully time would heal these wounds.

"Since we're being all touchy-feely here," Samantha said, "I do have to congratulate you also on your success. Between fending off an elite force of UAA soldiers and also helping find the cure for *The Disease*, you also did a good job." She smiled. "Not as good as me, but good enough."

The two passed by a few more armed police who stood their post, watching for any suspicious activity. Not only were they making sure no further terrorist activity occurred, but they also had been assigned to keep all media off the premises. Since the announcement of the cure, Neurono-Tek had been inundated with calls and requests for interviews. Alex and Samantha's faces were plastered everywhere, making them both instant celebrities. Not that either wanted the status, but after their discovery, fame was an inevitable consequence.

Samantha joked previously that she would rather be attacked by a bunch of necroids again than be swarmed by a pack of reporters. She said it would be safer.

"You know," Samantha went on to say, "I still don't understand how you found that genetic code within the Old Testament. The whole thing sounds a little far-fetched to me."

"You can't argue with the results," Alex admitted. "Stranger things have occurred—like the other day when you told me you were left speechless. Now that's completely unexplainable."

"Laugh all you want," she said. "If it weren't for me, we'd be walking through a pile of rubble around here right now."

"Hey," Alex said, "don't forget who had the only viable gene in their genetic code that could produce the cure for *The Disease*."

Though Alex joked about the situation, she did acknowledge that he did posses the only remaining, viable gene that could cure *The Disease*. At one evolutionary point all humans must have possessed the same functional gene. Those who didn't would have been killed off by the original retroviral infection long ago when *The Disease* first afflicted mankind.

Over the past week Samantha and Alex both had wondered how many other latent viruses lay dormant in the vast human genetic code. It was a theoretical question, but after the recent events, a pertinent one.

"Yes Alex," Samantha added sarcastically, "you are the greatest person who ever lived. Without you we'd all be dead."

"That's all I wanted to hear," Alex said with a smile.

"Aren't you late for that meeting with your old friend Albert Rosenberg today?" Samantha asked.

"That's where I'm heading right now."

"Don't forget to tell him what I said about women running the world," she said. "Tell him things would be better that way."

"I'll make sure I keep that in mind," Alex laughed. "Any other novel insights you want me to tell him while I'm there?"

"Well," she said, actually pondering the facetious question, "since he now runs the world, could you put in a good word for Neurono-Tek?"

Samantha's request had been a sincere one. The deadline had passed, and because no one was able to repay their enormous debt back to The New Reality, Albert Rosenberg and his company assumed control of their respective countries. No bullets were fired, and it occurred without one casualty. What many great leaders and generals had attempted to accomplish through might, Albert obtained through brains.

As he was now in control of essentially every country in the world, Albert created a centralized New World Order government with himself in control at its helm.

"I think I'll have a few more things to ask him than that," Alex said, surmising Albert's reason for summoning him.

CHAPTER 46

"IT'S ALWAYS A PLEASURE to see you Alex," Albert Rosenberg whispered.

He could barely complete the sentence without gasping for air. Speaking had become an exhausting task.

Albert looked much sicker than he expected. Alex surmised he had only days, if not hours, to live. As Alex looked upon the man lying in his bed, he could not help but remember all that Albert had accomplished throughout his life. Innately brilliant, well spoken, and with a keen eye for business, he had not only taken over the largest company ever created, The New Reality, but also had created a New World Order government. No other person could come close to the man in intellectual stature or cunning.

"It certainly has been too long," Alex responded.

"How's that Stratoskimmer doing?" Albert asked.

"Other than a few bugs, it's flying real smooth."

Different men and woman stood around Albert. All wearing executive suits, they obviously were there for business reasons and not to console him during his finals hours of life.

Instead, it appeared as if a board meeting had been conducted prior to Alex entering the room.

Alex recognized most of the people around the bed. They were all-too-familiar faces as each had been a high-ranking governmental official in their perspective country around the world. France, Greece, and Iceland's finance ministers were but a few who instantly stood out among the crowd.

Most would assume such disgraced governmental officials would have no place in The New World Order that Albert had created. They were the cause of their country's economic collapse and had no business remaining in office. If they could not execute proper fiscal responsibility in their own country, how could they do it globally?

However, the whole thing made sense. Albert was even more brilliant than Alex had ever imagined. The endless governmental spending, the unbounded borrowing, and the massive accrual of debt were all carefully planned by Albert Rosenberg.

These men and woman standing around him had Albert's and the New Reality's best interest in mind the whole time, not their respective countries. They must have been surreptitiously working for him like some sort of double agents and knowingly led their countries into an economic path of self-destruction. By increasing their dependence on foreign loans from Albert, they set into motion a financial situation that was destined for utter bankruptcy.

Ingenious!

And the entire plan had been carried out in front of the world. Everyone clearly saw the debt and wayward spending of their countries mounting, but nothing was done about it.

Alex could not hold Albert totally accountable for what he had done because few had the insight or initiative to actually try to stop it. The cries of fiscal responsibility were not heard or suppressed as the momentum of larger government and increased spending gained speed.

"I'd like to personally thank you for cleaning up my mess," Albert said with a little more gusto.

Alex raised an eyebrow. "I think that was more than a little mess."

Albert knew playing coy with a man of such intellectual prowess would be counterproductive. Alex most likely already discovered or figured out everything that he had done and probably knew more about it than his closest advisors. He admired Alex and saw much of himself in this young man.

Albert smiled. "You know what my only wish is?" he said, not expecting an answer, "I wish that we had a chance to run this New World Order together." He gasped for air before he could squeeze out another thought. "It would have been wonderful."

Alex did not want to contradict Albert, especially now in the man's final hours, but he would never want to work with him under any circumstances. The man was ruthless. His rise to power had been one filled with deceit, betrayal, and death. The ends did not justify the means. And even though Albert procured everything he ever wanted in this world, Alex did not respect the methods he went about doing it.

Alex kept quiet and only acknowledged his comment with a smile.

Albert sat up slightly in the bed. His skeletal frame became more apparent as the sheets rolled down below his chest. The effort took all of his energy, which forced him to gasp for air as a result. A nurse quickly came to his side and placed a small pellet underneath his tongue. The labored breathing slowly subsided.

"I am impressed with how you found a cure for *The Disease* and escaped from the UAA," Albert finally said. "They were certainly outstanding feats."

"But why Ari Lesmana and the UAA?" Alex asked. "What purpose was there in dealing with them?" He had already made the connection but wanted to hear it directly from Albert to confirm his lingering suspicions.

Albert mustered a smile. He recognized Alex already knew the answer but humored him anyway. "If you must know…" He coughed a few more times and spit up a bit of phlegm into an awaiting napkin held by one of his nurses.

"Ari was nothing more than a puppet," he went on to say. "Someone that I could control and manipulate at my slightest whim. The man served his purpose but in the end was expendable."

The men and woman around Albert stood like statues, listening to the conversation as if they were not there. Whether they were wrapped so tightly around Albert's finger that they were not allowed to speak or were just biding their time until the old man croaked, Alex could not tell. He would, however, ascertain their motives before he left.

A nurse put another pill under Albert's tongue. He then took a large breath and said, "Plus, I could not risk compromising the delicate situation in the Middle East. You see," he said after taking another large breath, "the other reason why I funded Ari Lesmana's rise to power was to solidify the UAA's control over a politically unstable area. His personality and rhetoric made them forget their differences and see themselves as one. Now with a new sense of national pride, the citizens of the UAA will be easy to rule with my puppet government in place."

"But Ari brought the UAA to the brink of total economic collapse," Alex interrupted.

"I was prepared for such an event," Albert responded, "and in fact expected it to occur. History has taught us that his fascist policies were doomed to failure since their inception. It was simply a matter of time before the collapse occurred. All I had to do was stop it before the process could no longer be reversed."

Albert's last words weakened him to the point of exhaustion. He closed his eyes for a few moments and began to drift into sleep. One of his advisors came to his side and knelt down next to him. Alex recognized the man as a senior member of the British House of Lords. His name was Stanley Wright, and he had made much press as of late with his public support of the New World Order.

"Let us cut to the chase," he said with a distinguished English accent. "We have invited you here in order to present you with a most auspicious opportunity. You see, with the imminent passing of our dear Albert Rosenberg, we have no one to lead The New World Order."

"Why not you, Mr. Wright?" Alex asked, wanting to clearly show that he recognized the man's identity."

"Oh no, don't be silly. We here are meant only to be seen and not heard."

I'd like to not see or hear any of you, Alex thought.

"We have been working with Mr. Rosenberg to create this fabulous New World Order, not to run it. Don't you see what we have accomplished?"

"Yeah, I see," Alex scoffed. "You created disease, economic misfortune, and an overall moral decay of the entire planet."

"You miss the big picture," the Englishman insisted. "We have created for the first time ever a universal bank with a unified society under the economic rule of The New World Order. Isn't it magnificent!"

Before Alex could answer, Mr. Wright added, "And the best part about it is that we want you to run for its presidency."

"Run?" Alex gasped. "What do you mean run?"

"The people will decide who they want to lead them," Albert

said, finally awakening from his short slumber. He wished to continue but words could no longer emerge from his mouth. He looked at Stanley Wright to continue.

"You see," Stanley said, "in order for The New Order to be legitimized internationally its president must be elected through a proper vote."

"You take over the world and now you want to bring its fate to a vote," Alex scoffed, suspicious of their true intentions.

"The world must believe that they are in control of their fate, not us," Albert said with a large breath. "Even if it is not true."

Stanley placed his hand on Albert's shoulder and added, "Mr. Rosenberg is correct."

Alex understood the method to their madness but still disagreed with their decision. "What if the world chooses wrong?" Alex commented, fully knowing their response.

"You don't think that we would leave our future up to mere chance," Stanley insisted. "Oh, no, my boy. We have handpicked candidates and no matter who comes out on top, The New Reality wins."

A woman on the other side of Albert added, "Your face has been all over the news. People know—and more importantly respect—you."

"You would win," Albert struggled to say. "This all could be yours."

Ruler of the world did have a nice ring to it but Alex had no interest in politics—especially those of Albert Rosenberg and The New Reality.

"If I wanted to be publicly humiliated," Alex said with a grin, "I'd go back to high school. I'm a scientist, not a politician. Neurono-Tek and the scientific community need me."

"The world needs you," Stanley insisted.

Alex shook his head. "I'll pass." He pointed to the men

and woman around Albert. "If you all want somebody who will run The New World Order with professionalism, common sense policies, and an uncanny knack for getting things done correctly, why don't you go solicit my favorite governor? He'll be the perfect candidate."

"But we want you," Stanley reiterated before Alex explained any further.

Alex looked over at Albert. The old man rested on a few propped-up pillows, laboring with each breath. Despite his terminal illness, he still kept all of his mental faculties.

Albert had invited Alex there for a reason, and it was not to offer him an opportunity to run for the president of The New World Order. He knew Alex would never accept such a proposition, despite his feigned insistence. His motives were much more subtle and lost among his cronies standing around him. He had them all assembled not to convince Alex to run for office but to show him the faces behind The New World Order. He wanted Alex to know who the true people were pulling the strings behind the economic institution that he created.

Alex understood Albert's true reason for bringing him to his mansion during his final hours. He needed someone outside the organization to know its inner circle just in case there were any future problems, catastrophic events, or possible coups. Albert's death would obviously bring about some instability and he knew only Alex Pella had the intellectual capacity to quell any future problems that could ensue within his organization.

"I'll pass," Alex finally said. "If any of you need me, I'll be back at Neurono-Tek. Where I belong."

"Please reconsider," Stanley requested.

Alex gave Albert a quick smile. "Rest in peace, old man. You have nothing to worry about."

Albert nodded and then closed his eyes, most likely for the final time.

Download a reading discussion guide at
smartino.lightmessages.com.

THE AUTHOR

Stephen Martino holds an M.D. from the University of Pennsylvania and is a neurologist in New Jersey. When he is not working, he can be found with his five children doing homework or cheering them on at a soccer field, basketball court, or dance recital. Martino is a member of the Knights of Columbus, a Cub Scout den leader and is an active public speaker, helping to educate the local community and healthcare professionals on the signs, symptoms and treatment of stroke. *The New Reality* is his first novel. Visit his website at martinoauthor.com.